INTO
THE SAVAGE
COUNTRY

Center Point
Large Print

**This Large Print Book carries the
Seal of Approval of N.A.V.H.**

INTO THE SAVAGE COUNTRY

Shannon Burke

CENTER POINT LARGE PRINT
THORNDIKE, MAINE

This Center Point Large Print edition
is published in the year 2015 by arrangement with
Pantheon Books, an imprint of The Knopf Doubleday
Publishing Group, a division of Random House LLC.

This is a work of fiction.
Names, characters, places, and incidents either are the
product of the author's imagination or are used
fictitiously. Any resemblance to actual persons, living or
dead, events, or locales is entirely coincidental.

The text of this Large Print edition is unabridged.
In other aspects, this book may vary
from the original edition.
Printed in the United States of America on permanent paper.
Set in 16-point Times New Roman type.

ISBN: 978-1-62899-508-4

Library of Congress Cataloging-in-Publication Data

Burke, Shannon.
Into the savage country / Shannon Burke. — Center Point Large Print
edition.
pages cm
Summary: "Young William Wyeth leaves St. Louis for a fur-trapping
expedition in 1826 and finds himself unwittingly at the center of a
deadly boundary dispute among Native American tribes, the British
government, and American trapping brigades"—Provided by publisher.
ISBN 978-1-62899-508-4 (library binding : alk. paper)
1. Male friendship—Fiction.
2. West (U.S.)—History—19th century—Fiction.
3. Large type books. I. Title.
PS3602.U7555I58 2015
813'.6—dc23
2014050342

For Charlie and Nicholas

Nature is loved by what is best in us.

—RALPH WALDO EMERSON

BOOK ONE
The Voyage Out

I was twenty-two years old and feverish with the exploits of Smith and Ashley. I followed their accounts in the *Gazette* and the *Intelligencer* and calculated their returns and dreamed of their expeditions. The fur trade was warring and commerce and exploration, and above all else in my mind, it was adventure. But the trade was also notoriously unprofitable, a fool's errand—everyone knew that—and I'd resisted joining a brigade for more than a year.

St. Louis had five thousand inmates as I called them back then. The French lived on the north side, on the high ground. I was living on the south end at a boardinghouse—a withered old widow for a landlady. She made it hot for us, bawling at any racket or laughter and particularly at me for bringing bloody pelts back, which, it is true, she had reason to complain of.

On the morning this narration begins, June of 1826, an acquaintance named Blanchard appeared beneath my window, calling up to say he was off to visit a Canadian half-breed who brain-tanned hides. The Canadian, he said, would increase the value of pelts more than she charged to tan them, and wasn't hard to look at, either.

"I'll join you on such a worthy venture," I called down, and a moment later was striding carelessly through the mud and muck of Market Street with Blanchard, hardly suspecting that little errand would change my life.

As we passed the Rocky Mountain House, a bellowing roar blasted from the doorway, and a French trapper named Goddard tottered out, waving a trade gun, breathing Taos Whiskey.

"Give an honest turn for the firearm, Blanchy?"

Blanchard needed a musket, and with Goddard falling down drunk, thought he'd get the better of him. Blanchard went into the alehouse and I went on to the half-breed's alone, not displeased to cut out the competition.

I don't know what I expected from Alene Chevalier—a feather in her hair and dancing around a bonfire or some nonsense like that. Not at all. She was foreign, to be sure, but French, with a quarter native blood that showed in her hair and eyes—a petite woman with olive skin and a long skirt and a shawl that she wore buttoned to her neck with a silver clip at the throat and her hair tied up with a wooden clamshell. All very proper and European in her manners and setting me in my place, though not uninviting, either. She trod that middle ground between warmth and propriety that the French have perfected and has never been replicated in our maidens, who seem to me to be either bawdy or puritanical.

"I'm Wyeth. A hunter," I said. "I have deer and muskrat pelts."

"Let me see," she said.

She had a bit of a French accent. Enough so you knew she was foreign, though not so much that you couldn't understand what she said. She ran her small hands along the first pelt slowly then flipped it over with an abrupt, practiced gesture. The administrators at the tannery were suspicious of native pelts and she wanted to maintain her reputation and did not take in furs that were old or poorly skinned or damaged.

"Twenty-five cents a pelt."

"Done," I said.

"Not much for bargaining, are you?"

"Not when I have a maiden to bargain with," I said, trying to be gallant, though she smiled thinly at that bit of nonsense. She was calculating the profits in her mind and by not bargaining I'd lowered myself in her estimation.

I carried the pack of furs along a hardened dirt path to the back of her cottage. She had a workshop beneath a pine scaffolding with willow hoops stacked in a row and a heavy pole at hip height for the scraping. There was a tub of mashed brains that looked like pink paste and a wooden flask of oil with a cork stopper and a basin with ash and murky water and a compressor with a pulley system and weights. I noticed she used a dulled carving knife to flesh. Also, a buffalo rib, a stained pumice rock, and a beveled deer antler. I saw indications of additives to the paste like liver and bone marrow and fish oil and pine nuts and wild rhubarb. I took note of all these ingredients, though I did not know the quantities or the process used to mix them. By her reputation, and later by the quality of the furs, I knew she had refined the process.

I heaved the pelts into the hard-packed clearing and she lifted soaked pelts from a basin and hung them on a wooden beam and put the first of my pelts, hardened and stiff, into the basin. Then she took one of the soaked pelts and sat on a smoothed log and stretched the pelt onto a willow hoop, affixing it with deer sinew and a curved wooden hook. She saw me watching, and said, "My father was a voyageur for the Northwesters. I learned from him."

"Is he with Hudson's Bay now?" I asked, but she shook her head, and by the way she did it I knew he was not with that company, or any other.

"Consumption," she said. "Two winters past. He battled the Ree with Ashley. Went on the winter march to the Medicine Bow. But it was the elements in St. Louis that took him." She made a drinking motion.

"The same ailment's taking my father," I said. "A farmer and man of property in Allegheny

County, Pennsylvania. Least it was two years ago when I last spoke with him."

It was a maudlin way to put it, but I said it in a careless tone, as I wanted her to think I was rugged and indifferent to the gales of life, and that we were two of a kind. If she saw the connection, she did not remark on it.

She finished with that first fur and when she reached for the second I knew I was meant to leave. I started back around the cottage and when I did she set her pelt aside and went through the doorway and I saw her writing out a ticket on a little pink slip of parchment. There was no need to give a ticket and, later, I thought she went through that bit of theater because she'd heard the sound of education in my voice and wanted to show she could read and write as well as any college professor—that neat cursive hand, the polite, precise sound of her voice, that Frenchified way of hers. She mistook me for a gentleman and didn't want me putting on airs, which, if she'd known me, she need not have worried about, as I worked as a laborer in a warehouse along the river.

I went on my way and seven days later I was back in front of her little cottage with my pink ticket. She met me at the door hauling a neatly bound pack of furs, rocking her slight body back and heaving the pack and carrying it, duckwalking, to the porch. I'd been thinking of conversation all week and come up with nothing but banalities.

As I paid she said, "You won't be long for St. Louis. *Les vrais gentlemen ne restent jamais ici.*"

"*Où est le vrai gentleman?*" I said, and she laughed, and said, "*Ici même, j'espère. C'est bien ce que je crois, oui.*"

"Not all would call me a gentleman," I said. "Talk to Professor Stanton at Temple. I put a fish with a pickle in its mouth in his desk. I won't be let back. So it's into the savage country for me. My education will be in the notable wonders of the far west."

"You'll join a brigade to the fur country?"

"Up to the Green River," I said boisterously. I did not believe I'd join a brigade at the time. I said it to be gallant, but I saw disappointment settle. She'd imagined I was a gentleman hunter with a carriage and a fortune, not some cast-off ne'er-do-well with no family or home to speak of. Something in her closed off to me.

"It's a hard life," she said.

"But an exciting one."

"The excitement ends quickly. The difficulties don't," she said.

I considered countering with some saucy remark, but she had been born to the life and undoubtedly knew it better than I did.

"Thank you, ma'am," I said, and slung the furs on my back and thought that was that. I was not a gentleman and she had decided against me in her mind.

14

I walked out the gate and when I looked back I saw that she'd gone through the cottage and was out behind collecting the willow hoops and stacking them with a clacking sound that followed me down her dusty street.

The memory of that short conversation stayed inside me all day.

The next day General Ashley arrived on a keelboat, and all of St. Louis gathered to greet him. Even at the advanced age of forty-six Ashley was a formidable figure, dashing and romantic in a way that has died out now—hair turning silvery and a nasty-looking scar across his forehead and at ease carrying a sword. It is true that he was drunk for much of his political career, but it is also true that he'd braved many hardships and faced enemy fire without retreating and he did it all with dash and verve that maybe is not necessary for that life but certainly makes it more palatable. The state had made him a brigadier general for running the militia during the war and he'd supplied the gunpowder for the militia, a tricky bit of business given that he approved the contracts himself. It landed him in court later, but he survived that scandal with most of his fortune intact and put the remaining money into the fur trade. Like nearly all who invested in that blighted business he lost his fortune, then was lucky enough to make a portion of it back on the shoulders of Jedediah Smith,

William Sublette, and David Jackson, those immortal trappers and adventurers who have lent their names to the rivers, streams, and mountains of the west and will live on as long as this nation does. These men enabled Ashley to get out with dignity if not with the riches he had once commanded.

At the time of which I'm speaking, the spring of 1826, Ashley had sold the Rocky Mountain Fur Company to Smith, Sublette, and Jackson, but stayed on as the hiring and purchasing agent. Like many connected to the fur trade, Ashley cursed the pelts for ruining his life and soiling his reputation and draining his finances and vowed to cut his losses and forgo even wearing fur hats, but those were idle threats. Despite the endless hardships and the constant setbacks there was nothing like the fur trade for camaraderie and adventure and excitement, and once the trade got its hooks into you everything else was pale and lifeless and seemed an imitation of life, rather than the genuine article.

After vowing to leave the business for the hundredth time, General Ashley was floating in on the deck of a keelboat, a foot up on the prow and that white hair blown back and a bear prowling behind him, chained to the mast. Ashley pretended he didn't know what sort of romantic figure he cast. He knew all right. Smith and company were shrewd when they kept him on as their hiring agent. The sight of Ashley on that keelboat coming on the heels of that reproof from the pretty tanner blasted the last of my hesitation. I had boasted to Alene that I'd join a brigade, and as it turned out, it was true. I would do it. I walked straight to the agent's storefront on Market Street and told them they could have me if they wanted me. You practically signed your life away if you were taken on as a camp hand. I did what I could to avoid that servitude. I lied about what I'd done and got Blanchard, who had joined me in my folly, to verify all my mistruths. We were taken on as company trappers, which right away was a better position if you could afford the equipage, which I could.

I spent the next week securing my traps and filling my possibles sack. I bought a J. Henry long rifle from Blanchard, as he'd gotten the musket from Goddard. I stocked up on all the necessaries: lead, a ladle and mold, a Sheffield knife, and a mirror for shaving so I'd look good for the squaws, as I'd heard they would call a bearded man *dogface*. I bought several parchment notebooks with vellum covers to record my observations. Like so many of my fellow travelers I planned on writing my memoirs if I survived and retiring on the glories and riches reaped from my misspent youth. All of us who signed on that year were puffed up with self-importance, as the Treaty of 1818, which had established the western boundary of our nation, was scheduled to be renegotiated, partially along trade lines, and the heart of the sales pitch for the various brigades was that a young man could make a fortune while battling the Brits and the mighty HBC and save Oregon Territory and New Caledonia for the nation. The trapping brigades were commerce and patriotism and battling and adventure and it was all westward ho, young man, out into the savage unknown, and other nonsense like that.

In truth, few of us had any idea what lay ten miles beyond St. Louis.

On my last days in the city I labored over a letter to my father, half justification for my misdeeds, half apology. I had parted from home two years earlier after a dispute over a piece of property. I could hardly blame my father for keeping the land from me, as I had done little to merit the gift and much to make him reluctant to pass it on, but he'd given my brothers their share on their eighteenth birthdays and he did not give me mine, and I'd accused him of stinginess. He blamed my restless nature for the delay. I called it favoritism, and our battle escalated. I left cursing him, and him me, and I had not talked with him since.

Now, two years later, I was leaving the States for at least a year, and probably much longer, and I meant to make it up before I departed. But while in the act of trying to amend my half-hearted apology I received a letter from my sister, sent months earlier, informing me that my father had died. I knew he was sick and medicating himself with the drink, but I did not think the illness would kill him. I probably thought he would never die and would be there at my funeral still casting aspersions. But no, there it was in print: dead and buried in the family plot, and it was like my whole insides collapsed. We'd had our battles, to be sure—no one could deny that—but I had not thought they were permanent. I admit that I bawled like a child.

The storm of grief lasted about an hour—it was furious, black, and desolate—but once it passed I realized I felt lighter. It's a hardhearted thing to say but the sad news of my father's death gave me a feeling not of victory or of dancing on his grave but of being cut loose from a past that was a blot on the mind and on the conscience, and as a sign that I was meant to do what my father had never dared. Since I was a boy I'd known I was made of different stuff from my brothers. They were born to the plow and pew while I craved the forest and woods and the vast, wild spaces. For better or for worse, I was fated to test my mettle in the west. If I didn't make a fortune, I thought, I would live my life up to the hilt and satisfy that inner craving and have something to talk about in my dotage.

I wrote to Mother that I was sorry I had not been

there for her during father's passing and that she'd hear from me again when I made my fortune (and I could imagine her saying, "Well, that's the last we'll hear of him"). And that was that. The final strand to the past was severed. I was cut loose on the world, and within a week would be off to the savage country.

I selected a pony from the company stock that I paid for from my future riches and I bid my adieu to all my companions in the Rocky Mountain House, and then, three days before my departure, I was walking the waterfront when I came upon two men battling, one an Italian sailor with an oiled black mustache, and the other Henry Layton, the son of Gene Layton, who owned half the warehouses along the waterfront. Layton the younger was an infamous bachelor: a twenty-four-year-old dandy considered to be the most intelligent, unpleasant, and mischievous young man in St. Louis. It was in keeping with everything I knew about Layton to find him with his jacket off, surrounded by drunken riffraff, battling with a laborer. Layton and the Italian exchanged blows for several minutes until Layton connected with a crosscut that snapped the Italian's head back. Layton, being hot, jumped in to stomp the deckhand after he'd fallen and had to be dragged off, frothing. It was an ugly scene, and I wandered off thinking this a fitting ending to my stay in St.

Louis—a dandy with the world at his fingertips stomping on an Italian deckhand.

That night I cleared out my room and left a pile of muskrat innards on the floorboards, like a turd. I put the innards on a scrap of deer hide so as not to stain, but I did leave it. The landlady had let me feel her tongue one too many times when I had no means of striking back, being her tenant. I left feeling vicious and wild and later remembered that pile of offal with a sick feeling. That sad old lady who was hanging on in youthful St. Louis and who took her bile out on the reckless young men who must have reminded her of her dead husband. I ought not to have left that nastiness. I know that now. That memory is a stain on the generally happy recollections of that time.

The next afternoon I stopped to bid Alene Chevalier farewell. I was decked out in my new leggins and deerskin and meant to steal a kiss before my departure, but as I neared the cottage who should be inside her fence but that blackguard Henry Layton, face bruised from the battle with the deckhand and the knuckles of his right hand scraped and swollen. Horace Bailey, a complacent, fat fellow, worth at least half a million, stood with Layton, both of them in black tailcoats and white cravats. I would have turned aside if I could have, as the show of money has always made me wilt. It has taken half a life to contain this feeling, but I have never quite extinguished it. I immediately regretted my deerskin and moccasins.

"William Wyeth in leggins like a booshway of the west," Alene called. "Come parley, you savage. You know Henry and Horace?"

I steadied myself, strode forward, and held out my hand. "Hello, gentlemen."

Layton, who was a quick-witted fellow, played it off rather well.

"This blackguard watched me battling yesterday and did not come to my aid."

"You needed little aid for stomping the man as he lay in the dust," I said.

"Tried to stomp. Unsuccessfully," he added, laughing. "But how good of you to mention that part of it, Wyeth." He turned to Alene. "I tapped a laborer with my riding crop to save him from being trampled and the damned rogue cursed me for saving his life. My temper was high, I admit, and I carried the battle beyond the boundaries— for which I would have apologized if given half the chance. Don't imagine I damaged the fellow. He was dancing a jig on the deck of a keelboat an hour later, waving a bottle that I had sent over, and thanking me for the diversion."

"True," Bailey said.

Motioning to my deerskin, Layton said, "What brings you here in that costume, Wyeth? Are you off to hunt squirrels and water rats?"

"I depart at dawn for the western drainages. I came to say goodbye."

"For how many seasons?" fat Bailey blustered in a gruff voice.

"A year, two, maybe three. I'll take the measure of it and see."

"Which company?" Layton asked.

"Rocky Mountain."

"Bravo, Wyeth. Up to the hilt."

The Rocky Mountain Fur Company was considered to be the most recklessly aggressive of the trapping companies.

"I hear it's magnificent country. Fertile and beautiful and savage and the whole world thirsting after it. I envy you. Truly," Layton said in that half-mocking tone of his so I could not tell if he jested.

"I'll end up some savage's pin cushion, no doubt," I said.

"But you'll have done it," Layton said. "It's what I ought to be doing, but"—he flicked his belt hooks—"these damnable straps are like shackles."

"Then take them off," I said, and expected some jesting remark, but he only nodded and said, "True. My enslavement is my own doing."

He cast a glance at Alene as he said this, and I noticed with a small satisfaction that she turned from his gaze.

"My enslavement comes only from my own ambition," I said. "My family thinks me faint-hearted and vacillating. I will show my worth in the savage country, and return a gentleman with a fortune."

"A fortune will hardly be sufficient to make you a gentleman," Alene said, laughing, and Layton checked to see how I took this barb.

"It will be sufficient to thrust beneath my brothers' noses and show them that they were wrong about my deficiencies."

"Or that they were right, which is why you succeeded," Layton murmured, but seemed to approve of what I said.

I thought there could be no benefit in idling, not with the two dandies spectating and speculating on my station in life. I moved to make my departure.

"I'll return in a year or more," I said to Alene. "If I survive, I'll bring you a native's headdress and a gourd of water from rivers that flow into the Pacific."

"When you return, you'll have been in the trapping country for at least a year," Alene said. "I'll be too timid for you."

"I'll be just brave enough to come for no reason," I said under my breath, and she laughed—a light, cheerful sound. It was the one thing I'd said without preparation, and the one thing that went off well.

Furtively, Alene took something from her pocket wrapped in a pink slip of paper like that on which she wrote her ticket. Inside the creased parchment there was a Saint Christopher medallion on a silver chain.

"Take this," she said. "Many don't come back."

She moved to affix the chain herself and I could see the places where her hands had been scrubbed raw and I smelled rosemary. I had to stoop, as I am a tall man, and she was hardly five foot. For a moment, as she put the chain around my neck, the tight brown coils of her hair were on my cheek and I felt her firm fingers on my shoulder, and the others watched with envy, which was satisfying.

"Don't forget me while I'm on my travels," I said.

"It's you who'll forget me with the squaws," she said, laughing again, a light sound that I remembered later. I turned to her companions. Bailey waved a pudgy hand. Layton stood straight, clacked his heels, and saluted from the porch.

"Westward ho and all that, Wyeth. When you return I'll come to hear of your adventures."

That was good-natured, I admit. I held a hand up as I turned, an attempt at offhand gallantry, and departed. I walked to the loading flats along the river and stood on the banks with the geese flying overhead and a keelboat's sail unfurling and accordion music drifting by and let my new situation settle into me. Now I am cast out of all society, I thought, belonging to no one, on the cusp of everything, the world's great heart beating inside me. . . .

I cringe now to think of all that youthful nonsense, but it warms me nonetheless.

After that minute of foolish reverie I went on to the warehouse where the recruits slept and where I had moved since leaving the lodging house. Buffalo robes lined the dirt floor with lanterns hanging from wooden hooks in the rafters and just outside the door an enormous iron cauldron on a *trois pied* burbled. Men sprawled playing bucking the tiger and I lay on a robe and looked at the ceiling planks where a moth darted. A veteran trapper with a gnarled beard and wearing deerskin leggins and jacket wandered over and sprawled out next to me, smoking a blackened calumet that he'd undoubtedly traded for on the trail. He said nothing until I looked at him, and he nodded and I asked him which brigade he was from.

"Andrew Henry's," he said.

"What was your take?"

"Two packs or just under. Hundred and fifty-two pelts a man."

I did the calculations. That was a fair sum.

"How many in the company total?"

"Eighty-four."

"How many gone under?"

"Seven. Four from the savages. Two from bears. One starved or froze."

He didn't say their names. Just how they died. Seven men out of eighty-four in a season. That was about average or even below average. He lay

26

there smoking quietly. You could feel the wilderness in his gestures. He was aware of everything around him and was comfortable with silence.

"You going back up?" I asked after a long while.

"Nope. One fifty-two. That's it for me. You going up with Smith?"

"Yep."

"You ever been up?"

"Nope."

He reached over. "Good luck to you, son."

"Good luck to you here in the city."

His calluses were like hardened mud. He could have squashed my hand if he liked.

"Good night," he said.

For the next four months the fifty-six men of the 1826 Rocky Mountain Fur Company brigade hauled a keelboat fifteen hundred miles up the Missouri. It was terrible, soul-crushing work, and in the first three weeks we lost sixteen men to defections. It was only the memory of my father's dismissive words that kept me from joining those deserters. For fourteen hours a day we pulled on that cordelle or poled in mud flats, baked by the sun and hardened by constant exertion until our bodies became all browned skin and wiry muscle, and the notch in the shoulder where you leaned on the pole had a permanent divot and discoloratio
At dusk we'd pull up along some mud bank
collapse, sleeping where we fell in the dirt

27

I had imagined escapades in the wilderness and romantic dashes across the prairie on wild ponies, but for those first weeks I was nothing less than a galley slave, and it was not until the eighth week of my servitude that I got a real sight of the western prairie.

It was August 1826, and for once there was favorable wind and draft. The sail was unfurled and the voyageurs, as we jokingly called ourselves, were handed weapons and ordered to hunt. The horses, which had been driven along by handlers, were saddled up and the next thing I knew I was riding through a dry runnel on horseback. I crested a hilltop to see sparse grass and the sunburned vastness of rolling land spread out in all directions. The locusts were droning and droning and a single bird flew silently in the distance and the white sky seemed very far overhead. It was as if the world had suddenly grown much larger than I had ever imagined and though it was grand, it was also solemn. The feeling of the prairie was of being at the cusp of a great mystery, infinite, overwhelming, and bewildering, and above all else, absolutely solitary. The utter isolation of the place settled into me.

The favorable wind lasted for three days, and for all that time we hunted and dashed back and forth over the sparse land. On the morning of the third day we saw smoke to the west, and a kid from Ohio named Ferris, Blanchard, and I rode out to investigate. After an hour of scrambling up and down those thorny, rock-lined runnels we came across a smoldering Mandan village with the dead sprawled everywhere, heads bloated and blackened with their eyes bulged out and an awful smell. The bodies were stripped and animals had been at them. At a rock-lined well we found a naked boy with a prickly pear shoved in his mouth. He was missing his left hand and later I saw the hand, like a small black flower, stuck in the branches of a cottonwood.

Blanchard, who was showing himself to be a tedious blowhard, acted as if the natives were nothing more to him than dead beasts. "Looks like this one's got his manhood shoved in his mouth!" I remember him crying, as if it were a carnival spectacle. That, and other unpleasant commentary, lowered him in my estimation.

Ferris countered Blanchard's indifferent affectation pointedly by covering the native boy with a deerskin he found in one of the lodges. I can picture Ferris now, nineteen years old, as small and frail and boneless as a doll, setting rocks gently around the edges of that deerskin, as if the wolves would not dislodge them as soon as we left. My sentiments were with Ferris, and I even moved to help him in his labor, but the sanctimonious way Ferris futilely tucked up the corner of the covering made me think he secretly himself above us. Ferris's father, we'd all was a physician and a man of wealth, and Ferris had paid a lump sum to be taken on, as they'd not thought he'd make it halfway up the Missouri. The knowledge of this pampered upbringing along with his self-satisfied manner damned him in my mind.

The three of us rode back to our encampment that afternoon and reported what we'd seen. Smith put up double sentries for the night, and the next morning the wind shifted and we went back to hauling on the cordelle. The memory of that massacre faded, but the feeling of heaviness and solitude from the prairie had lodged inside me and expanded and spread and became entangled with a sort of hesitation or uncertainty. I felt as if the enormity of the land were squeezing me and that I was dissolving into the utter silence and implacability of that immense, monochromatic, edgeless place. This oppressive heaviness and strangeness washed over me bit by bit until I understood what I was feeling: I was afraid. Afraid that I would not measure up to the others, and that I would fail in the tests that inevitably lay ahead. Afraid, too, that I would be slain in some lonely place with no one to mourn me, as my father had predicted. I was sure the others around me were real outdoorsmen, mountain men, all of them. Gruff, talented, and indifferent to hardship. All that late summer and into the fall these fears 'immered inside me and mingled with the feeling of solitude and isolation and utter vastness of that great burned country.

By early November we arrived at the juncture of the Missouri with a large river that flowed to the south called the Yellow Stone. It was here that the hauling ceased and we unloaded the keelboat and prepared to encamp until the spring season.

Fort Ashley, which was positioned just downriver from the juncture of the two rivers, was three low sheds half sunk in the dirt and surrounded by incomplete palisades of sharpened cottonwood trunks. Ashley, Smith, and a few others slept in what we called the commissary. The rest of the men slept outside the palisades in a wooded area to the south of the fort in lodges of deerskin and sailcloth pilfered from the keelboat.

One morning in November, a week after we'd arrived at the forks, we were woken in our encampment by the call, "Absaroka! Absaroka!"

Ashley stumbled from the commissary, bare-headed, and motioned to the south where forty Crow on horseback approached, black dots on a snow-covered hillside.

"Fingers off the triggers," Ashley called. "They come to barter powder for sustenance. We'll eat well tonight as long as you corncrackers don't blast 'em."

The Crow trading party rode down the snowy slope and pulled up at four hundred yards and saluted us. We saluted back, though in a paltry way, as we were conserving powder. The natives continued down, and when they arrived we saw their pack animals were stacked with smoked buffalo and deer meat.

The natives, curious about everything, were soon wandering among us, fingering all our personals, and at times looking to pilfer. It was the first time I'd seen the western natives up close. They wore sheepskin pants and ankle-high moccasins with fringes and fur hats and buffalo robes held at the neck with bear-claw clasps. They exuded an air of foreignness and savagery and most of the greenhorns kept their distance, but Ferris, I noted, mingled with the natives, putting on an air of affected and annoying friendliness, all the while scratching in a vellum notebook much like my own. I thought he took notes for his own memoirs, which I resented immediately, but when I drew close I saw he was not taking notes but making very quick and accurate sketches of the natives. He'd already done half a dozen. I even recognize myself in one, much to my disapproval.

Later, Ferris sat cross-legged in front of an old brave who had been blinded in one eye, repeating phrases in the native dialect.

"*Sho da chi*," he said slowly, which means "hello" in Crow. "*Sho. Da. Chi.*"

Blanchard found this horribly affected, and mimicked in a mincing tone, "Show dahhh cheee . . . Showww daaahhh cheee!," which sent the men snickering, as they thought Ferris imagined himself to be some Lord Byron of the wilderness.

Ferris ignored our ridicule, and while conversing with the one-eyed savage, took out a pair of reading glasses with one lens missing. Ferris put the broken glasses on the one-eyed native with a sort of pomp, which I understood was done as a jest. The other natives, seeing their one-eyed comrade wearing one-eyed spectacles, thought this was about the most amusing thing they'd ever seen. The natives leaped and hung on each other and laughed loudly, and Ferris stood there, grinning and rocking from foot to foot, childishly pleased with his prank.

Later Ferris showed them how the lens could be held at an angle and used to start a fire. This impressed them immensely. Ferris gave the glasses to the one-eyed savage, who returned Ferris's generosity by giving a triple-thickness buffalo-hide shield, intricately ornamented on the edges and wedged with bits of glass to reflect the sunlight. It was a wonderful, much envied piece of native artistry that we passed around to examine, and that brought us all down a notch.

There were songs that night, and feasting, and a second-year named Bridger tried to break out a bottle of Taos Whiskey that had been stowed in a hollow gourd. Smith and Ashley swiped the bottle, as they did not want drunk savages in the encampment.

I went to sleep with the murmur of conversations in a strange tongue filtering into my brain, and the next morning when I stumbled out of my lodging I saw the natives had already departed, the last ponies still visible on a far slope. As they reached the crest of the ridge they turned and saluted, the crack of rifles searing across the snowy flatlands in a way that left a feeling of emptiness afterward.

When they'd passed out of sight, I realized that Ferris had also stood watching their departure and was still standing there when I turned back to my lodge. He did not acknowledge my presence, but I had the feeling he knew I was there, and that however long I stayed, Ferris would make sure he stayed longer.

In the following days I noticed that Ferris questioned all the old-timers on the various tribes— their habits and customs and the location of their villages. The veteran trappers began mockingly calling Ferris "the White Indian." At the same time they started calling me "the Professor" because I carried a quill and parchment notebook. I resented being grouped with Ferris, and to combat the impression of being a fainthearted schoolboy, and also the doubts within myself, I made sure I was always the first out on our expeditions around the fort, and the first up to trap the nearby drainages, and in early December I made secret plans to trap the hills to the north of the fort. Smith had prohibited the greenhorn trappers from entering these hills, claiming they were full of Blackfoot, which only made the prospect more inviting.

During an unusual warm spell that felt more like fall than winter, Bridger and I slipped off and headed into the forbidden hills which were increasingly rocky and lofty to the north and west of the fort.

Bridger was a sturdy fellow with short-cropped hair and a ruddy complexion, and though he was as ignorant of book learning as the day he was born, he possessed all the accomplishments needed west of the Mississippi. He had a fine shot and was an excellent tracker and hunter and was as comfortable sleeping on rock as he was in a feather bed. He admired me for my education, and I admired him for his knowledge in everything that mattered out west.

After half a day of crossing drainages and scrambling up rocky hillsides we established our encampment at some hidden spot beneath towering pines and spruce, and immediately started off toward some drainages with our traps clinking, making a racket like we were the only living creatures for miles. We were about a quarter of an hour from our encampment when a shadow detached itself from a pine tree and vanished into the gloom with the sound of fading hoof beats. It happened so fast that I hardly understood what I'd seen but Bridger was already wheeling his pony, bolting after the native, brandishing his weapon. I understood I ought to follow, but in my surprise I managed to drop my pistol. By the time I'd retrieved it, Bridger had already vanished. I started out after him, following his tracks, which I lost.

After a quarter mile, I'd stopped to listen for them when a wolf wearing a leather harness padded into the clearing. The wolf's harness was painted with eagle and bear sketches and had feathers dangling and I understood I must be very close to a native encampment. I backed my horse into a shrub, trembling and panicked, though there was a very small voice in the back of my mind that was saying: Well, now you'll have a story to tell back at the Rocky Mountain House. The vanity of my youthful ambitions for glory touched a corner of my mind even at that moment.

Then I mounted and rode as quietly as possible back toward our encampment. I imagined Bridger bound and being roasted alive at that very moment, but I told myself correctly there was little I could do about it.

I picketed my horse two hundred yards from our encampment and crept forward until I saw the meat hanging on the trees. I was just about to enter the clearing itself when a native stepped into view. He was less than twenty yards from me and was dressed almost identically to the veteran trappers in the brigade. He was wearing a trapper's buckskin jacket and a buffalo robe and a beaver hat and leggins and fur-lined boots. He carried a Northwester musket and his horse was painted with the same buffalo and bear emblems as the dog's harness. The native had a pistol in his belt and what looked like an I. Wilson blade. He stood in the middle of the campsite and looked at the lodge and the hanging meat and the smoldering fire. We had left a fleshing knife stuck in a log. The native pried the knife out and tested the blade then used it to cut a strip from the hanging meat. He licked his fingers, pocketed the knife, jumped on his horse, and rode off through the gloom while I crouched in the shrubbery, too frightened to move. I waited for several minutes, then stole forth and collected our lodge and robes, knowing he'd return. I packed everything as best as I could and dashed off.

An hour later I arrived at a promontory that overlooked the juncture of the two rivers. From that spot I could see the snowcapped mountains and the two wide valleys with the rivers converging, and beyond that, the smoke from our fort rising into the late-afternoon light. I saw a rider with a pack horse moving toward the forks and I knew that was Bridger. So he was alive after all, I thought, and stood there grinning, feeling as if my heart had been clenched in a fist and suddenly beat freely again.

By dusk I was galloping across the flats toward the half-completed palisades of Fort Ashley, having recovered my nerve by that point and trying to pretend the whole thing was just an afternoon stroll for me. All the men came out of the lodging to watch me arrive, including Bridger. I rode in and told carelessly of how we'd given chase to the natives and been split up when we'd almost ridden into the heart of their encampment.

"Should have blasted the lot of 'em," Blanchard said.

A veteran named Pegleg gave a withering look. "He'd have had the whole hunting party testing his hump ribs with their blades. You did right keeping still."

The others began asking all manner of questions.

"Were they Blackfoot?" "Did they move with the British?" "Did they have long guns or trade guns?" And in the midst of this, that irritating Ferris asked, "Did you see his moccasins?"

"His moccasins?" I asked in the most derisive tone I could muster.

"That'd tell you if it was Bloods or Blackfoot," Ferris said calmly. "Most likely Blackfoot, given the slopes."

"He was wearing brocaded Wellingtons like

Chapman sells on Market Street," I said, which sent the men guffawing.

"How many were there?" Smith asked.

"I heard many horses. At least fifteen. But there could have been many more."

"Double sentries tonight," Smith said. "And if they're spotted send Peggy to invite them to trade. Don't fire unless they do."

Before Smith went back into the fort, he put a hand on my shoulder and said, "If you'd lost your scalp that would have been something to put in your memoirs."

"That it would," I said.

"Stay on this side of the slopes from now on," he said.

Smith was a fine, sturdy fellow, and if anything, he marked it in my favor that I'd had the pluck to strike out on my own, though he'd forbidden it.

The next day I noticed Ferris riding up to the edge of our encampment, scanning the slopes with his spyglass, but the natives had departed, and he did not see them as I had.

Two days later the real snow began, and for the next weeks we packed ourselves inside the commissary. Our supplies grew low, and our tempers irritable. The one diversion was that an elk had been spotted in the lowland south of the fort. Smith offered a reward of one silver dollar to the man who brought it down and late in the afternoon on the last day of 1826, I found myself riding alongside the high-toned Ferris, whom I had done my best to avoid, and who I felt was always silently competing with me.

As we rode toward the lowlands I saw a water bird over some unfrozen shallows, and pointing it out, said, "Duck."

"Goldeneye," he said, though from that distance identification would have been impossible. Another time I pointed to tracks and said, "Deer."

"Mule deer," he corrected, though that was obviously what I'd meant.

We rooted about aimlessly for half an hour, the sun lowering, until it was dim and shadowy, though the river, which was still sunlit, looked brilliant and blue when glimpsed from the gloom of the forest.

We arrived at the riverbank and Ferris leaped off his horse and drank with a cupped hand, then climbed back up the bank and was switching his halter from one hand to the other when his mare bolted into the woods, halter dragging.

"Pauline, you beast!" he shouted.

The mare stopped thirty yards off, and I thought, Bad rider.

"Now that all the creatures know we're here," I said boisterously, "might as well hold a powwow and start a fire."

"Not that we were cautious coming in," Ferris

returned, and then quickly laughed at himself. "Blast it, Wyeth. Help me catch my horse."

Ferris had dropped his rifle. He retrieved it and blew snow off the pan. He refilled the pan carefully, I noticed, taking his time, but even as he did, windblown snow dusted the pan again. He saw he would need to refill the pan a second time, but not wanting to keep me waiting, he left it as it was and we started for his mottled mare, which stood thirty yards off. Ferris took several steps toward her, then considered the situation and scanned the woods to see what had startled her. He saw nothing. I looked, too. I saw nothing. He took another step and looked again and we both saw it at the same time: a large moose in snow-covered thickets not thirty feet from where we stood. It was a full grown male, taller than a horse. I could see the nubs on its head where it had recently shed its antlers. It was standing utterly still in dense shrubbery. Except for two curls of steam from its nostrils it moved not a muscle. It must have been there the whole time, but great hunters that we were, we hadn't seen it.

My rifle was on my saddle horn, a mistake I would not make again. Ferris raised his weapon slowly. He aimed and pulled the trigger, but the gun flashed and misfired. In an instant the moose burst from the shrubbery, gave a snorting roar, and charged straight at us. I leaped for my gun but my pony sidestepped and by the time I retrieved my weapon the moose was on Ferris, who swung his gun like a club. The steel clattered on the beast's forehead without effect, and Ferris was pitched out over the bluff.

"Pauline, you devil!" I heard him shout as he tumbled down the bank.

I aimed to fire but the moose was already in some shrubs. It came into sight again a hundred yards off as it cut down the slope to the water. I ran to the edge of the bank but it had vanished from sight. Ferris's rifle had slid out ten feet and was lying on thin ice. Ferris stepped out after it and broke through the ice up to his knees. Meanwhile, far down the bank, the moose arrived at the riverside and turned back, gangly legs churning white ice chips, heading straight toward Ferris, who was stuck with wedged ice in the shallow water. The moose was blasting right toward him along the edge of the river. Fifty yards away. Then thirty.

"Good God," Ferris said, reaching for a branch to use to defend himself.

The enraged creature was twenty yards off when I fired. It was a good shot. It was not a hard shot. But I did manage to hit the thing. The beast toppled forward, cracking the ice in shallows ten feet from where Ferris stood knee-deep in frigid water.

"What corncracker said it was an elk?" was the first thing Ferris said, laughing.

"I believe it was Peggy."

"The damn corncracker," he said.

His voice was steady ten seconds after I fired.

Ferris dislodged his legs from the ice, retrieved his rifle, and laughed at himself.

"Lost the horse," he said. "Filled the horn in snow. Damned careless. And then scrambling over that ice. I must have looked like a fool."

"You did not look like President Adams," I said.

"Man of the Wilderness, western trapper, Walter Ferris, trampled by a moose two miles from the fort. The great hunter!"

"We both missed the moose sign," I said.

"Real booshways," he said derisively.

"The heirs to Lewis and Clark and General Ashley," I said.

I thought Ferris would make some excuse for what had happened. He didn't. He just laughed and went on deriding his own carelessness.

Well, you misjudged him, I thought. Might as well admit it. He's a fine fellow.

We dressed the creature and took what sustenance we could and left the rest on high tree branches. An hour later, with just a blue light on the rim of the snowy world, Ferris and I rode back across the lowlands toward the encampment. I think we both thought we were able hunters—greenhorns, to be sure, but not incompetent—and we'd almost been done in by a moose two miles from the encampment.

"Obliged for that shot," he said as we rode in.

"Not at all," I said.

He didn't mention it again and I didn't mention it again, but I'd shot the moose as it charged at him, and he'd thanked me for it. That was enough.

We rode on through the purple light with the sterile beauty of the icy mountains to the west and the stillness and vastness of that land resounding inside us.

We spent that night in the makeshift commissary, telling of our hunt. Ferris reveled in the ridiculous aspects of it, and the veteran hunters laughed and stomped and slapped our backs so we almost fell over, and I understood that we'd stumbled upon the best method possible of gaining acceptance into the brigade. With the veteran trappers, nothing could be more persuasive than to risk our lives needlessly and revel in our ignorance.

Ferris, as it turned out, was not some mincing dandy but an entirely good-natured fellow and a natural outdoorsman, interested in all the people and creatures and industry of the west. During the long idle hours that winter I told Ferris of my unfortunate parting from my father, and he told me how he had also shattered his father's hopes, leaving a physician's apprenticeship behind, though, being a more even-keeled fellow than I was, he did it with his father's grudging acceptance. We spoke of our mutual admiration for the western mountains and bragged of the magnificent lives we'd lead once we returned and of the fortunes we'd command, and in general made asses of ourselves. Several years later I would have a withering view of our blown-up expectations, but as I grow older I scoff at these romantic sentiments less and less. It is the yearnings of boyhood that add flavor and dash to a life that can very quickly lower to necessity. But I do not want to speak of this lowering. I am writing of the trapping land and of that glorious life that flamed up for a time in the western mountains, and of how, by luck, we came to play a small role in the great events swirling around us at the time.

The winter passed quickly and in mid-March, just before the real thaw, the company was split up into five brigades. Every man in the company hoped to be sent to the Bighorn Mountains, as a brigade in the Bighorn the year before had taken out ninety pelts in half a season, which was considered an enormous sum. Two brigades were sent to the Bighorn, but not ours. Another went to Pierre's Hole, and one to the eastern slopes of the Tetons. But Smith, Pegleg, Blanchard, an old-timer named Glass, Bridger, Ferris, and I journeyed south for rumored trapping lands north of the Wind River Mountains. For three weeks we rode over terrain that was not even mapped and arrived at the mountains where Ferris and I first practiced the trade that would employ us for the rest of our youth.

I do not mean to go into all the particulars of the trade, as the catching and accumulating of the pelts would make dreary reading and is only superficially connected to my story. Suffice it to say that we learned to sleep out on buffalo robes and to eat only what we killed and to wake at night and stand sentry and watch the darkness and listen to it with our weapons ready. We learned the different kinds of silence: those that held danger and those that did not. We learned the various methods of trapping fur-bearing creatures and came up with our own recipes for castoreum. We learned to flesh and prepare the furs so they would not spoil. We learned how to build a cache. In short, we learned the job of the western trapper—perhaps not as well as the veterans, but adequately and with what energy we could muster, and we had a fine time of it.

In mid-June, near the end of the spring season, after three months of industry, Smith, Pegleg, Blanchard, Glass, Bridger, Ferris, and I were gathered on an east-facing slope at the southern edge of some high, snow-covered peaks, surveying a group of thirty natives riding across the lowlands. We had been watched by natives sentries, seen their villages from afar, and had noted the location of their trapping parties, but we had not had any close encounters with the natives since our visit from the Crow the previous winter. These natives were dragging lodges and moving with many horses, and from our hidden spot up in the mountains we could see they were converging behind a low hill. Much dust was raised from behind that hill but we could not see the gathering spot. In the spyglass we could see dogs and children dashing around the ponies.

"Don't look like a war party," Pegleg said.

Bridger nudged Glass, nodding toward Pegleg. "I know what he's thinking."

Pegleg stuck his thumbs in at his waist. "Whatta you say we go down there and see if there's any squaws looking for conversation with a gimpy old trapper?"

"You willing to get scalped for the opportunity?" Smith said.

"I'm willing to risk it," Pegleg said cheerfully. "Dragging lodges and bringing the pups. That ain't no war party. Maybe we fill out our map on the drainages to the south. Whatta you say, Captain?"

Smith watched through the spyglass again. Despite the fact that he carried a Bible, which would have been considered a sign of weakness in another man, he was thought to be the bravest and most reliable captain in all the west. We waited for his verdict.

Smith collapsed the glass, unpicketed his horse,

and said, "Guns on the pommel. We see anything we don't like, we make a dash for the hills." Then turning to Pegleg: "And if you meet any squaws they don't come back to camp."

"Of course," he grinned. "Won't take long for Old Peggy."

In that region the higher elevations were tree-covered but the flatlands were scrubby and arid, and as we moved down the slopes we emerged out of the tree cover and onto barren hills. The natives did not change their bearing or speed when we showed ourselves. We rode on down to the flats and a brigade of French trappers, riding down the same slopes, veered when they saw us and joined our party. We all went on together, fifteen of us now, and eighteen horses. We rode across a salt pan and onto alkali flats where there were many white-rimmed pools of clear water with black pollywogs and translucent water bugs wriggling inside. We reached the small ridge that had blocked our view of the gathering and when we crested we saw, spread out beneath us, at least two hundred white-skinned lodges with fires in front and smoke racks set up, and Ferris, who could tell the natives from their accoutrements, scanned the gathering, and said, "Crow, Mandan, Hidatsa. Even a few Gros Ventre, I think."

On the north side we saw what we thought were white trappers around two large fires, entirely unmolested by the natives.

"Ain't no war party," Pegleg said. "Got the whole Indian nation here."

We picketed our horses, and for the next three hours Ferris and I wandered through the encampment, Ferris sketching arrowheads and moccasins and shields and dresses. We met or at least saw many of the famous native chieftains from that time—Raven's Beak, who was carried around like a pharaoh on a wicker chair, and Long Hair of the Mountain Crow, whose hair, when it was unwound, reached eleven feet and was like a bridal veil. We saw Red Elk for the first time, a Blackfoot leader who was traveling with the Gros Ventre. Ferris thought there must be some temporary truce if Red Elk was in that encampment surrounded by his enemies, and I made a point of studying the man, as he was known in the mountains as being the most clever and savage of the native chieftains.

Red Elk was five foot eight and stocky rather than lithe, with no native artistic flourishes on his body. He carried a wooden cudgel and a Northwest trade gun and was accompanied by eight or ten arrogant men, who paraded and bragged and jostled their way through the other natives, but I noticed Red Elk was reserved in manner, and rarely spoke unless he was spoken to. He struck me as a cautious, stern man, not given to sociability or jesting, and mostly avoided by the other natives.

By mid-afternoon we'd left the encampment, and all the men, native and trappers alike, had spread out in an enormous ring around some white, clayey hills. Ferris, Pegleg, Bridger, and I were waiting with a mulatto named Moses Branch, who had wintered with the Crow and had casually agreed to sign on with our brigade as a translator, trapper, and scout.

Branch was six foot three and all sinew and muscle, a marvelous physical specimen. He dressed like a native with feathers dangling from his beaded hair, but he spoke in a half-cultured St. Louis accent, and could read and write better than most of the men.

As we waited, Branch twirled and caught his Sheffield knife and threatened to roast a weasel that Bridger was trying to tempt from its den. I sat back on an elbow and recorded my observations. Ferris sketched.

After an hour idling, there was a high keening from the direction of the encampment, like a coyote's yips. We stashed our personals and leaped onto our horses. A moment after that there was a second keening and in an instant, all of us, at least a thousand men, started up the white hills on our horses.

As we crested the highest of the hills we saw that the land to the north was as different from the alkali plains as Ireland is from the Sahara. Below us was a lush, grassy lowland, ringed by higher ridges, and in this lowland there were at least five hundred buffalo, unaware until that moment that they were surrounded by a thousand men on horseback in a giant, converging ring.

As soon as the buffalo came in sight the natives began bellowing and caterwauling and a few fired their weapons. The buffalo leaped up and in an instant dashed off with a deafening thunder that literally shook the earth.

At the far end of the valley, a few miles away, there was a second herd of buffalo almost as large as the one we were chasing, also trapped inside the ring. We could see this second herd, tiny wavering dots against green hills, moving silently toward us.

The two groups of buffalo, the north and south herds, converged slowly, and after five minutes the two herds arrived on the same grassy plain. When the group of buffalo tried to turn, a pistol was fired. The men shouted and jeered and waved their arms. The buffalo ran on, the two herds nearing each other. They were a hundred yards apart, then fifty, then thirty, and then . . . a shrieking and grunting and shaking of the earth as the huge creatures struck one another. Beasts were sent dashing in every direction, spinning out, swirling, in a living, dusty explosion. Pegleg, Bridger, Branch, Ferris, and I, trying to keep ourselves equally spaced, charged toward the point of impact. A small herd of buffalo spun off in our direction. Thirty bulls. Gigantic, lumbering beasts, bearded, black-eyed, horned, the size of small elephants. The creatures tried to veer but were penned in by other beasts coming behind. Pegleg was at my side. He raised his weapon and, as he rode at full speed . . . Bang! He fired. One of the bulls in front of us fell and the charging beasts turned at the last moment and charged back in the direction they'd come.

Hundreds of arrows were flying and rifles were detonating and flickering all up and down the line. I raised my gun and entered a chaos of men and beasts and dust and smoke. I could hear voices in many different languages, yelling and cursing and crying out. Beasts swirled around us and among them men were shooting and spearing and hacking and stabbing and slashing. A desperate native with a broken arm, on foot, dashed about among the beasts. I made a grab for him but he was swept away.

A minute later I found myself on the crest of a low hill. I realized I had never discharged my weapon. Beneath me, in all directions, the bulls were rearing and snorting and charging off, pursued by natives and trappers alike. Men tagged the skins of dispatched buffalo with slashes from their blades, then aimed their weapons at the countless wolves that had slunk into the killing fields. In all directions women were gutting and skinning the great beasts. I saw Red Elk disputing with one of the Gros Ventre who apparently believed the bull Red Elk marked to be his kill. I saw Red Elk finish marking the beast then turn and very calmly smack the Gros Ventre across the skull with his cudgel. Afterward, the Gros Ventre lay alongside the beast, unmoving.

In another direction, near a shrub-lined drainage, a short, squat trapper with a handlebar mustache paced about a buffalo that had so many arrows sticking from it that it resembled a porcupine. This was a free trapper named Max Grignon with his companion Bouchet. The two were trying to provoke the injured beast into chasing them. Bouchet grabbed its tail and Grignon was jabbing its side with a section of spear he'd found. When Grignon stuck the blade in, the poor creature writhed and finally, after repeated jabs, rose weakly and lumbered after Grignon, the many arrows rippling and sending streams of blood down its thick pelt. Bouchet was dragged behind in the dust by the tail, laughing in a high-pitched tone. The buffalo stopped after only a dozen yards and made a halfhearted effort to dislodge Bouchet, then collapsed, blood pouring from the innumerable arrow wounds. Grignon walked back to the beast, looked it in the eyes, placed his pistol against the creature's head, and fired.

Ferris had taken refuge near me. I noticed he also had not joined in the hunt.

"Waste of meat," he yelled out over the sound of shooting.

"But a glorious hunt," I said.

He did not comment. I saw he did not agree. He did not think it was glorious. He thought it was a useless slaughter. A part of me agreed, but I was not indifferent to the hunt, either. I could not be so close to the men engaged in that sport and not want to join in. Everyone, it seemed, had gotten their bull. I had not. And a feeling of absolute misery quivered inside me.

Nearby, a young bull was flushed from a dense patch of foliage, and I was off in an instant, up the side of a nearly vertical hill, pursuing the bull.

As we neared the crest of the rise I let go of my reins and raised my rifle to fire. Just as I did the bull veered back toward me and I thought it odd for the creature to turn back after fleeing so desperately, but understood after a moment that there was someone coming over the rise on the other side. I thought I ought to lower my weapon, and then I thought, No, I have chased this beast. This one is mine. Let them lower theirs.

I kept my weapon raised, and just as I was about to fire I saw that it was Bridger coming up over the rise. Either the jolting of the horse or my own ineptitude made me shoot low. At the same instant Bridger shot. The bull was at the same height as his gun. If he'd hit it, all would have been well. He missed. I was close enough to see the blanket wad come from Bridger's muzzle. At the same instant I was thrown back and the world slowed and stopped. The smoke from my discharge hung overhead. A calmness and resignation flowed into me.

I am slain, I thought.

I felt my body hit and roll and wrench across the clayey soil.

The next thing I knew I was being dragged over grass by Pegleg who had a bloody piece of flesh stuck in the waist of his leggins.

"Gimme your paw, Wyeth, you ain't a virgin no more. Help me, boys."

Glass bent to one arm. Bridger, who was bleeding from the head, grabbed my legs, and was almost bawling.

"All you did was gutshot him," Pegleg said. "Now if you'd hit him a little lower he'd have room to complain."

They set me on a buffalo robe. My gut and my legs were wet with blood. I tried to sit up but could not. I was strangely chilled but felt little pain. Bridger knelt at my side, gape-mouthed, with a sad, dumb, cow-like expression.

"How are you, Wyeth?" he asked. But before I could answer, Ferris arrived, jerking Bridger away and shoving him to the ground. I believe he would have stomped on him but Branch stood between them.

"Vanish," Branch said to Bridger.

Ferris knelt next to me. "How do you feel?"

"Never been better," I said faintly.

I felt cold water splash my gut and something squirming at my side—black tadpoles flapping. That was Pegleg, who'd brought a hatful of water.

"Wash without the fish," Ferris said in a derisive tone that was not normal for him. A while later I felt the pressure of Ferris's hand gently prodding my stomach, pushing something in. A sort of faintness welled as he did it. And then I did faint.

When I awoke there was a native staring down at me, holding a wooden cudgel with a little hair on the end. It was Chief Red Elk. He stood over me, feathers dangling off the braids of his hair, sweat streaks on his cheeks. I thought perhaps he'd come to watch a white man die, or to cudgel me. But he did neither. He just stood there looking down at me and after a moment he turned and wandered off without a word.

Ferris was returning with Pegleg waddling behind him holding a glowing iron ramrod from a military rifle. Ferris knelt next to me and pressed my hand.

"Turn away, Wyeth."

"What?"

"Look somewhere else."

I turned my head. I had a view of the grassy lowland where hundreds of dead buffalo were spread, some of them skinned. Thousands of vultures and magpies flapped about and pried at the innards, torn red nastiness in their beaks, leaving trails of drippings across the grass. The unskinned beasts, huge red lumps of gore, attracted masses of skittering wolves that slunk about the fires and smoking racks.

Ferris wedged a doubled halter between my teeth, and then, without warning, Pegleg stuck the glowing iron into me.

I woke again to the sound of wood creaking and willow branches being bent near my head. I had been moved to the riverside.

"You're still alive after Pegleg doctored you?" I heard Captain Smith say. "That's a first."

"It was the greenhorn Ferris that did it," Branch said. He had the deepest voice in the brigade, so I knew it was him. "Plucked a two-inch strip of deerskin that had been blasted from his shirt into his gut. Sewed him up like a moccasin."

Ferris hovered over me, bathing my wounds in salt water and wiping a salve of oil and castoreum over my gut and then covering it. By the way he did it I could tell he had done it many times before and I remembered he'd grown up assisting his father at medical procedures.

A gourd was pressed to my lips and I drank. Bridger stood nearby with a forlorn expression. He was a bighearted, sturdy fellow and I thought I ought to forgive him before I died, but then I was asleep and there were bizarre memories of early childhood with the looming shape of my father and a wavering prism light on a wall. I must have slept through a day or several days, for the next thing I knew it was daytime again but the sun was on the other side of the sky, and I was in a boat. With my head turned I could see a pack of pelts wrapped with deerskin with the word gentry written in charcoal on the outside and I thought it must have been prepared by Sam Gentry, a trapper from Ashley's Hundred of 1823. I remember considering this. Sam Gentry. I had heard he had a cache in the area we'd been trapping, and I thought they must have unearthed the cache while I slept and meant to transport it.

When I woke again I was on the shore of some wide, shallow, braided river. A gourd rested near my head with twine wrapped about the neck. I shook the gourd and heard water in it. I lay listening to the riffle of water two feet away but I could not sit to drink and could not pull out the stopper though I practically wept with the effort. When I woke again rounded river-bottom rocks slid across my back. Pemmican had been placed in my mouth and I was chewing. A gourd was pressed to my lips and I drank. The river had broadened and was swifter. I could feel it carrying us along. I heard water splashing. I gathered my forces and tried to sit. Ferris appeared overhead, holding a wet, roughly hewn oar.

"So you had a mind to pull your weight for once," he said.

"You're one to talk," I said weakly, and that sent the men cackling.

"Is Bridger here?" I asked, and when I heard he was I tried to sit up to forgive him for shooting me but did not have the strength.

"He's coming for you?" I heard Pegleg say, and that sent men all up and down the river guffawing again, happy as children because I was alive and talking.

I could hear swallows chittering and, momentarily, saw their dark, curved shapes as they cut and soared overhead in the patch of sky above me. There were hoots and calls all up and down the river, men wishing me well, telling me to take a paddle, and I understood that Smith had ended the spring season early and allowed the men to carry me back to safety. It must have been a blow to the business side of his arrangements to let them scatter like that, but no matter, that was the trapping life.

My father had predicted I would die a lonely death in a desolate spot with low companions, and he had almost been proved right, but it was these same "low companions" who were going seven hundred miles out of their way to save me. And as I lay there and listened to the swallows chittering and the cheerful men calling to one another from boat to boat and felt the smooth river-bottom rocks slide against my back, I knew I was in the most beautiful country on earth and in the care of the most lively and good-natured companions a man could ask for, and that I'd done the thing up to the hilt, like I'd vowed, and that despite my father's predictions, I was alive.

BOOK TWO
The Settlement

Fort Burnham was a U.S. Army encampment just upstream from the juncture of the Missouri and the White River. The fort had ten-foot-high palisades and four-pound guns and room for two garrisons. Inside the palisades there was a blacksmith and commissary and a powder room, a hospital, and a storeroom with fifty sacks of grain and enough sustenance for the entire company for nearly a year. In 1827 eighty men were stationed at the fort on eighteen-month tours of duty. It was considered a hardship to be stationed in that desolate stretch of country where there was little hope for conflict or possibility of advancement, far from civilization and also far from the trapping regions. The soldiers spent their time farming and clearing land and improving the settlement, which was originally called Fort Burnham, and later, when the fort was moved five miles downstream to the juncture of the White River with the Missouri, and the town overgrew the garrison, the settlement was called Smitts Bend, as it is called today.

The garrison of U.S. soldiers, which was under

General Burnham's command, lived in the original fort at the very high point of the ridge that ran up the middle of the loop of the river. Half a mile beyond the settlement there was an infirmary for natives dying from smallpox, an illness that had ravaged the easternmost tribes and would sweep across the entire continent, decimating the native populations. There was a half-mile stretch of prairie, a barrier between the sickness and the town, and then a few square blocks of low wooden structures with wood-shingle or sod roofs, containing a general store and a dry goods store and little cottage houses with hardened mud between the logs, all with very thin, translucent deerskin or cloth in the windows instead of glass. Many of the cottages had half sunk into hills and were little more than caves with earthen roofs. Though this settlement would be considered paltry now, it was the only "civilization" for five hundred miles.

The doctor at the fort, Isaac Meeks, was a tall, stooped, awkward man with bifocals and a protruding Adam's apple, a scratchety high-pitched voice, and a broken thumb that had healed incorrectly so he had imperfect usage of his left hand. Meeks was a nervy bore around women, but he had a marvelous curiosity about everything in the west, and was wonderfully concerned about the natives and their sickness. Two or three times a week Meeks walked to the infirmary where foreign nuns cared for natives who were dying at an astounding rate, dying of mild sicknesses that hardly affected the whites. The doctor treated the natives as human beings, an attitude which set him apart from much of the settlement. He tried poultices and bleeding and quinine and even the sweat lodges and medicine men. Nothing worked. The natives grew sick and died and it cast a shadow over the good doctor's life, though some at the fort seemed to consider the death of the natives as good riddance or even God's judgment.

It was the summer of 1827 when I arrived at the settlement, wounded and near death. The men secured a lodging for me with Smitts the innkeeper and assured my care with Dr. Meeks, extracting a promise from me that I would join them on the spring hunt, not adding "if you survive," though I am sure this was in their minds. They started back the seven hundred miles toward the trapping lands and I was left to my sick bed.

I do not remember much of my recovery, as I was wracked with fever for weeks, but as it turned out, I did live, and within a month I was out of danger.

During my recovery I lived in a one-room cabin next to a dry goods store, paying for everything with IOUs and treated like a rich man, as Ferris and the others had greatly exaggerated the size of our returns, hoping to assure my adequate care.

Once I was healthy enough to move about,

Smitts did everything to keep me in the settlement rather than have me and my supposed riches move on to St. Louis. I enjoyed the luxury of sleeping as late as I wished and riding leisurely out to set traps in the nearby creeks and lowlands. I trapped the White and the small braids of the Missouri, and hunted in a loop of the great river, which made an enclosed hunting grounds. Each night I played a sort of billiards on a rough pine board with Plochman, the owner of the general store. The talk in the settlement was always of the encroachment of the Brits on American land and the greediness and devastation British brigades left behind, and the worry that the only thing standing between St. Louis and the British Empire was the garrison at the fort and a few trappers.

Apart from playing billiards with Plochman, I spoke almost daily with General Burnham, who was eager to extract every bit of information from me about the land and the natives to the west. He was always peppering me with questions, asking me if I'd seen this or that tribe, and how I distinguished one tribe from another at a distance, and how many poles they used in their lodges, what sort of wood and fiber they used, how many feathers in their arrows, what kind of horsemen they were, and whether they carried firearms, and if so, of what sort, and if I'd worn their moccasins, and if not, if I'd seen them, and how they compared with some other tribe's moccasins, and a thousand other questions of that sort, most of which I hardly knew the answers to. It seems strange to me now that the man who seemed most appreciative of the natives and their way of life was the one who was out there to wage war against them.

I was injured in June. By late August I was completely recovered. I could have returned to the brigade but I did not, and at the time I said I was still too weak to travel, but it was lassitude and not weakness that kept me in the settlement. Every morning I'd set a few traps, and then wander down to the river and wash myself, spending hours in the roiling, sandy water. I'd clamber out stiffly afterward, hopping from foot to foot in the soft mud, letting myself dry in the sunlight, then stepping up steep bluffs through tall grass and wild onions to view the tan-colored grasslands spread out in all directions.

I am recovering, I told myself. That is why I cannot return. I'm still too weak.

It was only gradually that I understood it was not a physical injury I was recovering from but, to my shame, a mental one. For weeks after my physical recovery, in the hot, dry days of late summer, I reconstructed the moments leading up to my injury. I was pursuing the young buffalo up the steep hill. I was waiting to shoot and then I saw the blanket wad come out of Bridger's gun. I hit the clay and was jolted. The event repeated itself endlessly in my mind, as if I was trying to discover a flaw in the memory, until in the end I understood that I was grappling with the realization that I had almost died and someday I would be dead. That was it. That was the length and breadth of my great realization. I was not immortal. I would die someday. My youthful mind could not quite comprehend it.

It took me about six weeks to understand and to overcome this sapping lassitude, and by then it was too late in the year to join the brigades for the fall season. Regardless, by that time I had found something else to divert my interest, and that was probably the best remedy of all. I have found that questions about death are never really satisfied with the intellect, but they can be neatly conquered by distraction.

I had been in the settlement for six weeks and was making my first visit to the infirmary. Smitts and Plochman would not even allow natives in their stores, yet the young soldiers were constantly visiting the infirmary, as all had heard this unlikely structure held the settlement's only real attractions. There were the nuns and the nuns' Italian and French helpers and a woman called the Widow Bailey who excited much speculation among the young soldiers.

The native infirmary was half a mile south of the town, in a long, low structure built into a hill with a rock chimney at either end. The shutters were kept open during the summer, and the two wings of the infirmary were connected by high walls, making a rectangular courtyard between them. The walls of the courtyard had doors embedded into them that allowed children to enter and exit without being exposed to the illness.

On this day, August 1827, I walked south along the top of the bluff, crossed the high point where the road dwindled to not much more than a path, and walked down toward the double-winged building where the sick natives were cared for.

I heard moans and murmured native dialects and the clink of cupping glasses inside the infirmary. I entered a long, low room with makeshift cradles made from straw baskets. On the east side there were pallets with impossibly skinny natives, some of them asleep, others hacking into tubs of murky water. Scalpels were tossed into porcelain basins. There was the smell of chemicals and death. I tipped my hat to Dr. Meeks, who said, "You shouldn't be here, Wyeth," and I agreed with him as I furtively surveyed the room's attractions.

I ducked through another low door into a courtyard where native children sat in rows in a sort of classroom. A woman in European clothes scratched at the dust with a wooden stick. She was drawing the letter C with the stick and the children were drawing with their fingers or small twigs in the dust.

"*C* is the third letter . . . *C*," the teacher intoned.

She had a French accent, and dark hair cut short and pulled back with a wooden clamshell that gave me a strange feeling. Then there was a flip in my mind, a kind of vertigo. I realized the teacher was Alene Chevalier, the Canadian tanner whom I'd conversed with before I left St. Louis. She was dressed in black and wore work boots that were too big for her small feet and her skin was so dark from the sun that I had mistaken her for a full-blood native.

She saw me in the doorway, let out a brief shout, but recovered almost immediately. "William Wyeth. Upright and interrupting my classroom," she said.

"My apologies," I said, and stood there grinning foolishly, not able to contain my happiness at finding her there.

She motioned for me to go, which I did, but only after she assured me she'd follow in a moment. She went on with the stick, scratching in the dirt. "*C* . . . the third letter is *C* . . ." I walked back through the infirmary and out over the hard-packed dirt and waited near the path.

I was grinning and pacing back and forth with all manner of hopes and fancies surging inside. We were hundreds of miles from St. Louis and I'd been in that settlement more than six weeks and somehow I had not seen Alene or known of her existence there. I realized she was the woman they called the Widow Bailey and was in black because she was in mourning.

My mind went back to the last time I'd seen her and how she'd stood in front of her cottage with Henry Layton and Horace Bailey.

Blast the dandies, I thought. She must have married that pork-eater Bailey.

I stood there, piecing this together, while a few natives slumped in the shade and watched me. Five minutes passed. Children straggled from the courtyard and started for the Indian camp. Then Alene came out, wiping her hands of dust.

"So, you're here," I said jovially. "The Widow Bailey."

"Yes. And I knew you were here. I came to see you during your fever. You don't remember. They weren't sure you'd live."

"And now you're disappointed that I have lived," I said.

"I was pleased to hear you'd recovered," she said in a measured tone. "I apologize. I meant to visit."

"You were hoping to pilfer my buffalo robe and moccasins," I said.

"Yes. They were such high quality." That stung a bit. "Not properly fleshed," she said. "You did it?"

"I traded with the Crow."

"You traded with the wrong Crow. Not properly fleshed," she said again.

Though her composure was in keeping with her black dress, I could not contain my happiness.

"Well, this is good luck," I said. "Not the circumstances, of course, but I'm pleased to find an acquaintance in this godforsaken place. And you . . . you're in mourning. For . . . Horace Bailey? Am I right?"

She nodded. "We were married two months after you departed."

"Congratulations."

She bowed her head. "He died four months after that."

"I'm sorry."

"Thank you."

She kept her head lowered. There was a long silence. I waited for her to explain her present situation. She did not.

"But—how did you end up in the settlements?" I asked.

"Horace joined the regiment."

I could hardly imagine that fat dandy Bailey as a soldier. I started to say about three things, then merely said, "I'm sorry to hear of his demise."

"Yes," she said. "He was forced out of St. Louis by his creditors and his father. He participated in some underhanded dealings arranged by Henry Layton. You remember him?"

"He was with Bailey the last time I saw you."

"Horace lost his considerable fortune, or at least the part that he was allowed to access, all because of that blackguard Layton. Despite his circumstances, we agreed to be married. His father arranged for Horace to become an officer, and he came out here to separate himself from St. Louis and its low occupants and to recover what was left of his good name. Now it's killed him."

She said all this bitterly.

"Was it the natives?"

"A fall from a horse. He was hunting."

I was trying to be as grave as possible and was putting on a horrible show of solemnity. Blast the lazy man, I thought. Gambling in some business venture with Layton, then having his father arrange an officership and falling off a horse and stranding Alene out in the settlements with patched clothes and dusty hair.

"And now you have chosen to stay?"

"I have no means of leaving," she said evenly. "He had only debts. The doctor has offered me an occupation. And the children need me."

"His family was wealthy."

"His family had cut their ties with us before he died."

"Because of his debts?"

"Because of me," she said matter-of-factly.

She had a quarter native blood.

"I knew his father slightly," I said. "My initial impression was of an arrogant, heartless man. Now I have another reason to dislike him. I'm sorry to hear of all this. I offer what assistance I can."

"I ask for no assistance. I will be glad for your friendship."

I could think of nothing more to say and she did not offer any word of familiarity. Slowly the position she was in settled inside me. She had taken on Bailey's rich-man's debts without the rich family to buffer her. The cuffs of her pants were frayed. She was wearing a patched winter jacket though it was summer.

"I must return to the children," she said after a moment, though I'd seen the children straggling away to the native encampment. "I will call on you in town. Do not come here again. Because of the illness." She added, "I'm glad you've recovered."

"I had until about five minutes ago," I said, holding my hands over my heart. That made her laugh, though briefly.

"I will see you in town, William. Don't be such a fool as to come again."

I waited until she'd entered the courtyard, then walked back to the settlement.

So, Alene Chevalier had gotten married to a dandy from St. Louis who'd lowered himself to take her on after losing everything else, then had gotten himself killed while hunting. I remembered how she'd cut me when Layton and Bailey were with her, and now I understood why. She was angling for Bailey and had not wanted me to interfere. She had succeeded in her venture. She'd married the gentleman, which was a wonderful match for her and ought to have secured her future, but Bailey had managed to get himself killed at the worst moment and left her without his fortune but with his debts. Now she was stranded in the settlement.

It was a comedown for her, to be sure, but it left the door open for me. I think a more compassionate man than me would have noted the possibilities of the situation, particularly as I was flush after the half season.

Back in the settlement I heard the whole story from the blacksmith Higgenbottem, a stringy mulatto who worked bare-chested and made wonderful beaver traps for a dollar less than they cost in St. Louis.

"From what I heard his friend Layton killed some ship's captain in a duel in St. Louis and Bailey acted as his second. In return Layton invited him into a land deal. Bailey signed the deal and funded it, and when it was found to be fraudulent, Layton battled in court, and Bailey, blasted by his father, did the brave thing and made a dash for the territories. The first day in he tossed two gold coins in the dirt. Didn't even get off his horse. 'Make me twelve traps.' Twelve. As if he could even keep track of half that number. On the second week some barefoot urchin from Frankfurt, Kentucky, stole a silver shaving kit. Fancy thing with his initials. Bailey demanded satisfaction. The kid could not have been more than sixteen years old. I'm not even sure he knew what he was agreeing to. The next morning they met out on the mud flats. The boy, being from Kentucky, knew how to handle a weapon. He fired and grazed Bailey's neck. Bailey fired in the air. An honorable gesture, given that he'd just been shot. Afterward, Bailey shook the kid's hand and gave the shaving kit as a token. Don't know what to make of the dandy. Throwing the money in the dust like some blackguard. Then firing in the air like an honorable man. And then giving the shaving kit. I suppose he would have turned out all right if given half a chance. In three months he had lost his gut and was learning to use his weapon. Said he was having a wonderful time. He'd gone out hunting with only a native scout and one other soldier. Had a skirmish with the Sioux. Then came across an elk and while getting after it his horse stepped in a badger hole. That was it for the horse and Bailey. The widow's a half-breed they say but she seems like a Frenchy if I ever saw one. Can read and write like any professor. She said she'd teach me."

"Imagine that," I said.

"I got no mind for it."

The mulatto doused a glowing horseshoe, sizzling, in a barrel of water.

"Four soldiers have proposed. She turned them all down. 'In mourning,' she says. Some say she's trolling the waters. I say these waters aren't deep enough for her. You have a mind to try your hand at it, I see."

"Why not?" I laughed.

"Yes. Why not? All the same . . ."

The next morning I was outside the infirmary again, ignoring Alene's advice not to visit. After some minutes of idling Alene came to the door and waved me off. She did not walk out to greet me but started sweeping up and a moment after that a mustached nun who put beaver traps around the fruit trees in the garden to keep the children from taking the apples, a nasty creature with a small, pinched mouth and a dry-looking tongue, writhed her way out to the road where I stood.

"The general warned the soldiers from coming."

"I'm not a soldier."

"Then even worse. You're a beastly trapper. She's in mourning for Sir Bailey."

"I know her from St. Louis."

"I don't care if you've known her from the cradle. There is sickness here. You think you're the first to come? Not the first. And not the most promising. And one would-be suitor already dead from the illness. I'll talk to the general. Go away. Go!"

She shooed at me and behind her Alene half seemed to protest, but not loudly. She was showing sense in keeping me away from the illness.

"I'll see you in town," I yelled.

"Good day, Mr. Wyeth," she called faintly.

A few wasted-looking natives sat along the wall in the sunlight watching her dodge my advances. They cackled among themselves and it was irritating, to say the least, but I had little choice other than to retreat. I went back to my lodgings and mulled it over. Alene was there, penniless and desperate, and for the first time in my life I had some money, yet it seemed she would not even speak with me. Given the exaggerated tales of my fortune, many women would have made up to me out of desperation, but Alene was the exact opposite. She did not want to appear to beg, and that made me all the more determined to offer assistance.

One of my father's main complaints of me was that I had no ballast, always looking off to the horizon, dashing here or there without forethought or consideration, as ill prepared as I was enthusiastic. If he had seen me that fall he would have felt that flawed impulse had borne full fruit. I went from being flattened and deflated over memories of my injury to puffing myself up in a blissful daze, drunk with dreams of my imagined future with the Widow Bailey. Gauzy schemes filled my idle mind.

Late summer now: Dry grass, and the drone of insects, and I was near the high point of the ridge, stepping up the steep drainage to the white stone bluff that overlooked the Missouri, when I saw that Alene already occupied the space. She was clearly annoyed to be caught there by herself and began moving away before I arrived.

"I'll leave you to the view," she said.

"I'd rather you stayed and admired it with me," I said in an awkward way that was meant to be gallant.

"I have my work with the children," she said.

"It is not work that sends you away. You know that," I said. "I see you struggling, Alene. There are those who'd come to your aid if you'd let them."

"At what cost?"

"At no cost."

"It is not my experience that aid comes from men without a price."

"You have grown bitter from your experience."

"I've grown practical," she said. "I appreciate your commiseration."

There was a savagery in the *commiseration*. She started to go, but I held a hand out as if I'd detain her. She moved to walk past me. I tried to take her hand and she slapped me, hard, so there was a white light in my head and a tree on the horizon passed across my view twice. She was hurrying away through dry grass. All around there was the metallic droning of insects.

"Well that's blasted," I said. "All because of fat Bailey."

I laughed to myself, falsely jovial.

"A woman of principle," I said out loud.

I walked back to town with my cheek burning and a dull resignation simmering. Up to that point I'd seen her physical attractions and understood her to be a western lady with an able tongue and fine manners. A catch for any young trapper. But that slap drove appreciation into me like a spike. I understood that her husband's death was not a mere inconvenience for her. She was attempting to mourn him and was enduring hardship honorably. My attentions were only increasing her hardship.

Three days later I saw her exiting the dry goods store carrying a tiny quantity of flour. She put a hand to her cheek with some of her past jauntiness.

"You've recovered, Mr. Wyeth."

"Barely," I said.

"I am pleased to see you're not slain," she said.

"But I am," I murmured, so low I'm not sure she heard. She paused to see if I'd tarry, but I did not. I hurried on with my heart pounding and my hands shaking and that was the model for our future relations. I began to address Alene as Miss Bailey and did not try to stop her in the road and did not idle near the infirmary.

She does not want your companionship, I thought. Most likely she never did, and she certainly does not now. She is in mourning. Leave her to it.

In my free time I began to pore over maps of the west and my mind returned to the fur country. I made preparations for joining a brigade in the spring.

Mid-fall now, and the nights were cool and in the morning, if it was clear, there was mist over the river. Several fully laden keelboats passed the settlement on the way to St. Louis and every afternoon the men would gather in front of Plochman's and discuss the encroaching of the Brits and the diminishing of fur-bearing creatures of all sorts, along with the various American trapping companies that were springing up like mushrooms in St. Louis. Often during these discussions Alene hurried past, giving a slight wave or nod, but never stopping to talk. Plochman would whisper that her inheritance had been contested by Bailey's family and that they vowed she'd receive nothing, or he'd inform us that all she bought was on credit, but despite her poverty she would not take charity. Smitts and Plochman and their wives consulted on various schemes, wondering how to help her, and one day that fall an idea presented itself to me.

Fort Burnham had no official trade with the natives like the Hudson's Bay Company had at Fort Vancouver and Flathead Post. Unlike the British, the American government, in a mis-guided effort to avoid conflict with the natives, discouraged all trade of any sort. This stricture was foolish and shortsighted, but it meant there was much opportunity for an individual in buying and selling trinkets and pelts. Many of the soldiers tried their hand at the trade but they were handicapped by not knowing a good pelt when they saw one and not having spent enough time with the natives to understand their customs. With the natives you had to be patient, smoking the pipe and spending a whole day bartering to get what you desired. Also, because of the amount of time needed to negotiate with the natives, the general discouraged the soldiers from making a side income. I knew a good pelt when I saw one, I knew the basics of tanning, and I had learned a great deal about the natives in my half season on the march. All that was to my advantage. So that fall I took up bartering for pelts and made nearly as much as I'd have made in the mountains, at a tenth of the risk and a twentieth of the effort.

All through that fall Mandan and Sioux natives would show up at my lodging in twos or threes, bare-chested and tossing furs down with disdain, demanding powder or balls or vermillion. These natives I traded with were not accustomed to our manner of exchange and did not know what was expected of them, and the pelts were often of the worst quality and close to unusable, though they'd act as if they'd just brought me a king's ransom. There was always much bickering about how much they'd receive and accusations that I favored Americans over the natives. I did not. At least, I think I did not. Often the natives did not care for their furs in the proper manner. They took beaver who were too young or in summer when the furs were thin, or acquired the furs at the proper time but left them out in the elements and ruined them, or scraped them too thin or patched holes incorrectly. I advised the various natives I traded with on what they could do to improve their rate of return, and a few times got Alene to speak with them, as she was known as a medicine woman among them. I thought that might have some impact on them but it did not. They'd listen silently, haughtily, and go on treating the pelts carelessly. This is not really part of my story but it seems my difficulty with this group of Mandan and Sioux was indicative of relations between the natives and the Americans as a whole. The natives took on some of the trappings of our civilization, covetous of our knives and guns and horses, but they never really took on our system of trade enough to use it to their advantage. They participated in the trade without forethought, always leached by it, never benefiting.

The fall passed. The beaver and deer pelts piled up in my room until I had somewhere between sixty and eighty pelts. That would be an enormous number of pelts for one man a few years later, but at that time I thought I'd have gathered a far greater number out on the trail, though I'm not sure this is true.

Six weeks had passed since that slap on the bluff. The first snow had fallen and melted, and a few mornings afterward there was a hard frost. The dawn was very cold and very still. Every straw-colored blade of grass glistened, white with frost. I loaded the deerskins on my pack horse and led it out to Alene's sod cottage beyond the infirmary. It was half dwelling and half hole in the earth, with the wind howling through visible gaps in the roof and a single window of untreated deerskin that let in a weak light. Hardly a lodging for a lady.

She must have heard my horse, and not wanting to invite me inside, came out with a buffalo robe wrapped around her shoulders. I loosened the straps on my pack horse and the bound wrapping fell to the ground.

"Native pelts," I said. "Deerskin. Can you tan them? I'll pay you. And if you can use them to make shirts or leggins you could sell the finished product to the soldiers and we could split the profits."

"I have no paste," she said.

"I have arranged with the Sioux scouts to bring the brain paste, if you'll agree to tan them, at the normal price, with the normal quality. I have found no tanner who can preserve the hides as you did in St. Louis."

This was not an exaggeration and she knew it. I could see her making various mental calculations.

"And the willows?" she said, half unconsciously.

I had not thought of that.

"I can cut willows in the marshes and be back by evening."

"At what price?"

I thought of saying at no price and then saw her ragged clothes and the buffalo robe flapping at the door and her proud manner.

"Five percent discount."

She nodded and said, "Yes. I'll try. If I can acquire the paste." And then, after a moment. "Thank you."

"I will thank you if the quality is as before," I said, and heaved the pack and walked it through the low door and into a dirt-floored lodge where I saw bits of straw on the floor and a few chickens pecking about. There was a straw mattress in the corner and a rough-hewn table and a single candle with the drippings hardened on the round, ridged lid of a tin. I dropped the pelts near a broken wagon wheel that leaned against the wall and met her outside.

"A soldier named Gadaira will bring the materials tomorrow."

"I will start as soon as he arrives," she said faintly.

I rode straight from her lodgings down to the river to cut the willows. I made a drag like the natives did with two poles and buffalo hide strung between them and the willow saplings thrown on top bound with deerskin. I hauled the willows up from the river and dumped them in front of her cottage and did not go in to say hello and did not stop by for all that week other than to accompany Gadaira when he delivered a capped barrel that had held powder, heavy now with buffalo-brain mash gathered by one of the wives of a Sioux employed as a scout by the general. Alene wanted the barrel not at her lodging but at the infirmary, as she would do much of the work there.

I rolled the barrel through the front room and into the sunny courtyard as she'd directed and saw the willow hoops were already stretched with pelts, and the children, eager to help her, were setting the furs in the sun to dry after the soaking.

Two weeks later I came back and the pelts were stacked and wrapped and somehow compressed. The pelts, which had been stiff and rigid, were now pliable and scraped thin and smoked so they would not return to rawhide after they got wet. I paid her what she asked and no more and with no swaggering, though I admit, this was more by calculation than by lack of feeling. When I held the coins out she snatched them up and stashed them in a deerskin pouch around her neck.

"Thank you," she said.

"Thank you for doubling the worth of my pelts," I said.

Over the next week I brought her more skins and there was the usual conversation of commerce: payments, numbers of pelts, and supplies.

The next week I ventured to loan her a book. I offered *The Scottish Chiefs*, but she did not seem to think much of Porter.

"Do you have any Richardson? Radcliffe?" she asked.

"The general's wife has a copy of *Clarissa* and all of Radcliffe. I'll get them for you, if you like."

Alene tried to hide her eagerness, but said, "That would be kind, William."

Two days later I brought her a copy of *The Castles of Athlin and Dunbayne* and *The Italian*, with promises to bring others later.

She devoured these books eagerly. She was a great reader and despite her long hours of labor kept each volume for less than a week.

This exchange of books and of pelts went on all that fall, and then one day in early November she told me to stop by the infirmary. I waited several hours, then rode by when I thought the classroom had let out. It had not. She only had a moment, and came hurrying out to meet me so I hardly had time to get off my horse.

"Bend down," she said.

"What?"

"Oh, you ignorant savage. Bend your head."

I bent my head so it was near hers and she slipped a hat over my ears. It was a round hat made from a processed beaver pelt, simple but expertly made and very warm. She must have gotten the pelt from Gadaira because it was not one of mine.

"That should keep your big head warm this winter," she said.

I did my best not to smile foolishly, at least not until I was out of sight of the infirmary.

I suppose everyone knew I courted Alene with this commerce. I'm sure she knew it herself. Yet I thought little of my chances. I told myself that she was in mourning for a very rich man and that she was the heir to one of the largest fortunes in St. Louis. Despite her present conditions, I thought there was little reason for her to consider me. I imagined she found me diverting and harmless, and yet, with every interaction my feeling for her grew and my disdain for my own faint heart increased. At the time I thought another man would have at least attempted to penetrate her defenses and it was only my shrinking nature that made me delay, though I think now that this is not true. There are men who are persuasive with women, but I think these men make love to women who are ready to have that effect put on them. Alene was not ready to be courted, so my shyness was fortunate and maybe even persuasive in its own way. But just because I did not woo her does not mean I did not want to. All that time I was awash in a mixed haze of self-deception and longing, terrified that I would show my heart too openly but equally terrified that another might sweep in and conquer her while I stood back being cordial. I suppose there may have been some basis in that second fear.

A few days before Thanksgiving I noticed an expensive black thoroughbred in Smitts's stables. I dismounted and walked past the stables and on up the boardwalk and into what we called the tavern but was really just an open area with rough-hewn tables and high stools at a plank-wood bar and a few bottles on a shelf below the rafters. A man with riding boots, muddied to his knees, sat with his feet spread, and a heavy glass on the table next to a bottle of Taos Whiskey. A pistol rested on the table and a shotgun on a chair nearby. The traveler had long, dark hair and a black riding jacket of an expensive cut. I noticed he had not bothered to wipe his feet before he entered and there were chunks of drying mud around his expensive boots. The traveler turned as I entered and held a hand up and said, "William Wyeth, western adventurer, I heard you graced this lovely settlement. How kind of you to call."

By his voice and not by his rough appearance I realized it was Henry Layton, the St. Louis dandy, now somehow transported to Fort Burnham.

Layton had changed greatly in the sixteen months since I'd last seen him. He'd lost a fifth of his weight, and his smooth cheeks were now covered with a dark beard. He sat laconically, exuding a casual arrogance.

"I hear you've been keeping Bailey's widow company. Damned honorable to respect her mourning, Wyeth."

"I've respected it much more than I'd like," I said, and he laughed loudly.

"Alene will make gentlemen of us all despite our protestations. She had only started her work on Bailey. Damn the poor whapper."

"I was sorry to hear of his death," I said. "You were friends."

"Hardly," Layton said dryly. "We shared the same bottle, nothing more. We had some unfortunate business dealings that he blamed me for. Unjustly. All of the money and none of the grit. But he's dead now. No reason to speak of his shortcomings. Alene resented me for judging him honestly. I am sure you know that already."

"I do not know her thoughts," I said. "She is in mourning. We are not intimate."

"You can't blame that on her mourning," he said. "Mourning is a time for rich widows to weigh their options."

"She's hardly a rich widow."

"She will be, though not without a fight. I have

brought her correspondence from Bailey's family in which they refer to her as 'the Squaw.'"

"That was generous of you to read it."

"It *was* generous of me to bring it. Damned generous. I diverted five hundred miles to come here. And damn the misplaced morality, Wyeth. How is she?"

"She's surviving."

"I have heard that surviving is the only word for what she's doing. She is tending to sick natives, exposing herself to infection, and has gone back to tanning pelts while Bailey's sisters eat off Imari plates, bickering among themselves about which barouche to buy. She is the rightful heir to Bailey's fortune, which was considerable. There will be a scandal when my letter arrives."

"Does she know this?"

"Of course she knows it. She'd rather wallow in some obscure dust pit than fight for what is hers. I have no such reservations. Sit," he said again. He waved to Smitts. "Bring Wyeth a glass. I haven't had a conversation worth a nickel since St. Louis. I don't know what Wyeth will rate, but in this settlement he'll have to do."

I hesitated, and he added impatiently, "I was insufferable in St. Louis. I know that. Against my nature I have been forced to reform. My presence in the settlements is proof of that. I hear you have traveled the western mountains. Talk to me, Wyeth. I'm dying for conversation."

He kicked a chair out and after a moment I did sit.

"You were injured. Tell me the story. I imagine some heart pounding and gallant act. You were wounded while dashing across a desert waste and battling hostile savages."

"I was shot by another trapper while hunting buffalo. And I missed the beast before I was shot."

"Bravo, Wyeth. A truthful trapping story. We will need to amend that."

Smitts arrived with a glass and Layton poured me a drink.

"Where were you? In the Tetons?" he asked as he poured.

"No. South of there."

"Do you have a map?"

"No."

"Could you make a copy from memory?" he asked casually.

If I had not understood it by his presence there, I understood then without a doubt that he had joined the fur trade in some capacity.

"I could not draw a map with an accuracy that would make it useful," I said.

"Can you describe the land?"

"It was rolling hills. Sparse in the lowlands. Lush farther up. Snowy on top in midsummer. Three days' ride from the southern border of the Mountain Crow."

"And there was much game?"

"In the mountains, yes. But we almost starved several times in the lowlands."

"There was beaver?"

"In the high drainages but not before. It was very sparse on the way up. And it would all be much less fertile now that we have been there."

"They were great mountains?"

"Higher than any we'd seen before. Passes closed far into June."

"West of the Great Lake."

"Not so far as that."

He opened a notebook and wrote for several minutes.

"You're on your way out west now?" I said when he'd finished scribbling.

"I am."

"The season will be over before you arrive."

"I make preparations for the spring season," he said. "I have been financed by my father and he wants a return on his money. I'll give him a return or I won't return. That's my motto. Tell me, you lodged with the natives?"

"We traded with the Crow. We did not lodge with them."

"Are they openly hostile?"

"The Crow are not. Nor are the Sioux. Though you cannot leave your weapon uncharged with any of them. The Blackfoot are aligned with the British and will attack any brigade that is vulnerable and even some that aren't. The rest are opportunistic. But I traveled at the edge of Crow land for nine months and we had no battles. When our guard was kept up, we felt relatively safe."

"And what precautions did you take?"

"Never being unarmed. Two sentries at night. Picketed the horses and cached the furs when necessary. We trapped in groups of four and always showed openly that we were prepared for attack. Always assume you're being watched."

Layton made a few more notes, and at the same time, with his left hand, fingered a chunky looking pistol with a cylinder above the trigger. I had never seen anything like it. I searched for the firing pan and did not see it. Layton grinned, pleased with my interest, and slid the weapon over.

"Collier," he said. "Automatic."

He drew the pin out. The cylinder was on a spring mechanism and it popped open and fell to the side. I could see many chambers. Each contained a cap and ball.

"It's self-priming. Powder is automatically released from the chamber into the firing pan when the hammer is cocked. It can fire eight times without reloading."

"Does it work?"

"That was my question," Smitts asked. He'd wandered over and was pouring for us as he inspected the pistol.

"You think I'd have carried it out here if it didn't?" Layton said.

He pushed his chair back and slid a full glass to me. I took the glass and Layton took his and the three of us walked out back. Behind the inn were rolling, snow-covered hills with bits of tan grass sticking up and a single cottonwood thirty yards away. Layton held the gun up and fired three times—one, two, three—in rapid succession, each shot within several inches of the other. Layton handed the Collier to Smitts, who touched the barrel, then shook his hand out. Smitts aimed and fired twice and held the gun out to me. I took it. I could feel the heat coming off the cylinder. I aimed at the tree and as I put pressure on the trigger the cylinder began to turn. I released the pressure. The cylinder slid back. I put pressure on it again and again it began to turn. I pulled the trigger hard and the cylinder fired. I pulled again. It fired again. All of this without reloading. I handed the pistol back to Layton.

"Three hundred dollars," Layton said proudly.

"That much?" Smitts said with mock admiration, and caught my eye at Layton's boasting. Layton understood that he was being mocked by Smitts, and was instantly furious. Smitts stepped away slowly, seeing that it could be dangerous to tarry.

"I'll have your supper prepared when you're ready," Smitts said.

"I'm awaiting the delicacies," Layton said

unpleasantly. Then to me, as Smitts entered the inn, "I have forgotten about the lovely companionship of settlement clerks."

Layton reloaded his weapon and as he did, slowly his anger receded. I had started back for the inn, but Layton called, "Are you up for a ride, Wyeth? My time is short. Show me the sights of your vast metropolis."

"There are many wondrous sights," I said.

"Then we should begin at once," he said.

I considered refusing but could think of no plausible excuse, and so a quarter of an hour later we were mounted and moving down the sloped sides of the bluff to the flatlands at the end of the loop and then back up to the high point on the ridge with the great gray river meandering far off to the west. Layton did not know the land at all, but after twenty minutes of riding he began to spur his horse ahead of mine. He was a fine rider with that wonderful thoroughbred, but he caused himself much backtracking by assuming he knew our destination when he did not. And yet, despite this annoying quality of riding foolishly ahead when he had no idea where he was going, the dandyish parts of his personality were mostly suppressed while we were away from the settlement. Other, more favorable qualities emerged. There was a steel and strength and grit in Layton that I had not expected and he seemed alive to all the flora and fauna and the muted winter beauty of the prairie. And he did not gab at all as we rode, which surprised me. I thought perhaps his recent hardships had helped to improve his nature. But he did have that damnable quality of wanting to lead when he did not know where he was going. I judged him a capable man, but proud, and with many irritating qualities.

By the time we arrived back at the settlement it was getting dark and Layton said, "I'll be staying on for a week and then traveling to the trapping regions, where I have business to conduct."

"What business could there be in the mountains in winter?"

He did not answer directly, but only said, "You'll know soon enough. Come by tomorrow, Wyeth. We'll ride again."

We parted and I started off to tell Alene that Henry Layton had arrived in the settlement with some mysterious "business." I planned on making it sound haughty and ridiculous, but halfway to her cottage I changed my mind. I knew she'd hear of Layton's arrival and of his business, but I thought it would not be me who encouraged their meetings. In St. Louis I had seen Layton on her doorstep, and I remembered how Layton had snapped his belt hooks and said his shackles were his own.

I started back to my quarters and when I passed Smitts's lodging house I saw Layton in the doorway, bent over in imitation of an old or enfeebled man, making all the merchants in the settlement burst out in derisive laughter. I laughed, too, and despite myself, I was glad for Layton's arrival, if only for the novelty it presented.

The next afternoon as I trotted past Alene's cottage I saw her knocking icicles off the roof with a piece of wood. It had snowed half a foot the night before and the world was white and sparkling and all shapes were silhouettes against the blinding snow.

"You saw an old friend last night," she said as I rode up.

"Yes. And by the prints that lead here I know you must have seen him, too."

"Oh, yes. He graced me with his presence this morning, pretending to come for my benefit, the bereaved widow, but that did not keep him from making his own proposition."

I held a hand to my cheek. "Did you give him your usual answer?"

"I would have struck him with more than my palm if I had the chance, but he is quicker than others. And his assault was halfhearted at best. He knows what I think of him. He's a vile man. He ruined Horace on purpose to punish him for our marriage."

I gave her a skeptical look, as this seemed far-fetched even for Layton.

"Perhaps he simply meant to aid Bailey at a desperate time," I said.

"It is true he framed it in that way," Alene said. "But it was an ill-advised scheme and meant to ruin him. I am sure of it, though Horace would never have believed it. He pitied the vile fellow."

"I can hardly imagine Layton warranted that emotion."

"Horace knew him in his youth and spoke gravely of a father perpetually engaged in business and a doting, frivolous mother. The poor little prince with all he desired in the world except his father's approval. Being the petulant creature he is, when Layton realized he would never please his father, he set out to displease him immensely, which he had great success at."

"I am brimming with compassion for the poor dandy," I said, and noticed with satisfaction that Alene held laughter.

"Layton had some moderate hardships, to be sure, as have many others," she said. "But others brave their hardships stoically. Layton seems to have made it his life's work to take his bile out on the world, which I'm sure you saw yourself. I heard you went riding with him."

"I have little to complain of on that account. He has a magnificent horse and is a fine rider, though he was constantly spurring ahead when he had no idea where he was going." Alene laughed at that.

"I don't believe he's taken instruction from anyone in his life. Or taken into account another's sentiments."

She seemed to be referring to something in particular, and I said, "Did he bring you news of St. Louis?"

"Oh, yes, wonderful missives from Horace's family. Layton tells me of their meanspirited slander because he thinks it will anger me into shortening my mourning period."

"Did he tell you the purpose of his journey here?" I asked.

"Business," she said, mimicking his manner.

"Did he elaborate?"

"Not yet. But he will. Layton is too full of self-regard to keep a secret for long. And he believes any plan of his a monumental development in the world. He is preparing some venture in the fur trade. There is no other reason for his presence. Do you not agree?"

"I'm sure of it," I said.

I owed her payment for treated pelts and handed her a lump of coins. It was necessary to step close to hand her the money, and as I did I heard a distant cracking sound. The old hag who lived on the south wing of the infirmary, which was in sight of Alene's cottage, was knocking snow and icicles from her doorway in an energetic, disapproving manner, casting disparaging glances in our direction.

"You make friends wherever you go, William," Alene said.

"I don't know why I oughtn't be seen as friendly. I am not here on bended knee with roses. Tell her we are engaged in profitable industry."

"She is under the bewildering impression that there can be no profitable interaction with a trapper."

"Slander and defamation," I said.

"She has her opinion."

"And what is your opinion?" I asked.

"Trappers are admirable men," she said without hesitation. "Admirable, but who will always put their desire to wander above all else. It is an exciting life for those engaged in the industry, but an unsatisfying one for those left behind."

"But they are left behind only temporarily," I pointed out.

"But that temporary absence can stretch to years. I endured that life of waiting as a child. I will not settle for it now that I can choose otherwise." She said that last part emphatically. I felt she was telling me something and I made a note of it.

"Well, I don't plan on spending my golden years on a buffalo robe," I said. "And, anyway, the business cannot last. They say the land will be trapped out in a year or two."

"They said the same in my father's time."

"I do not know what they said in his time, but it is true now," I said.

The hag was now bashing ice in a basin.

"I am off for the lowlands," I said. "If I manage to kill a goose I will bring it to you."

"Don't trouble yourself."

"I won't know what to do with it otherwise. It will only trouble me if you refuse. I will return later," I said, and rode off.

All day I ran the implications of that conversation over in my mind. She was critical of Layton—that was certain—but I also noticed that her manner was quicker and livelier that morning than it had been since I'd seen her in St. Louis, and for the first time in the settlement she did not seem like she was in mourning.

If there had been any doubt before, I understood clearly on that day that Layton was there in the settlement for Alene and was my enemy.

Over the next week Layton brought a feeling of liveliness and wicked merriment to the settlement. It was like a piece of St. Louis had been set down in Fort Burnham with all its vividness, glamour, prejudices, and vice. The men would gather around Layton to hear him talk of his business ventures, his pranks, his feuds with various men, and his affairs with women. Men who would not spend a dime on liquor suddenly were paying for Taos Whiskey and cherry brandy. The few women in the settlement put on silk dresses because a gentleman from St. Louis was passing through. Layton seemed to be in secret negotiations with Smitts about something that Smitts appeared very eager to pursue, so I knew it must involve a large sum of money. Layton's bill at the lodging house must have made Smitts's year, as an entire entourage of mule drivers and scouts arrived three days after him. These drivers and packers were always hanging about Layton, laughing loudly at his jests, and gave an undercurrent of menace to the half threats that were sometimes laced in his conversation. One of these mule handlers was the trapper Max Grignon whom I'd first seen tormenting the wounded buffalo at the surround on the day I was injured. I will have the misfortune of speaking of Grignon further. It should suffice for now to say that Grignon was the chief mischief-maker among Layton's men, and seemed to be involved in underhanded dealings with the local merchants.

Layton's stay stretched on for two weeks and he entered into every corner of life in the settlements. I admired his energy and enjoyed riding with him, finding his conversation to be consistently lively and engaging, though there was also an undercurrent of unease inside me whenever I was with him, and an unpleasant residue remained after we parted. It was as if I sensed I was being conned, though I could not have said in what way. I found myself resisting him in my mind, a resistance that was strengthened by conversation with Alene, who at least claimed to loathe Layton above all others, though she seemed fascinated by him as well.

On the day before he departed, Layton and I sat across from each other at Smitts's lodging house, a bottle between us.

"You mean to join a brigade in the spring. Am I right?" he said.

"If I find one that'll take me," I said.

"Well, keep your dance card clear. I'll be back in late winter and we'll earn our fame and fortune together. Meanwhile, try to look after the widow. She has false ideas about me and will not take assistance if she knows it comes from me. She'll see the truth in time, but I fear it will be too late to help her. She's a fine woman. Better than Bailey deserved, God rest his soul. He was a weak-willed man."

"Will she get his money?"

"If she had any sense she'd have returned to fight and have it now, but she's afraid to be seen as profiting off his death and refuses to fight them during the mourning period. Others aren't so delicate. I will do what I can from here. But try to keep her alive, Wyeth."

I began to say it was hardly my place to say I would do anything for her, but something in the way he said it—he was genuine—made me say I'd do what she'd allow.

"Well, make her allow you to do more, Wyeth. Don't be such a scarecrow."

This was an epithet my father had used.

"I will take your example and not be," I said, and that stung him.

His temper rose, but he mastered it and smacked his hand on the table.

"Blast it, Wyeth. I will not quarrel with you." He rapped the table with the butt of his pistol. "Smitts, you blackguard. Our bottle is empty! Are you an innkeeper? Smitts!"

We had two more drinks together and made a lively time of it, and when I went to pay my bill Layton had already paid it. He was good in that way.

As I was passing back through the tavern I saw Layton handing that muttonchopped Grignon a blue envelope that I could see held money.

"Tell her it came from the Baileys and that the envelope was soaked and only the money remained. Don't mention my name. And leave before she opens it."

Layton had not said any of this as quietly as he could have, and later I understood that he wanted all present to understand that he was aiding the widow with money. That was Layton in a nutshell. He could buy you a drink and do a good deed, but he could not do it without others knowing he'd done it.

Layton left the next day and once he was gone I hardly knew what I thought of him. Some men, despite their good deeds, are a drag on the soul and dampen all humor. Layton was the opposite. Though undoubtedly a scoundrel, he made the heart beat faster and filled the air with jesting and wit and the force of his personality, and he carried in his being an undeniable spark of intelligence and life, if not goodness.

As I get older, despite the destruction such men sometimes cause, I value that spark for its own sake.

The crackle and smell of cooked fat dripping into the fire, baked apples with cinnamon, sweet potatoes and pumpkin pie, walnuts that had been brought up on the last keelboat, and bread from native flour. With the money from the furs, Alene had repaired her cottage, installing an oven with a crooked pipe going out through the roof. She'd put buffalo robes on the floor and hidden her bed behind sailcloth that she'd arranged artfully into a kind of canopy. After the renovations she'd invited Meeks and me, her two friends in the settlement, for dinner.

Meeks, that garrulous, awkward physician, seemed to have no interest in her as a woman, and filled the conversation with mixed trivialities and private fascinations. At the time I thought of Meeks as an old man, but he was only forty, and I wonder now if he was in love with her, and if he showed his affection through apparent indifference to her appearance and garrulousness that bordered on banality.

"Have you seen the buffalo herds? Magnificent. And the plovers when they flap overhead? I rode out once to see them as they passed the tip of the great loop. It took a full hour for them to go over. Wondrous sight. It darkened the air. And it reminds me. Curious thing. I was out near the native encampment and as I passed I saw our visitor, Henry Layton, conversing with the squaws."

"I'm sure it was conversing he was up to," Alene said.

"Yes, that is what I imagined," Meeks said. "Wreaking havoc among them with disease and unneeded babies. But I misjudged him. He was giving them money."

Alene gave Meeks a strange, fearful glance.

"He had gone hunting with their husbands and was repaying them with meat and coins for trivial errands. I can acknowledge an admirable gesture when I see it, even if it is done by an apparent scoundrel. He is a strange man."

"That he is," Alene said leadenly, and my heart sank. If Meeks had plotted to find a subject of conversation more irritating to me than Layton's unexpected philanthropy, he could not have come up with one.

After the meal, Meeks went out to smoke his pipe and Alene sat near me and said, "I need you to be truthful, William. Under the guise of it coming from Bailey, did you give me money in a blue envelope?"

"No," I said.

She retrieved the envelope from a box under her bed. It was the blue envelope that I had seen Layton give Grignon.

"It was this envelope. Are you sure?"

"I am sure it was not from me because . . . it was from Layton. I saw him give it to Grignon to give to you."

She kept her head down and held very still.

"You're surprised," I said.

"I wouldn't be surprised by anything Henry Layton did, either good or bad. In St. Louis he took a hundred dollars of his father's profits and gave it to some dirty girl walking the streets. Two weeks later he killed a companion over a silver pocket watch that he thought the companion had broken. Afterward he joked that his friend would be alive if he'd bothered to wind the watch after he stole it. He takes a delight in confounding expectations. I suppose he thinks I'm like that low woman, requiring saving, and that he can add me to his collection of surprising stories. Do others know?"

"Many others," I said reluctantly. I told her how it had been done in the open.

"Oh, that horrible man," she said. "And with him gone there is no means of returning it. Damn him."

She folded the envelope and slid it in her bodice, and I understood that Layton had done what no one else had been able to: make her accept charity.

"He did it with the best intentions," I said, half reluctantly, and she said, "He has only one form of intention and that is self-serving. He says he means well, and perhaps he does at the time, but there is nothing steady or consistent with him. And when he is in a dark frame of mind he is incapable of not trying to use whatever good will he's built up to his advantage. I have seen it over and over. He destroys all who are close to him. He will destroy you, too, if you let him."

I laughed loudly. It seemed an overly dramatic way to put it. "If he is such a devil as all that, undermining my flimsy character is hardly a worthwhile challenge for him."

"It is not for the challenge that he would do it."

"Why then? He's a rich man. I'm a lowly trapper. I have nothing he values."

"I can think of one thing," she said.

I opened my mouth to ask what but just at that moment Meeks came bumbling in and Alene changed the subject. I wanted to brain the poor fellow.

An hour later, as we were plodding through the dry snow with the cold stars spread out overhead, Meeks rattled on about the crane migration and the native maneuverings beyond the settlement and the growing barrenness of the trapping lands and the hope for the next summer's harvest, and I wanted to strangle him to shut him up so I could consider what had passed.

As soon as I was back in my lodgings I fell onto my bed and went over the situation in my mind. Layton was a wealthy, charismatic, forceful young man, and I thought by the lively way Alene spoke of him that she must be at least half in love with him. But then I recalled that she had said that I had something Layton wanted, and I imagined she was acknowledging her friendship with me.

I lay there with a warmth and heaviness flowing through me. She considered me seriously. I thought she did. But she was also charmed by Layton.

Snow tapped lightly on the windowpane.

As Grignon was the one who delivered the money to Alene, and as he plays a role in this narration, I will describe him more fully now.

Max Grignon was a waddling plug of a man with buck teeth that rested on his lower lip, a thick red mustache, and muttonchop sides. He wore a soiled black vest every day, even on the march, and spoke in long, elaborate sentences. His manner was peripherally formal and polite, but beneath this formality he was a cunning, under-handed, mean-spirited rogue. Once I saw him reach behind Smitts's bar, uncork a bottle, drink from it, then put it back furtively. Afterward he grinned at me and held a finger to his lips to silence me. I would not have told Smitts what I'd seen, as I do not go telling stories for trivialities, but there was no need to make me an accomplice in his petty theft, and I remember thinking he'd gone out of his way to involve me, which was the sort of thing Grignon was always doing. Like many accustomed to underhanded dealings, Grignon could not conceive of anyone acting from anything other than the lowest instincts. In short, I found him to be a wholly disreputable fellow, and my judgment of Layton lowered because of his use of this unpleasant and greedy man.

Grignon stayed in the settlement two weeks after Layton's departure, trailing mischief and discontent wherever he traveled, and then one day he vanished without a word of parting, to the relief of everyone.

Two days after Grignon's disappearance, Ferris, Glass, and Bridger arrived in the settlement. It had been almost six months since I'd seen them and they were decked out in native garb, with beaded hair and caps fringed with wolverine or coyote fur. Ferris leaped off his horse and embraced me, and laughed afterward, seeing my expression, as he smelled like a beast after hibernation.

"You were once the same, Wyeth," he said. "Let me wash and we'll split a bottle."

Ferris went to secure lodgings and took a long time in his preparations. I waited, grew impatient, and walked across to the stables where I found Ferris collapsed in straw with half a bottle of Taos Whiskey in the crook of his arm.

I helped him to his room and he slept all afternoon and it was only near supper that he rose and staggered across to my lodgings.

"Sorry, Wyeth. Was overcome by fatigue."

"And a bottle of whiskey," I said.

"Just a taste," he said. "It's the first I've had in half a year. Set me reeling."

We made arrangements to go hunting the following morning, though I only half believed he would awaken, as he was still well-seasoned when we made the plans.

The next morning I overslept, assuming Ferris would as well. When I woke I looked out my window and saw Ferris standing in the frozen road in his moccasins with a robe about his shoulders. I was up in an instant, feeling like a blackguard for keeping him waiting. Fifteen minutes later the two of us had set out for a patch of lowland to the west, where Ferris had spotted a large bull on his ride into the settlement.

Our route toward these lowlands took us on the path near the infirmary, and we passed Alene on her way into town.

"Are you off to raid the Sioux?" she called to us.

"To hunt the savage creatures," I said. "We'll bring you hump ribs for your larder." And then motioning to my companion, "This is Walter Ferris. Back from the western mountains."

"I gathered," she said, as she had heard they'd arrived.

"Pleased to meet you," he said, and reached from his horse to take her hand.

"Your companion promises me hump ribs," she said. "Do you share his confidence?"

"I have confidence that we will be lifting a bottle tonight," Ferris said. "That is the only thing I am sure of."

"An admirably cautious forecast," she said. Then, "I hold no stake in your partner's judgment, so I appeal to yours. Take care not to tarry in the hunt. The weather's changing."

"By the time it changes we'll be roasting buffalo steaks over Smitts's fire," I said.

"Or raising a bottle to our empty larder," Ferris under his breath.

"Make sure that you are raising those bottles and not out in the lowlands," Alene said.

Ferris wheeled his horse in a jaunty manner. "We'll return early. Come raise a horn with us."

"I'll need to come early if I expect to see William upright," she said.

"That you will," Ferris said. He held a hand up. "Until tonight." We rode off with unnecessary vigor as Alene was watching us, and when we were out of sight of the settlement Ferris gave me a knowing look. He had heard of Alene in St. Louis, but he had not known she was in the settlement.

"I see you continued the hunt even after you left the drainages," he said.

111

"If it is so, it has been a particularly meager sport," I said. He glanced to check my meaning, and I said, "She is in mourning."

It was a cold, clear, windless day, the snow dry and glistening. On arrival at the lowlands we did not attempt to hunt, but spread out buffalo robes and lay on a snowbank with a robe on top and one beneath, gnawing on bits of jerked meat and passing a corked gourd between us.

"You wouldn't believe who we met on our return from the mountains," Ferris said.

"Henry Layton," I guessed.

"Yes!" Ferris said. "A thousand miles from St. Louis, and he's wearing an ambassador cap. I thought I'd died and woken up on Market Street. Pegleg asked him if he had porters on the march."

"Did he take offense?"

"He knocked Peggy's hat off and said, 'Hadn't thought of porters, but I'll be glad to consider you for the position.'"

"What'd Peggy do?"

"He swung his rifle around, but Layton had the draw on him with his pistol."

"It's a Collier," I said. "Repeating. Can fire eight shots without reloading."

"Yes. He mentioned that afterward," Ferris said dryly. "Not that he'd have needed more than one bullet at that range. The rest of us were scattering, but Pegleg pretended he was only checking the firing pan."

I laughed at that, imagining Pegleg's feeble attempts at dissimulation.

"Ten minutes after turning his gun on Pegleg he tried to hire us," Ferris said. "Including Pegleg. Apparently he's forming a brigade in the spring. He says he'll pay three dollars a pelt. The others didn't believe it. I can see the three dollars if he intends to make it up on the transport. But what mountains does he imagine we'll trap? Did he tell you?"

"No. And I'd hardly believe anything Layton said. He's a damned scoundrel, though I admit he's an entertaining one. We've had some dealings because . . . his companion married the Widow Bailey, who you just met, and was then killed in the settlement last March. He brought Alene's correspondence."

I told Ferris how we'd ridden together during Layton's time in the settlement, and how, on the last day, I'd seen him give money for Alene, which she'd accepted.

"It is hardly charity if it is done in the open for all to see," Ferris said heatedly. "It's more like coercion and self-aggrandizement. The damned blackguard. When we met him in the native encampment he tossed a coin to a native boy. Some ungodly sum that I'd have gotten down to scramble for myself. He shouted, 'Water, water!' "

"What happened?"

"The boy took the coin and got the water. But he would have done it without the coin. That's the sort of thing you can do in St. Louis. Not out here." Ferris hesitated, then said, "The widow seemed a fine western lady. Was she won over by his beneficence?"

"Not by his money. No," I said. "And she seems to hold her dead husband's death against him. She paints him like he's the devil, but she's flustered when she's around him."

"And you've made your own advances?" Ferris said after a moment.

"I made an attempt. She slapped my face so I saw double."

"Did you counter?"

"I did not at first. And then"—I hesitated, remembering how she'd made clear that she would not settle on a man bound to a brigade—"I countered with . . . nothing."

"Oh Wyeth."

"What?"

"Renew the assault."

"She's in mourning."

"Mourning is preparation for marriage. The widow has tamed you."

"She has showed me my manners," I said with some heat. "And if I make an attempt and am wrong she'll think me a scoundrel."

"If you do not she'll think you perfectly respectable," he said, with derision. "She is in her ninth month of mourning. That dandy Layton will slip ahead and—"

Ferris stopped. He'd heard something. We both turned to the south where a large buffalo, up to its belly in snow, lumbered out of the pine forest. The great beast plowed forward, then stopped suddenly. It had scented us. It snorted. Slowly Ferris reached for his gun, but the ice on his robe cracked sharply when he moved and the bull bolted. In an instant Ferris and I were up on our horses, dashing through a heavy winter snow, up and down through the channels in the lowlands and out onto a windswept patch of ice that was a shallow branch of the Missouri.

Once on the ice the beast pawed and fell and stood unsteadily and fell again and wheeled as if it would charge us and slipped and fell and tried to get up and slipped once again. Ferris and I dismounted. It hardly seemed fair to shoot the beast when it was helpless like that. We watched for a full minute, but the beast merely grunted and flailed and could not move. Finally, we both raised our guns at the same time and fired. The beast lurched and tottered and stood still and Ferris reloaded rapidly and fired again. His first shot and his second were within an inch of each other, just above the shoulder, the exact spot aimed for in a bull, which fell heavily.

"Why, you're a regular green jacket," I said.

"I'd have missed the beast entirely on the third

shot," he said, though as I found out later, this was untrue. Among his other accomplishments, half of which he'd hidden from us, Ferris had the best shot in the brigade.

I heard a cracking sound out on the ice. I heard water glugging and more cracking and the bull began to sink.

"We should have waited until it was off the ice," I said.

"It's you who were hasty."

"I was hasty?"

"Yeah. You. Hasty in shooting but not in anything else," he said, and I gave him a dark look.

Meanwhile, the beast sunk bit by bit into the water. Ferris stepped off the bank and tested the ice gingerly with one foot. I strode halfway out towards the fallen beast. I motioned for Ferris to follow.

"The ice held a buffalo. It'll hold us," I said.

"You show some sense there, Wyeth."

"I've been known to," I said.

It had started to snow, coming fast at moments and then clearing suddenly with patches of blue showing here and there overhead. The low clouds moved very fast. Ferris and I walked out to the bull and stood there, far out on the ice. We could just make out our picketed horses on the bank, gray silhouettes through gray veils of snow.

The buffalo had sunk to about a third of the height of its body and then hit the shallow bottom.

Bits of dirt spiraled in the icy water. I measured the water's depth with a stick. It was higher than my boot tops. I cleared a spot on the ice then untied the binds at the base of my leggins and peeled them up and pried my boots off. I stood barefoot on the ice, hopping from foot to foot. Ferris grinned.

"How's it feel?"

"Balmy," I said.

I tossed my gloves back with my boots and edged up to the spot where the ice was cracked and then, carefully, stepped into the water. The muscles in my calves tightened and began to ache and then go stiff and numb like wood. I gripped the beast's fur with both hands and lifted my feet from the water and placed them on the thick, stiffening fur, then lifted myself up and plunged a knife in at the neck and drew it backward, wedging my feet on the bulging girth of the great beast, using all my weight as I sawed through the tough, thick pelt. The cut widened and the intestines toppled out and splashed in the water. I hacked at the hump ribs until I'd cut through bone and tossed them back on the ice. I found the gallbladder and punctured it. The green juices poured out around the blade. I cut the liver out and tossed it back on the ice with a slap, skidding, so it left a red streak and melted the snow around it and lay there steaming on the wet ice. I went for the heart—an enormous, squishy, rubbery thing, as big as my head. I cut the great vessels with a splash of warm blood around my hands. When I squeezed the heart, blood oozed over my hands and down my arms. I tossed it back onto the ice and it rolled and wobbled to a halt leaving a trail and a bright splash of red where it came to rest. I cut the choice pieces of meat from the breast. I cut out the tongue. When I was finished the ice was scattered with red gore and all around was that vast wilderness with just that spot of blood and tossed nastiness, a tiny stain in all that white world.

Ferris had started back for a deerskin on his pony that could be used to wrap meat when there was a whooshing sound. Blood and gore rained around me. Ferris slipped on the ice, but was up in an instant, scrambling. There was a native on horseback on the crest of the riverbank, a vague gray shape in the snow, lowering his weapon. I dropped into the water up to my thighs. Something splattered overhead and I heard the delayed pop of gunfire. Ferris rushed past and slipped on the ice and clambered behind the beast.

"Wyeth!" he yelled.

"What?"

"You alive?"

"I'm half frozen in this blasted water."

Over the edge of the ice I saw our horses fading into the snow, a caterwauling Indian driving them on. There were three more natives at the river's edge.

"On the bank," I yelled.

"What?"

"Three on the bank."

"I'm going to fire," he said. "When I do, get out of the water."

I heard the scrape of the ramrod as Ferris loaded his rifle. I heard the metallic click as he cocked the hammer. He was aiming. Three natives slipped behind the bank. I leaped out of the water, grabbed my gun, and skittered along the ice. Ferris fired and I saw the snow explode several inches from where the natives had vanished.

I joined Ferris behind the buffalo.

"You get one?"

"I think I scared them," he said.

We pressed ourselves to the buffalo. The ice had broken cleanly on the back end of the buffalo so we could lean against the beast and not be in the water. The ice bent as we stood on the edge but it was wedged against the buffalo's fur and did not break. I loaded my rifle.

"You wait a moment after I fire," I said. "Get them when they come up."

"Good plan," he said, not earnestly.

I pulled up to aim. Saw nothing. Just snow and the riverbank and the gore spread across the ice. Then, to my right I saw the three natives crouched in a declivity, loading their weapons. I fired and they dipped beneath the bank, and when one came up Ferris fired and they slipped back down again and then they all came up at once and fired and one of the bullets grazed Ferris's leggins. We were at a bend in the river and if the Sioux spread out far enough they would be able to get a shot from either side. Ferris reloaded. I reloaded, too. We pressed ourselves against that beast, making the most of the shelter.

"Too exposed here," Ferris said. "If the snow dwindles we'll be easy prey. We'll scramble to the embankment. You ready?"

"You can go first."

"You got the footwear for it," he said.

My bare feet were pale and bluish and looked shrunken to me. I could not feel them. Ferris gripped his rifle, then sat up and aimed.

"Go on!" he hissed.

It was snowing heavily. The bank was only a gray shadow. I turned and ran over the ice barefoot. It was like running on wooden stilts. I made the far bank and clambered up across rough ground. I threw myself over the rocky edge and while I was doing it I heard a shot. The smoke from Ferris's rifle drifted past me.

I positioned myself, peering over the bank. I saw nothing except the frozen river and the gray shape of Ferris huddled behind the bull.

"I'm loaded," I yelled.

Ferris bolted and all the while I scanned the far bank. I could see some of it clearly. Other parts were simply a gray silhouette. Ferris threw his rifle over the top and heaved himself up and landed next to me. We both put bullets in our mouths and looked out over the windswept ice and the lump of the dead buffalo. The snow came heavily for several minutes, blotting everything out, and then dwindled. We lay there, scanning the bank.

"You see 'em?" I hissed.

"No. Do you?"

"No."

"Sioux. From south of here," Ferris said. "You see the way their hair's inlaid with fur?"

"I failed to admire their coifs as they were shooting at us."

"I scoped them on the way in. It's them for sure." Ferris scanned the far back, then spit his bullets into his hand and said, "There they go."

Far off on a distant hill four natives galloped in the gray light with our horses driven in front of them. Ferris watched them then turned and looked at me. The blood was already freezing on the front of my deerskin jacket. He tilted his head and looked at the bottoms of my feet and said, "You don't feel that?"

"No."

"That's good," he said. "You don't want to feel that."

I felt a dull ache in my calf and after a moment Ferris held up some cactus spines. There was bloody gore on the end of the spines.

"You walked on a cactus," he said.

"Aw hell," I said.

He pulled some more spines out of the bottom of my feet and seemed to be shoving a few in farther so they wouldn't stick up. He looked me in the face again and said, "You're glad you don't feel that. We better cover those up."

With Ferris's help I hobbled back to the buffalo and washed my feet off and then walked along the ice to the place where my gloves and boots had been. The gloves were still there. I did not see my boots.

"Ferris," I said. "Find my boots."

"What?"

"I don't see my boots. Find them."

They were brogans, light and warm, that I'd bought from Smitts to wear in the settlement. I'd only worn them that day to show Ferris I had them. Ferris kicked around in the snow. He got down on his knees but the ice was windswept. If the boots were there, we would have seen them. We looked in the water and we looked on the bank. We saw footprints other than our own all the way up to the buffalo. I understood one of the natives must have crept up while we were on the embankment.

"They took 'em," Ferris said.

"They were good boots."

"At least you can't feel your feet," he said.

Ferris scanned the horizon then set his rifle on

the ice and stepped behind the buffalo and began working at a section of the pelt. I slid back into the water and clung to the top of the buffalo and my feet made a sucking sound as they sunk into the warm innards. Ferris cut two sections of pelt and cleaned them as best he could and tied the oval sections together with two long strips of deer hide. He wrapped the meat up and made a sort of sling that he could throw over his shoulder. All the while I had my feet pressed inside the beast. It was snowing harder and the gore was covered up now except for a certain grayness on the ice. When Ferris was finished I stepped down and stood on the sections of buffalo hide he had cut out. Ferris wrapped the hide over my feet then tied the hide off with the makeshift thongs that wrapped up around my ankle. Afterward Ferris found his deerskin gloves and put them on and I washed my hands at the edge of the water and got my gun. We were about two miles from the place where we'd been lying out earlier in the day. We'd left provisions there.

The skin that was wrapped around my feet had not been dried or cured. Ferris had bound the skin as tightly as he could, but once it froze on the outside snow worked its way through crevices. It took us an hour to get back to the place where we'd started the hunt. Our provisions were still there. Our extra powder and balls and our robes were there. Ferris got a fire going and I held my feet to the fire and when they started to warm up I groaned and tears came to my eyes. There were cactus spines wedged half an inch into the bottom of my feet and every time I bumped them I wished I was dead.

"I can leave you here and try to make it back," Ferris said. "If this is a real storm building, which I think it is, it'll be two or three days. You'll be all right with the robes and the wood and the provisions. Long as you can keep the fire going."

"And as long as those Sioux don't come back," I said.

He was quiet. He had not thought of that.

"They won't come back. Not with this storm," he said.

"The storm could end," I said.

"We could try to walk out together," he said. "Can you do it?"

"I don't know," I said.

"You decide."

"I'm not staying out here waiting for those Sioux. And you'll never make it back without me. You don't know the land like I do."

"I know it well enough," he said.

"Better we stick together," I said.

He was quiet, thinking about it. "We better get going then," he said.

Ferris made new moccasins from one of the buffalo robes. He wrapped the new buffalo-skin footwear around my feet and tied it off, more easily and tightly now because it was a treated pelt. By the time all of that was finished it was dusk. There was a three-quarter moon showing overhead and it had gotten colder. Tears from the eye froze immediately on the face. Deep breaths could be felt descending into the chest. The moon appeared and vanished many times and the clouds moved fast and low over the vast, snowy prairie. Snowflakes spiraled down among the dim trunks of trees.

We started off, Ferris carrying the provisions, walking ahead, and me walking in the path he plowed. It went on all night and over that time we said about twenty words to each other. It was only, "How are you, Wyeth?"

"Passable. You?"

"Sprightly."

And more trudging.

It cleared during the night and the hills were faintly blue with new snow. The stars could be seen down to the horizon and spread wide and vast over our heads. It was very quiet and for a long time it was still, but near dawn, the stars to the west vanished and it seemed to get warmer, and I felt sweat beneath my hat and then it was pitch black and began to snow, slowly at first and then more heavily. The wind began to blast in from the north, and we fumbled our way to the lee of two boulders and sat out of the wind in the darkness. We had hoped to beat the storm but we had not and we both thought we would have done better to stay encamped in the lowlands. Ferris's beard was completely frozen now, just a white mass in the darkness. We began to shiver and then stopped shivering and a while later Ferris stood and said, "Get up."

"We can't see anything."

"We'll freeze if we don't."

"I don't care."

Ferris leaned in, put his mouth close to my head, and screamed directly in my ear, "Get up, you stupid beast!"

It startled me. I looked at him, wide-eyed, then did what he said. I got up. But unsteadily, realizing that I wouldn't have been able to get up at all if I'd waited much longer.

We started off again. At some point the black night eased into a featureless gray dawn. We kept walking. Ferris pulled me along through snow-drifts and up and down the banks of frozen waterways. Around midmorning the snow let up and the wind seemed to die on the ground, though the clouds still moved quickly overhead. Through a part in the clouds a bar of sunlight slanted and flamed the vast gray landscape and, turning to see it, I noticed a rock pillar we called Chimney Butte to the north. I understood that we'd veered far from the settlement.

"How far?" Ferris asked.

"Four, five hours maybe."

He didn't say anything. We just turned back north, almost in the opposite direction that we'd been going.

The snow started again late in the afternoon. It stopped. We tried to keep on heading northeast. We'd get to a rise and see the chimney and adjust our course. We gnawed on frozen meat and ate snow. Ferris adjusted the weight so he had all the food except a tiny portion that I could eat as I walked. He was constantly checking on me, though it was me who guided us through the snow-covered land.

Just after dark we'd climbed a high ridge and were starting down the back end when Ferris said, "Wait," and stepped back up to the crest of the ridge that we'd just passed. He brushed his foot in the snow. He got down and was pawing at the snow.

"This is a road," he said.

"What road?"

"I don't know. A road."

There was only one road for hundreds of miles. It was four miles long. It went between the infirmary and the north end of the bluff. I told him this.

"Which way to the settlement?" he asked.

We'd come from the south so it was hard to tell if we'd walked up the east or west side of the bluff. I looked one way and saw snowy wilderness. I looked the other way. Snowy wilderness. We could see about fifteen feet.

"I don't know," I said.

"Guess."

I was pretty sure if I guessed wrong we'd die. We'd been walking for twenty-four hours. Our beards were frozen solid. It had started to snow again. We could not survive another night.

"I think we came up the back end," I said. "So this way. To the right."

Ferris turned right. I followed. I tried to keep up and could not. He waited. We started up. Again, I fell behind. I stopped. He came back and I said, "Go on."

"No."

"We're close. Bring help. Don't leave the ridge-top."

Ferris stood silently, judging if I could walk farther. After a moment he said, "Rest here. I'll be back."

I slumped in the snow and watched him walk off in that winter twilight. I closed my eyes. I was settling in the snow when I heard a far-off clink of metal. Maybe it was Smitts using an old horse-shoe to knock ice off the iron railing at the entrance to the lodging house. Maybe it was a stirrup on a metal runner of the doorstep. I only heard it once and it was very faint, but I heard metal on metal and it was in the direction Ferris had gone. I sat up. I crawled several feet then stood and staggered off in that direction. Five minutes later there was a pale glow in the snowy darkness that coalesced into an oil lamp. Then another lamp held aloft and the sound of doors opening. The distant call of voices. I saw the peaked shape of Smitts's lodging house.

"Here!" I called weakly. "I'm right here."

There was the sound of voices. Then Plochman took one of my arms and Smitts took the other. I was dragged toward the lodging house. Alene ran out with her hair uncovered and a knit shawl falling into the snow. Smitts stepped on the shawl with his snowy boots but Alene didn't notice. I knew how I must look—face frozen and buffalo gore up and down my front. I tried to say the blood wasn't mine, but my tongue wouldn't work, so I just raised a hand in mute greeting and was led into the warmth of the lodging house. They lay me roughly on the floorboards alongside the fire. Alene hovered over me, rubbing my face, opening my jacket. She cut the leather strips at my ankles and pried my makeshift boots off and I heard her gasp when she saw my feet. I reached over and she held my hands in her warm hands and blew on them, and I said, "If this is what I have to do to get to hold your hand, then, damn, it's worth it."

"Quiet, William," was all she said.

Sprawled next to me, Ferris, who'd saved my life, lay in front of the fire like a piece of wood, the ice frozen to his face just beginning to glisten.

In the morning Meeks gave me laudanum and cut into my feet and pulled the spines out. Afterward,

I slept and that evening when I woke I heard someone outside on the street yelling, "The damned crupper's going up my ass, you corn-cracker." That was Pegleg. I recognized his voice. I lay there, groggy, understanding that Smith, Branch, and Pegleg had arrived in the settlement. They had been trailing Ferris by several days. I lay back smiling and slept again and was woken by many footsteps on the cross planks.

A moment later the door swung wide and Ferris hobbled in followed by Pegleg, Branch, Bridger, Glass, and Captain Smith. Ferris had gray patches on his cheeks and fingers, but besides that, seemed to have recovered completely after only a day. I had not been inured to hardship by a full year on the march and I'd had my feet operated on. It would be weeks before I could really walk again. I sat up in bed and shook all of their hands.

"How are you, Wyeth?" Pegleg bellowed.

"Dandy," I said.

"Well, you're a hivernant now for sure. Shot up and half froze. We get you a squaw wife and you'll have gone whole hog."

"He's working on it," Ferris said.

"That so?" Pegleg said, and took a bottle from Branch and held it out to me. "Give her a horse and get on with it. You need any more romantic advice, feel free to ask."

I'd just managed to pry the cork off the bottle when Branch said, "You take as long to shoot as you do to drink I'm surprised you're alive, Wyeth. Let's hear of the battle. And give me that bottle." He snatched the bottle from my hand and tossed the cork aside, saying, "The battle and then the bottle."

"Wasn't much of anything," I said. "We shot a bull on the ice west of the bend. Shot it and it cracked the ice and sunk—"

"Should've waited till it got off," Pegleg said matter-of-factly.

"I would've but Ferris was hasty."

"He's been known to be so," Branch said, and that set them cackling, as Ferris was the most laconic in the brigade. The flask was handed to me again. This time I tilted it immediately.

"You call that drinking?" Branch said. He took the bottle from me. "Go on, Wyeth."

"I'd taken my boots off and stepped into the water and was gutting the bull when the natives stole our horses."

"And your brogans," Ferris pointed out.

"Yes. They stole my boots."

"Let's see those hooves," Pegleg said, and pulled the blanket back. My feet were huge with cloth bandages. Pegleg prodded at the bandages with the tip of his knife. Ferris stood in the corner, an arm behind the back of his neck, inhaling deeply as the tip of the knife touched the bandages. Pegleg turned and looked at him.

"You got something to say?"

131

"If I did I'd say it," Ferris said. Then, to me, "I'd have another drink, Wyeth. I think Peggy's set to go to work."

"I ain't set to do anything 'cept see how the doc's maimed him," Pegleg said. "Shame old Peggy wasn't here to help you out."

"Well, you're here now," Ferris said. "Still a chance to hobble him."

"Quiet," Pegleg said.

Pegleg knelt at my feet and I felt him snip the tied end of the bandage with his knife. Very carefully he unwound the dressings, which came away white and then yellowed and red and stiff. I winced at the tearing sound as the last strands pulled away.

"Go on, Branch. Offer him a drink," Pegleg said without looking up.

"No danger of him not taking it," Branch said, and the bottle was held out to me again. This time I took a full swallow. The bottle was taken away.

Pegleg peered at my bluish, bruised, swollen feet.

"Fine stitching," Pegleg said. "You sure old Meeks did this? I'd think he'd be talking too much to manage it. I believe you'll walk again."

"Don't know how you walked at all," Ferris said.

"I was thinking of the alehouse with its bottles."

"I don't doubt it," Branch said.

Pegleg wound the bandages back around my

feet. When he was finished Branch produced another bottle from the folds in his jacket.

"Go on. Have a swaller, Wyeth. You deserve it."

They stayed for an hour and by the time they were ready to go I was reeling. After they walked out Ferris lingered.

"I saw you groping the widow's paws when we were dragged in," he said. "Damn fine maneuvering, given the circumstance. I'd keep it up."

I put the back of my hand to my forehead. "I see the darkness closing in."

"I believe that'll do," he said. "My apologies for annoying you about her before we hunted. I could see it rankled."

It seemed like three weeks had passed since that conversation. I'd forgotten it.

"You were right, Ferris. I waste time on hesitation and trivialities and mewling about my position in society. I need to make my intentions clear and be done with it."

"Continue the assault. And whether you succeed or fail, recover quickly. I look forward to our hunt this spring."

"I wouldn't miss it," I said.

Ferris wished me luck, then departed, and I tried to get up and see them on the road but a stabbing pain shot through my feet and went all the way to my head. I held very still until the pain subsided to a dull ache. The whiskey glowed inside, fatigue crept up on me bit by bit, and I slept, dreaming of those long hours when we trudged through the icy darkness, my mind replaying the memory of that march, not, I think, puzzling over the event so much as educating myself. I had pushed myself to the edge of what was possible for me and my mind was teaching itself the limits of my body's endurance.

When I woke again it was dusk and there was a wicker basket on a chair near my head. I heard a rustle somewhere in the room and sat up.

"Hello," I said.

There was no answer. A figure rose from the gloom.

"It's me," I heard someone say.

I realized it was Alene. She was at the door. She was leaving.

"Where are you going?" I said. "I've slept all day. Stay."

She lingered in the doorway. I was struggling to sit up.

"Please, stay," I said.

She hesitated, then came over to the bed and placed the basket on the bedcover and helped me sit. There was a blue-and-white checkered covering on the basket. I pulled the corner aside and saw the end of a loaf of bread. I raised my hand to touch it. It was still warm.

"Smitts gave me the flour," she said.

"That was generous," I said.

She sat in a bedside chair and arranged the checkered cloth, and as she did, I placed my hand on top of hers.

"Thank you for coming. And thank you for the sustenance."

"You can thank me by eating it. We thought you'd perished."

"You were probably praying for my demise, hoping to take over the tanning trade."

"That was the first thing that went through my mind," she said, a little shaky in her voice because my hand was still resting on hers. I waited for her to push my hand away, but she did not. Instead, she turned her hand upright so my palm was on hers. I thought if she pulled her hand away I'd just say, "I don't blame you, shape I'm in," and make a joke of it. But she didn't pull her hand away and after a moment her fingers grasped mine. A few minutes passed in silence, without either of us moving, and in those minutes a great change was taking place within me and I believe within her, too. It was as if something that had seemed massive and immovable, an impossibly tangled problem, had suddenly shifted quite easily into a new and pleasing shape. After perhaps a minute, though it seemed much longer, I reached up and pulled her to me and kissed her. She withdrew afterward, flustered, and said faintly, "Don't do that, William."

"I've already done it," I said. "And you did, too."

"My mourning ends in three weeks."

"I think it ended right now," I said.

She tried to stand. I was still holding her hand and she was holding mine back. She looked as if she'd go but she did not go, and she did not let go of my hand. She sat back down. She started to get up again but didn't. Then she turned to me and bent and her mouth met mine.

"I'm going," she murmured. "In a minute."

But it was much, much longer than that before she left.

I was in bed for a week. Ferris visited for the first three days, speaking of the prospects for the new season, of the possibility for fertile drainages farther west, and showing me the progress he'd made in his sketchbook. He had much improved in his ability to capture the men in action, and there were wonderful studies of the pack train on the move and of men wading through streams with traps in one hand and guns in the other. There were many quick sketches of the native villages with accurate details. Even with my limited knowledge of art I could see he had progressed in his ability to capture the life and spirit of that country.

Near the end of the week, when it was clear I was out of all danger, Ferris, Smith, and Bridger reluctantly continued on to St. Louis, where they were securing supplies for the following season.

Glass and Pegleg moved into the barracks, and the mulatto Branch, who could not associate with the men of the brigade freely in the city or the settlement, rode off with a party of Mandan. After that I was free to spend every waking moment with Alene, which is what I wanted. She brought me books and fed me and read to me and pretended to tend to me, but as soon as we were alone she was holding my hand and kissing me in my bed and letting me brush her hair and draw her down to me and every day it was like some new and wonderful country was opening up a little more for both of us.

Three weeks later Alene's mourning period ended and we were officially engaged. By the way the town congratulated us, with a hint of fatigue, I could tell they were surprised it had taken so long and thought me a particularly slow fellow.

It was a "western engagement," which meant I could hold her hand, steal a kiss without reproach, and be in private with her with the door open. No one, except a few of the religious women at the infirmary, even thought to disapprove. All this was wonderful for both of us. I think some couples are meant for courtship and others are more comfortable once the initial courtship is over. Alene and I had a rough, uneasy beginning but were content with each other as soon as we were formally linked. This is not primarily the story of our love for each other, but if it were, and

I were concentrating all my meager powers of description on this great event in my life, I would not be capable of capturing how magnificent and wonderful I felt at that time, or what a monumental change it had on every aspect of my outlook and being. All who knew us thought we were a finely matched pair and saw me, in particular, as being fortunate. Alene was a strong, steady, reliable woman who would most likely receive a fortune. I had not wished for that fortune and if anything had resented it, as it meant I was the weak link in the match, though I knew if she received it I would benefit greatly. If there was any disturbance in our bliss it was not her past connection to Bailey but the unspoken prospect of the upcoming trapping season.

Alene and I had made plans to take the first keelboat out in the spring and to get married that summer in St. Louis, but she also knew that I had told Ferris I would join a brigade the next season, and in my heart, I yearned for that final season in the trapping country. I had come west to satisfy some restless craving, to sound the depths inside myself, and if I did not do the thing properly I feared I would never be content. I had pledged myself to Alene and I would have died for her, but if I did not make that final voyage there would always be a piece of me that felt I had not done the thing. Not really. Not the way I ought to have. I knew I was lucky to have joined myself to Alene, and yet I yearned for the western mountains.

In early January there was a celebration at Smitts's lodging house. It was considered the formal engagement party for Alene and me, and it was also a New Year's celebration for the entire settlement and its surroundings.

Alene wore a black cambric dress with a white ruffle and I wore a borrowed suit and tie and black boots. General Burnham gave a speech celebrating our great nation and Smitts toasted to the newly engaged couple. Then the tables were carried behind the lodging house and stacked among the heaps of snow thrown from the roof and the entire population of the settlement gathered inside for a dance, and for a few hours we were not a loose collection of ragged settlers and trappers stranded on the endless prairie but a bright hive of human activity, all dancing and whirling and stomping, a many faceted, candlelit blur. For most of the settlement it was a bright spot in the hardship and monotony of the long winter, and it ought to have been doubly so for me, as that was our engagement celebration, but I remember feeling only half involved in that dance, feeling as if I was stranded there on the edge of the wilderness but had not really entered into it.

At one point that night I walked away from the dance into the frigid darkness. It was a windless night, very cold, the white sparks of stars spread silently overhead. Natives had crept up and crouched in the snowy scrubland, watching, and I stood there watching with them, hearing the distant calling and clapping of the men and the faint stomping of feet and the *thump thump* of the drum, looking at that square of light in the open doorway. And it perhaps says something about me, and what I yearned for at the time, and perhaps what I have become, that it is not the celebration itself that I remember most but those minutes outside it, seeing this small white flame of life blazing up in the midst of that vast, savage darkness.

That was January. Three months later the spring trapping brigades began passing through the settlement, and despite my promises to return with Alene to St. Louis in the spring, I yearned to join them.

It was mid-March 1828, and from the top of a windswept hill I saw a party of riders to the south moving along the winding blue thread of the river. Later that day I walked into Smitts's lodging house to find Branch, Glass, Grignon, and Bridger sprawled on the rough-plank benches placed along the wall. As I moved to greet them two meaty arms encircled me from behind. I was thrashed about as if I were a child and thrown against the plank-wood walls so the whole structure of the lodging house shook.

"Glad to see you on your hooves again, old friend." It was Pegleg. That was the way he greeted me. "Grab yourself a horn."

I picked myself up from the floor. Ferris toasted me from the bar.

"I see you've survived Pegleg's greeting."

"Barely."

"And I hear you've made advancements in your conquest."

"I am engaged to be married," I said.

I told Ferris of our intention to return to St. Louis on the first keelboat and he congratulated me, but then said, "You will need to break that pledge and join us for a last season. We have all broken our ties to the RMC and are bound to Layton's brigade."

"Layton's!" I said.

"Captain Layton," he said wryly. "And he wants you to join."

"He is joining," I heard someone say behind me and turned to see Layton himself. I had not seen him for more than three months. He was sunburned and windburned and even more emaciated. He held his hand out, grinning.

"I hear you've successfully occupied the fortress of the Widow Bailey," he said. "Or should I say the Bride Wyeth?"

"You can say that when we return to St. Louis."

"Congratulations, Wyeth. This calls for a drink."

All this was said in an even, not particularly

jovial tone. He poured for me and said, "Ferris tell you where we're off to?"

"Not yet," I said.

"Wonderfully closed-lipped of you," he said to Ferris, then to me, "I've told others we're going north of the Tetons. As you know, those slopes have been trapped out three times in five years."

"And there's the Blackfoot," I said.

"And there's the Blackfoot," he agreed. "But we aren't going to the Tetons. We're going to the Wind River Mountains. The northern half. From the base all the way to the upper reaches."

"That's Crow land," I said.

"It's fertile, though."

"It's fertile because it's Crow land, controlled by Long Hair, and unlike a lot of the Crow, Long Hair hasn't let trappers into those hills. And when trappers have tried to go in they end up dead or running across the prairie naked with the natives firing arrows like they did to Sam Williams."

"We will not be creeping around and hiding in willows like Sam Williams. Wouldn't be possible. And I wouldn't be foolish enough to try. We'll walk in like men. I have made a treaty that will give us access to those mountains."

"A treaty with who?"

"Chief Long Hair, of course. I've just come from meeting him. The natives are in need of our aid. And we are in need of pelts. We struck a mutually beneficial agreement. There is a

Blackfoot chief named Red Elk. Have you heard of him?"

"I am aware of the existence of Red Elk as are all who have been to the west. I saw him at the surround nine months ago. I can't speak for his character, but I can say he was a sullen, arrogant-looking man and an excellent rider."

"Well, to our benefit the Crow fear him like no other. Red Elk has made an agreement with the Hudson's Bay Company who have armed him, and now Long Hair wants an agreement with us. I supply the necessary warfaring instruments that they need to fight Red Elk and in return Long Hair allows us to trap his land."

"Which drainages?"

"All of the Wind River Mountains."

"He doesn't control the entire range. Not even close."

"He controls enough of it and is in contact with those who control the rest and will bribe them with what I give him. Come see."

Layton glanced at Ferris, then walked from the bar and I followed him into a low-ceilinged hallway. Layton stood outside the door to a storeroom.

"You got the chief's daughter back there, bound up, ready to deliver?"

"I got something better than that," Layton said.

Layton opened the door to reveal shelves stacked with hempen sacks, glass jars that held honey, vinegar, and various crates. In the center of the small room sat a barrel of Taos Whiskey. Alongside the barrel were four long wooden crates. I walked to the barrel and thumped it. It was full. I eyed the rectangular crates set one on top of the other. One of the crates was pried half open and I saw brass plating inside.

"Pennsylvania long rifles. Twelve total," Layton said.

I let out a low whistle. Pennsylvania long rifles were hard to get even in St. Louis, and they were dearly expensive. I pried one end of the lid up and pulled one of the rifles out. Forty inches long with the wooden ramrod beneath the barrel. Beautifully crafted and perfectly balanced. I felt the rifle's heft and sighted with it, felt how the weapon rested neatly against the shoulder. I lowered the rifle, slid it back in the crate, and hammered the nails back in with a stone that stood behind the door.

"The whiskey. The rifles. Powder. Twelve bullet molds and lead. A few other gewgaws like mirrors and vermillion. My whole fortune right here," Layton said. "The Market Street Fur Company. This is your chance, Wyeth. If you enter right now as an investor I'll give you a percentage of the returns."

"How much of an investment?"

"Three hundred dollars. For that you'll get six dollars from your cut of the pelts and we split the cut of everyone else's and you get fifteen percent of the profits. Ferris did it. You could do it, too. Then you come back not with eight hundred or a thousand dollars but three to five thousand. Plus your stake in the company."

I had to bite my lip to keep from laughing. "Those are entirely unrealistic calculations, Layton. Not that it matters. Alene and I are returning to St. Louis."

"Those are your plans," he said. "Alter them. Send her back where she belongs. Take the last boat out in the fall."

"I wouldn't make the last boat out in the fall."

Layton gave me a skeptical look.

"Then tell Alene you'll be back in the spring. Extract a promise from her to wait for you, then send her off to St. Louis and meet her when you can. We have a chance to profit from the last untouched drainages in the west. A chance that will never come again. You can make your fortune and return like a man and not some pauper hoping to profit off Bailey's death."

"I am hardly hoping to profit off his death. You are speaking of your own intentions, not mine," I said.

Layton's eyes grew dark, but he mastered his anger. When he spoke again it was in an even tone, and offhandedly.

"I'm not talking about your motives, Wyeth. I am stating how it will be perceived by others. I am offering you a chance to blast that perception with six months of labor."

"It's eight and not six months. And at least three months of travel."

"Nevertheless, Wyeth, this chance won't come again. You know that as well as I."

I was quiet. My eyes strayed to the crates.

"What'll keep the natives from turning those guns on us?"

"Nothing except we know how to use our weapons and they will just be beginning to learn how to use theirs. And Long Hair has some sense," Layton said. "He knows the Americans and the Brits are going to keep coming. The one card in his deck is those untrapped lands. He's kept them fertile. He's now willing to part with the furs to protect the villages. We all stand to make a fortune from this decision, you more than any of us. I have debts that need to be paid. For a three-hundred-dollar investment you can increase your take ten or fifteen times. I could get anyone to join us, but I know you won't run like some flatlander, and Bailey's family is treating Alene roughly. I meant to do well by both of you by offering a partnership. If you return to St. Louis now, what will Bailey's family say to this linkage? Bailey was a gentleman."

"And what am I?"

Layton smiled. "A dirty trapper."

Fire came into my eyes, and Layton laughed,

and said, "Easy Wyeth. I am only saying how they perceive you. If you invest your money now you stand to profit greatly. Think about it. You get the entire profit on your take. You won't get that anywhere else. And if you sign on as an owner you get fifteen percent of the other three dollars' profit per pelt, minus expenses, and divided with the other owners."

"What other owners?"

"You, me, and . . . Ferris will be an owner, too."

"So Ferris has put in his money?"

"He will," Layton said.

I understood that Ferris had not invested yet.

"I have taken on debt at a foolishly high rate. If I can raise six hundred dollars right now, before I leave for the fur country, I can pay the worst of the loans. It will be worth the thirty percent reduction. You two will make more than I will on the season, though I will own the majority stake in the company."

"Must have been damned high rates."

"They were. But that is my problem. After we take in thirteen hundred pelts, we start to get paid back a percentage. All profit."

"And how many pelts do you think we could gather in a season?"

"We have eight men. Plus me. Three thousand pelts."

I laughed loudly. We had walked back to the bar.

Ferris was slouched with his feet stretched out on a chair. He looked up at us.

"Layton said he expects our returns to be three thousand pelts for eight men," I said.

"Nine men," Layton corrected.

"The average brigade is taking between a hundred and a hundred and twenty pelts a man per season," I said. "In a good year. Even in those southern drainages in the best conditions, Smith's brigade took in less than a hundred a man."

"They lost many due to hardships. That will not happen to us."

"You have no way of ensuring it doesn't," I said. "And it doesn't change the fact that the average is close to a hundred. If that."

"The country we are going into is the most fertile imaginable and we will have the most experienced and energetic trappers harvesting the furs and the most experienced captain to guide them."

"I'd hardly call you experienced, Layton."

"I am not speaking of myself. I have hired Jedediah Smith to lead us."

"Captain Smith is part owner of the Rocky Mountain Fur Company," I said.

"Smith has taken a leave from his company to guide our brigade," he said in a steely tone. "He is in a room above us as we speak."

I glanced at Ferris who nodded that it was true. Smith had signed on as the scout and captain of Layton's brigade for the season.

"You seem not to understand, Wyeth. We have complete access without harassment to the richest drainages in the west. I have forgone using camp hands, which will make the year arduous for those who sign on but will increase our profits. There are nine of us. I calculate we'll take in around three thousand pelts. Without our own profits, the remaining men will split around nineteen hundred pelts. So, around three hundred pelts each."

"They'll be splitting almost two thousand pelts. About three hundred and thirty each," Ferris corrected.

"Each paid about nine hundred—"

"A thousand," Ferris said.

Among his other accomplishments Ferris had a knack for figures. Layton had a habit of always overestimating his profits.

"Fine, Ferris. By your calculations, a thousand dollars each. The profit on those two thousand pelts is around six thousand dollars. Minus the twenty-five hundred expenses we're left with—"

"Thirty-five hundred," Ferris said.

"Exactly. You get fifteen percent of that."

"About five hundred extra," Ferris said.

"And then all the profits from your own pelts, including free transport," Layton said. "That's three hundred and thirty times six. Around—"

"Two thousand," Ferris said.

"Plus what you invested originally. So you walk out with—"

"About twenty-eight hundred dollars," I said.

"That's the least of it," Layton said. "It could be higher. Could be double that."

"Won't be double," I said. "It won't even be half."

"That is the most fertile land imaginable. Never touched," Layton said. "And part owners of a company that has returns like that is of inestimable value. Once you return, those shares of the company can be sold and will be worth more than any accumulation of pelts. You could come out with five or ten thousand dollars. Probably more."

Behind us Branch and Pegleg were throwing their knives at Smitts's new door. The intermittent thuds punctuated Layton's words.

"Who else is going?"

"Smith, like I said. And Glass and Bridger and Branch and Pegleg."

Pegleg heard his name, and turned holding his knife, and yelled, "You don't decide on your own to come we'll drag you out on a mule. You think we're letting you get hitched to a St. Louis lady? You're a trapper, Wyeth." He turned and hurled his knife.

"Grignon, too?" I said.

I had seen him sitting by himself at a table with a bottle, oiling his mustache.

"He's handy with a pistol," Layton said. "And he's been useful to me."

"Let me talk to my counselor," I said, indicating Ferris.

Layton hesitated, then, without a word, walked back to Pegleg and Branch. He took a knife and threw it at the door, hard. It lodged in the pine door and stood vibrating. I leaned in close to Ferris.

"Have you really promised all your money to Layton?"

"Not yet," he said.

"Do you trust him?"

"There are few people I trust less. But damn, Wyeth, I can't say I'm not tempted. It's not free and clear like before. The Hudson's Bay Company's been leaving wasteland behind it. There are two more brigades from Astor's company out this spring. There are Mexicans around Santa Fe. There are even Russians in California. All the fertile land's been trapped."

"And you believe his story?"

"I believe he has spoken with Long Hair. And Layton's right about one thing. The golden days are over. You weren't just in St. Louis, Wyeth. Dandies in ambassador hats everywhere, saying, 'Make way for the gentleman.' The returns are diminishing. It's never going to be like that first season. Way I figure it, the Crow aren't our enemies, the Blackfoot and the Brits are. And he did get Smith to lead the brigade, so there must be something to it."

151

"And Smith's in his room right now?"

"I know he's not down here drinking," Ferris said.

I asked which room he was lodging in, then motioned for Ferris to wait and went up the stairway to the second floor. I saw a narrow hallway with doors on either side and a window overlooking the snowy prairie at the far end. There were framed pictures and glass flumes over unlit candles at intervals. I stopped in front of the last room on the right. I knocked and heard Smith say, "Come in, Wyeth."

The walls there were very thin. I opened the door and there was Smith studying a hand-drawn map with a magnifying glass. He swung his legs around and stood and shook my hand.

"William Wyeth. In the flesh. Have you signed on?"

"I've been petitioned to," I said. "But I have other engagements. Tell me. Is it true we're to be let into all the Wind?"

"The entire northern half. Yes."

"And you believe Layton?"

Smith was a mild-spoken, cautious man. A teetotaler, a Bible-reader, a man of business, but also fearless, a natural leader, and a fine judge of character.

"You've found the point of weakness," he said. "The risk is in trusting Layton's word. I don't know that any of us would want to risk our life on it. But I'll tell you one thing, Layton hasn't done

152

any of the greenhorn conniving I'd expect from him, like get inferior powder or imitation guns. He's gotten real Pennsylvania long rifles. Real Taos Whiskey. Held up his end. I'm willing to take the chance."

"Layton's never run a brigade."

"He won't be running anything. He's paying me to run it."

"And the other men?"

"You saw them as you came in. Fine men that you know as well as I."

"And Grignon?"

Smith looked at me steadily. "Grignon is an underhanded scoundrel who is wanted in St. Louis for forgery and assault on a woman. But he is one man and I will manage him."

"You're sure you can."

"Grignon will not be a problem," he said.

I took this in silently.

"There are no sure things, Wyeth. But the land's becoming trapped out. This is the last, best chance of a big take."

"Or to get scalped by the entire Crow Nation."

"You have taken a fair assessment of the situation, Wyeth. I understand he is offering you fifteen percent stake for a three-hundred-dollar investment. If it were me, and if all my money were not tied up in another company, I would take the chance. We'd like to have you on with us. We leave in three days. Think it over."

Smith shook my hand and then I stepped out and shut the door and stood at the end of the hallway looking out over the snow-covered prairie. I could hear the men carousing below. I knew that Layton was capable of almost any underhandedness, but the worry about the money was fleeting. Money was not the real enticement. A brigade promised adventure and camaraderie. It promised another year in a wild, untouched country that was quickly changing. I knew the chance to hurl myself out into this country would not come again in my life. I wanted to take it. I knew I did.

I walked back down the stairs and sat next to Ferris at the bar. I turned and waved to Layton, who came over, grinning.

"I need to talk to Alene. But don't give away my spot."

"He's calling it *his spot* now," Layton said. He held his glass up triumphantly. "To three St. Louis ruffians out in the wild. We'll make our fortune and come back with riches and glory. To the expedition."

"To the Crow," I said.

"To Long Hair," Ferris said.

We all drank. Layton shook my hand and shook Ferris's hand, then walked back and picked up a bottle and jumped on the table.

"We got another two booshways teetering. Drink up!"

"Booshways? Where? I don't see 'em?" Pegleg shouted.

Ferris leaned forward and looked at me. "You better go talk to that pretty little maiden while you still got a working tongue. This party could go on a while."

I came home reeling and it was not until the following morning that I told Alene of Layton's proposition, which she took even worse than I expected.

"Layton has taken pains to court you, William. He has chosen you because he saw I was partial to you. Now he means to ruin you."

"I hardly think it would be worth the bother," I said, and Alene leaped off her chair in indignation.

"Layton is an undisciplined, spoiled, greedy, destructive man who possesses a genius for gathering men around him. It is not a bother for him to destroy others. It is what he does for pleasure. He has taken an interest in me and because I refused him he has set out to destroy any man I have affection for." I laughed, as all this seemed overly dramatic, but Alene's eyes blazed. "Oh, William, you only see the charismatic side now. The part when he persuades. When he wheedles. When he promises. When he uses all his charm and cunning and good nature and energy and cleverness to arrange things so men follow him, so they bind their lives to his. But when it is necessary for him to fulfill his promises he will feel the necessity as a form of bondage and he will wilt and turn sour and ugly. Then you will see the weak, contemptuous part of his soul. In St. Louis he ruined countless women. Countless. First seducing, then deriding. He killed a man in a duel—"

"I am not joining the brigade for Layton's noble qualities. He has hired reliable, capable men."

"And that Grignon. I saw him ride in, too."

"Grignon is only one man."

"One man, well placed, can cause inestimable damage. You must see that. If you are to break off our engagement—"

"I'm not breaking it off, Alene. I thought I was postponing it."

"If you are to break the pledge you made earlier this year and leave on a brigade and give all your money to an inevitably losing venture, I do not see why you must do it with the exact man I loathe above all others."

I could hardly find a response for this other than to say it was Layton who had arranged the most promising brigade, that Ferris and others I trusted had linked themselves to this brigade, and the idea of profiting from Bailey's death was poisonous to me.

"You are an able and likable man, William. You would thrive at any occupation you put your mind to. You have money of your own. Sufficient for a start in St. Louis. I will most likely receive an inheritance."

"Which I cannot be seen to profit from."

"It matters little to me, William."

"But it does to me," I said. "I hardly knew how much until this moment. I will succeed on my own and will know myself to be a sturdy and reliable fellow. From a young age I was told my wandering nature was a weakness. I mean to show otherwise."

"I feel you will prove your unreliability by trying so desperately to live against your father's false prognostications," she said.

"They will not be false unless I return to the drainages."

"They will be true if you break your word to me," she said.

We went round and round like that. She saw I was determined to go.

"At least promise me that you will return at the season's end," Alene said.

"Of course I'll return," I said. "I only leave to secure our future."

"You say that now. But I know what trappers are like when the fever of the hunt gets into them. I saw it with my father. Now I am seeing it with you. I will wait until the end of the season, but no longer."

I let out a deep breath and sat back in my chair.

"That is all I ask," I said. "I will return before

the heavy snows. We will reunite, spend the cold months together, and float back at the breakup in the spring."

"And if you don't return?"

"I will."

"But if you do not?"

"If I don't it means I have perished and I release you."

She took my hand and looked me in the eye. "You understand you are releasing me if you do not return before the new year?"

"Yes."

"Swear that you understand. Put your hand here." She pushed a Bible over. "Put your hand on it. I do not want there to be any misunderstanding. I'm sorry to do this, William. But trappers have short memories. I have seen it all my life. I saw it in my father. I had even begun to see it in Horace. And now I see it in you. Swear that you will return after one season. Swear I will not spend another winter alone."

I put my hand on the Bible. A sort of premonition hovered but I brushed it away. I said, "I swear I will return after the fall season and long before the spring thaw."

Alene took the Bible from me and set it near the window.

"I am sorry to sound defeated, William. I saw this happening months ago. Henry Layton has now twice ruined my life."

"He could be the means of enriching it," I said.

"How much you sound like Horace," she said.

"I may sound like him. But I will not end up like him."

"Those will be my prayers until I see you again."

A day later I bought a wooden hut with the last of my money. It had two rooms and a loft up top and there was a corral behind for horses. I acquired it from a Swede who was heading farther west for better land. Smitts arranged the transaction, completing it in a day with the Swede unable to sign his own name.

A day after that I moved Alene into this improved lodging and prepared for departure. I did what I could to console Alene, but I'd be damned if I knew how to explain my attraction to the trapping lands without making it rankle.

The next morning I was mounted early. A brief kiss, a wave, and I dashed off on my mountain pony. I looked back once and saw the pale light at the window of the cottage, small and insignificant from that distance. For a moment I saw the situation as it really was and not as I wished it to be—she had committed herself to me and I was leaving her to fend for herself for a year.

You're a vile fellow, I thought.

I almost turned back, but that inner restlessness and yearning, subdued for a moment, began churning again.

As I passed the infirmary the old nun, who had heard of my imminent departure, turned off the path and kept her back to me in a gesture of disapproval. I laughed loudly so she'd hear and spurred my horse, my thoughts of Alene receding and my heart bursting with anticipation at a final season in the savage country.

BOOK THREE
The Far West

My father had predicted I would die a lonely death in some distant drainage and I am sure if he saw me riding into Crow country with Henry Layton, a notorious idler and miscreant who knew little of the trapping life, he would have felt all his predictions were coming true.

To his credit, on the voyage west Layton did his best to remedy his ignorance of life on the trail. In a matter of weeks Layton had learned to balance and pack the goods, scout the land ahead, and manage his string of ponies, which were the main duties when on the move with loaded horses.

After six weeks of arduous and monotonous labor we arrived at the Crow village, which was situated in a flattened bowl at a spot where the Popo Agie flows out of the Wind River Mountains. Native sentries flanked our progress and all the men and women of the village came out to observe our approach. The brigade stopped. Smith, Layton, and Branch rode forward and disappeared into the village while the rest of us settled into makeshift fortifications. We waited for an hour. Then Smith returned, followed by ten natives.

"Let him have it, boys," Smith shouted.

We transferred our expensive goods to the Crow and, with much native fanfare, were allowed to proceed past the village and up into the mountains just as Layton had promised. This was in late April of 1828, a year of early thaw and light snows. Though still half frozen, the lower slopes were passable and many of the sunlit faces were already clear. The creeks and rivers and small waterways, at first, much to our disappointment, showed signs of being heavily overharvested, and for nearly an hour it seemed we had traveled six weeks and given away a fortune to hunt on land more trapped out than those we could have entered for free.

But the drainages were barren only in close vicinity to the native village.

After an hour we began to see signs of fertility, and then, all at once, there were fur-bearing creatures everywhere, in even the smallest of trickle of water, in plain sight of our horses, and completely unafraid of man.

Smith leaped off his horse and with an uncharacteristic burst of enthusiasm shouted, "Forget the fuel and lodging, men. Traps in the water!"

He divided us into groups of two, which was half the size of a normal trapping party, and gave us ten traps each, which was almost double the normal number. We set our traps that evening. The following morning eight men harvested twenty-seven beaver, which was an unheard of number for a single morning, and that began the most productive weeks of trapping I have ever encountered or heard of. For twenty hours a day we were fleshing, trapping, moving between various camps, and standing sentry. And though pushed to the limits of exhaustion, all the men were wildly enthusiastic at thoughts of our future riches. Or, I should say, all the men except Layton, who became increasingly ill-tempered with each gathered pelt.

Up until the time we arrived in the drainages, Layton had been an acceptable if not an admirable companion. But once we were up in the high country, and the exchange with Long Hair was accomplished, and the promises from Layton to the rest of us had been fulfilled, and all that was left was for us to harvest the creatures, then Layton's suspicious, uncertain, peevish side began to ferment. Layton was cheerful when he was industrious, but he did not have the practice of doing anything for very long, and he knew little of patience, endurance, or fortitude. And once he was idle, it was like some other part of his personality began to churn and rise up and possess his entire being. He became imperious about fulfilling his side of the bargain and suspicious that the men were not working as they ought.

I first noticed this irritating suspicion a week

after passing into the mountains. Pegleg was fleshing our first gathered pelts. Layton, who had hardly done anything all day, stood over Pegleg, watching his progress skeptically. After a moment, Layton pointed at the skin stretched on a willow hoop.

"Is that skin prepped?" he asked.

"You think it comes out like that?" Pegleg asked.

"All that gristle on it. I thought it had just been cut from the beast," Layton said, which caused Pegleg, who took great care with his fleshing, to look askance at the men. The skin was as finely fleshed as any pelt I'd ever seen. Either Layton did not know what a freshly fleshed skin looked like or he had hardly examined the pelt and just assumed the work was done poorly because he knew nothing of it.

Several days later, at daybreak, on a particularly frigid morning, all of us rose on stiff legs, shivering from cold as the fire had died in the night. It had been Layton's task to gather the fuel, and he had done it inadequately. Branch, who was the most adept at getting a flame going, had arranged some pine shavings that had pitch on them. He struck his flint. The tinder began to glow. Layton hovered, as desirous of warmth as the rest of us, and just as the flames began to rise Layton reached in and moved the tinder. The abrupt movements doused the flames. Branch made a displeased, grunting sound. He said nothing, but his meaning was clear. Layton had put out the fire.

Slowly Branch arranged the tinder again and again struck the flint and again nursed the ember into a timid flame and again Layton reached in and doused the fire.

Without looking up, Branch said, "Next time you'll lose a finger, Captain."

"If you'd constructed the fire correctly it would not be necessary to come to your aid," Layton said.

"Your aid has twice put out the fire," Branch said.

"The problem was with the arrangement of the fuel, not my aid," Layton said.

The custom of respecting the owner of the brigade ran deeply in all the men, and Branch said nothing, but Ferris could not contain himself.

"We are all of us shaking from cold because you did not gather enough fuel last night. Now you impede Branch's progress."

"Impede his progress?" Layton said in that airy way of his.

"Twice you have impeded it," Ferris said. "If our work was to debauch on Market Street we would ask your advice, which I am sure you would supply with admirable detail. But Branch needs to start a fire with a flint, which he is an expert at, and which you know nothing of, so leave him to his labor."

"Starting a fire is hardly labor," Layton said, and Ferris, under his breath, but audibly, said, "What would you know of that, Layton?"

Layton turned and looked at Ferris, who looked straight back at him. The men began to scatter and Layton's hand was already on his Collier when Smith, who had been following all this, exploded out of the deerskin flap of his lodging.

"Walter Ferris! Hivernant and Man of the Mountains!"

"At your service," Ferris said, turning to Smith as he approached.

"You are so eager to offer advice, perhaps you'd care to trap that little snowbound stream beyond the forks of this drainage. I noticed it has begun to run on the lower portion."

Ferris was shaking from the cold as we all were. He had not eaten that day. This drainage was very far and would keep him away until nightfall.

Ferris turned without a word and departed.

We had all seen what happened. Layton had kept Branch from starting a fire, and when Ferris pointed out the situation, he was punished for it.

This began a pattern that repeated itself several times over the next weeks. Layton's carelessness impeded the brigade. The men covered for Layton with hardly a protest. And only Ferris, the mildest in the brigade, pointed out the injustice. Each time Ferris was punished for resisting Layton's "managing," and the discord in the brigade heightened, as all the men sided with Ferris, except Grignon, who whispered to Layton about Ferris's discontent, further fueling Layton's suspicion that Ferris rallied the men against him. Layton rewarded Grignon's wheedling by sending him to the richest drainages, which annoyed the men even further, as Grignon was notoriously lazy and the worst trapper on the brigade, and these fertile creeks and streams were wasted on him.

And so, very quickly, the brigade, which had been well ordered and content up to that point, began to simmer with resentment. At the time I thought that Layton's distemper blinded him to the discord he was sowing. Now I believe that Layton riled the men purposefully, out of boredom and perverseness. He was one of those men who work excessively to prepare for success and worthwhile ventures and then sabotage their own creations in a self-destructive impulse. I have seen this a few times in other men, though never as strongly as I saw it in Layton that spring season. I cannot say I know the source of this impulse—perhaps it was due to a coddled upbringing or a contentious relationship with his father or an inbred sense of utter superiority to all men and labor—but I can say for certain that Layton overtly and insanely courted disaster that spring. And it was not only his father's fortune that he risked, but both Ferris's and my own.

And yet—and this is strange—I still believed Layton meant well. I believe he was proud of having arranged the brigade and the fortune we were gathering. He was not like Grignon, who was simply a blackguard. Layton had many fine and noble qualities, but these qualities were at times completely swamped by impatience, suspicion, and irritability.

The essence of the situation was that Layton had done a fine job arranging for us to trap in fertile land, but he needed to hold his tongue and let the men do the job for which they had been hired. But holding his tongue seemed the thing Layton was least capable of doing.

This was the situation in that spring of 1828. Layton and Ferris feuded daily. The men sided with Ferris, and discontent in the brigade grew. I looked for a time to speak to Layton privately, to advise him to moderate his tongue, but he was so constantly nervous and short-tempered and irritable that it was a full month before I found a moment to speak with him.

A windy day of low gray clouds, and Layton and I were scouting a steep-walled valley when we came across a path of shattered, crisscrossed tree trunks that went all the way up to the tree line. At the base of the cleared path we found a fifteen-foot pile of rock- and wood-filled snow, the remains from an avalanche. Protruding from the snow we saw the head of a wolf with a hare clamped in its jaws. The wolf and hare were partially uncovered from the ice by the spring thaw. Layton examined this oddity, imagining the wolf had been chasing the hare and set off the avalanche and they had both been caught by it. Diverted by this peculiarity, Layton's bristling imperiousness lowered for a moment, and I said, "Layton, I must speak to you."

"Then do it clearly, without mewling around it," he said.

"You need to be more careful in how you treat the men."

"I was careful in choosing them so I do not have to be careful how I speak to them. Do they demand I uphold proper etiquette?"

"They demand you treat them as men and not as servants," I said.

"They are employees of this company of which I am majority owner. It is their job to accept the treatment I choose to give them. These are the richest drainages in the mountains, just as I said they would be. And it is me who has secured them for the good of all. The men ought to be grateful for what I've done, not complain of it."

I had to bite my tongue before I spoke.

"We are all pleased with the richness of these slopes," I said. "But despite the fertility of the land the men won't accept unwarranted submission."

"Who is it complaining? Tell me. Is it Ferris?"

"I know of no complaint, and particularly not from Ferris, who would never complain overtly about any hardship. If you think that he complains of hardship you do not know him. He does speak openly of injustices and you punish him for it. If you continue in this manner, particularly in punishing those who speak up when it is warranted, we will lose our investment and all our labor will come to nothing."

He was quiet for a moment. In the silence I could hear the roar from a distant waterfall in that vast, snow-rimmed valley.

"In what way will we lose our investment?" he asked.

"By someone putting a ball in your back and the entire brigade scattering into the mountains with the pelts."

"A ball in my back?" he said in that imperious manner. "It would be the height of ingratitude and stupidity. I am their captain and we stand to make a fortune."

"The men care for riches, as we all do, but not at the cost of servitude. They are not footmen and carriage drivers, Layton. If you continue to treat them in the present manner they will forgo riches for the satisfaction of dumping your body in some drainage and taking the furs they have gathered to market themselves. You must hold your tongue."

By Layton's reaction I could tell the possibility

of them putting a ball in his back had never occurred to him. I think it most likely that Layton was so filled with his own mental turmoil that the men in the brigade did not register to him at all as actual living, breathing creatures. I had noted this dismissive quality in other men of the upper class, both British and American, though never so baldly or unashamedly as I saw it in Layton that month.

He paused, and after a moment he recovered himself and said, "If the men mean to mutiny I will sniff out their intentions and blast them before they blast me. My suspicions begin with Ferris. Thank you for warning me."

"I warned you to prevent confrontation, not promote it. Ferris is an owner, and is as unlikely to mutiny as you or I. It is injustice he cannot tolerate."

Layton ignored my words. He mounted his horse.

"If Ferris means to cause disruption he will feel my lash."

Layton dashed off and in the days afterward he was, if anything, more high-toned, irritable, and impatient, particularly with Ferris, which irked the men like nothing else.

The fortunes of the company seemed to depend on Layton considering the sentiments of the men who were employed by him, but as far as I could tell considering the sentiments of the men was the thing Layton was least likely to do.

It was a week later and Layton, Ferris, and I were on some high, slaty slopes when we came in sight of a large bear just as it slipped behind a tiny green shrub. We stopped at fifty yards, aimed our weapons at the shrub, and waited. We had run low on provisions other than beaver and that bear represented the first real meal in days. Minutes passed, and the bear did not appear again, though the shrub was hardly larger than the bear itself.

We were on a wide-open, treeless slope completely covered with black rocks with pinkish-colored lichen on the flat sides. The rocks were mostly plate-size and very loose, so every step, no matter how gentle, was accompanied by the clattering and sliding and skidding and tumbling of these rocks. Far below there were trees and the silent white froth of a distant torrent. Overhead, at the top of the slope, there were pine trees growing straight out of crags in the rock. But on the slope directly in front of us there were only a few scraggly thornbushes growing up here or there, and that vast plain of loose, flattened, plate-size rocks. It was an absolutely barren landscape. There was no possible chance the bear could have escaped from behind that lone shrub without our notice. We waited. The bear did not come out from behind the shrub. After ten minutes Layton motioned impatiently and took a step forward.

"Will we waste the day idling? Which of you is not afraid to join me?"

"We are both afraid to join you," Ferris said. "That is one of the great bears. What the men call white bears. Do you know what the natives do when they see a white bear?"

"I am sure you are going to educate me," Layton said.

"They go the other way."

"Well, I am not a native," Layton said. "I am an American from St. Louis and we are three men armed with long guns."

"Which will do little if the bear comes at us," Ferris said. "There is no way to stop the white bears once they are enraged."

"A well-placed blast will stop them."

"Perfectly placed," Ferris said.

"I was under the impression you had a fine shot," Layton said.

Ferris began replacing the powder in his pan. "It is adequate," he said.

"He has the finest shot in the brigade, if not in the mountains," I said.

"Then his mettle is not so great as his aim," Layton said triumphantly. "Perhaps if it were a contest to sketch the beast you would win that."

Ferris finished with his horn and capped it.

"If we must approach the shrub we should spread out and keep a distance. And if the bear charges, fire at the nose. If you aim higher the bullet will deflect off the skull. If you have a view of the flank fire at the shoulder to incapacitate it."

"Wyeth?" Layton said.

"It is foolish to get much closer," I said. "But I will move with the rest."

"Then let's go."

Layton stepped straight toward the shrub. There was a sharp clattering of rocks, as it was impossible to move furtively across that broken-up landscape. At each moment we expected the bear to burst from the shrub, but it did not, and as we neared we saw that at the back end of the ledge on which the shrub grew there was the opening to a cave. At first I thought it was only a grotto, but as I neared I felt the cool exhalation of moist, musty air. I saw the green plants all around the cave mouth. Layton stepped closer and peered into the darkness.

"We could fire into it," Layton said.

"And if we managed to kill the beast, then what?" Ferris said. "Who'll go in after it? You? Why don't we just drop you in on a rope?"

"You can mock," Layton said. "But I do not give up so easily as you. Perhaps we can dislodge the beast."

"It is not a shallow cave," I said.

"You don't know that," Layton said.

"I do know it," I said. "I can hear the distant grumbling of the beast and feel the exhalation of air. See the liverworts."

"The what?"

"The plants around the mouth. That is a large cavern that breathes."

Layton tilted his head and looked at the fernlike plants around the mouth of the cave. He felt the cool, steady stream of moist air. He set his rifle on top of a flat rock and found a stone the size of a teacup, lifted it, walked to the opening, and carelessly tossed the rock inside. We heard the rock rattling and clattering inside, the sound echoing out of the black mouth, growing fainter and fainter and then . . . Thump! It hit something. A loud huffing and growling drifted out.

It was indeed a deep cavern.

Ferris skipped some distance away, holding his rifle pointed toward the cave's mouth. Layton stood right near the darkness, peering in. We all waited. The growling faded.

"Wonderfully idiotic," Ferris said, after a long while.

"I am attempting to gather sustenance for the entire brigade," Layton said. "If we dislodge the beast we can each put a ball in it. That will undoubtedly stop it. Are you afraid?"

"Yes," Ferris said.

"I am not so timid as you," Layton said.

"You are magnificently more foolish," Ferris muttered.

Layton turned to me. "Are we trappers or are we sitting at the kiddie table at the cotillion? My God."

Ferris checked his rifle again and took a few more steps away from the mouth of the cave and positioned himself so he had a clear shot. I had backed up and positioned myself on the uphill side some distance from Ferris. Layton glanced back at Ferris derisively, as he had positioned himself farther than the rest of us.

"I see you have found a suitable position for yourself," Layton said to Ferris.

"He need not be so close as his shot is more accurate," I said.

"So he says," Layton jeered.

Ferris said nothing to Layton's taunts, but I could see he trembled with barely contained irritation. He lay his pistol on a rock and aimed his rifle at the cave. Layton stayed at the mouth of the cave. He picked up his rifle and checked it. Then set it back on a flat rock and looked around the slaty landscape until he found a boulder larger than his head. He lifted it.

"You boys ready?"

"You know this is a bad idea," I said to Layton.

"I know we need sustenance. And I am not weak-kneed like some of the men in this brigade. I do what is necessary."

Layton duckwalked with the boulder to the mouth of the cave. He set the rock down in a mincing, self-righteous manner that anyone would have found irritating. He brought his rifle closer to him. He checked the powder one more time. Then he gripped the stone and checked to make sure we were in position and stepped to the mouth of the cave. He heaved.

The rock tumbled and rattled inside the mountain and then . . . Thump! It hit something. A guttural roar arose from the cave mouth. A mad thrashing of rocks. Layton had hardly reached his rifle when the bear exploded outward and tore straight through the small shrub. It was a very large bear and in its fury it passed right by Layton, spinning him to the ground. The great beast lumbered toward Ferris, who fired. The bullet struck the beast's right shoulder and knocked it back, but it was up in a moment. Ferris fired his pistol. The beast was struck in the other shoulder but hardly paused. I fired and struck the beast in the neck. It reared and turned on me, but after an instant turned back on Ferris who was reaching for his knife, but too late. The bear swatted at Ferris who was knocked back as if he'd been made of straw. In an instant the bear was on top of Ferris and opened it's great jaws and—BANG—I fired with my pistol.

I had not braced myself and both of my hands struck my forehead. I stumbled backward. When I recovered I saw the beast still straddling Ferris. It raised one great paw. The claws were as thick as my finger and curled downward toward Ferris's face. It lowered the paw gently so the tips of the claws tapped faintly on the rock. A drop of blood fell from its mouth onto Ferris's cheek and then the thing tumbled sideways and rolled a few times down the slope and came to a rest with a clattering of rocks. Ferris leaped up, wild-eyed. Layton was standing near the cave mouth holding his rifle. I do not think he had ever seen a great bear up close. He had not understood that they are not at all the same creatures as the black bears. Ferris had fired twice and I had fired twice. Layton had his rifle and the repeating Collier but he had not fired at all. After a moment, Layton examined his rifle in a sheepish manner.

"Misfire. Damnable," he said in a self-conscious way that was not natural for him. "Wonderfully accurate, Wyeth. Didn't know you were up to it. I misfired."

Layton moved past us and down to the great bear, slowing as he got close to make sure it was dead. I stepped over to Ferris.

"Are you alive?"

"I believe I am," he said. Then, glancing at Layton, "Did he fire?"

"A misfire," Layton said again, hearing the question. But his voice shook when he said it. His skin was pale, glistening.

We all joined in the task of dressing the great beast and hanging the meat we could not carry in the trees. During the whole procedure Layton was diligent, agreeable, and reserved, which was not at all his normal manner. Whether due to a misfire or nerves, his gun had not discharged. At first Ferris and I thought we'd keep the story from the rest of the brigade, knowing how it would be perceived and understanding it would only cause trouble, but Pegleg, who was also hunting at the time, had been high above us on a ridge and seen everything. By that evening everyone had heard about our encounter with the great bear, had heard that Layton did not fire his weapon, and put the worst interpretation on it.

Ferris, Pegleg, Grignon, Branch, Bridger, Glass, and I were sprawled out against our packs in a small enclosure of shrubs. Glass, a silent, taciturn man, the oldest in the brigade, gestured with the nub end of his fleshing bone, and said, "Thinking you want to face Old Ephraim and doing it—ain't the same thing."

"He was afraid," Ferris said.

"Wasn't fear that made him hold his shot," Grignon said. "The two of you battle daily. So of course he didn't fire. He set the whole thing up and thought the beast would do his work for him. Anyone else would do the same."

"I wouldn't," Ferris said.

"Perhaps not," Grignon said, looking at the others and grinning. "But I'd hardly take Layton to be such a psalm singer."

"He could not have known the beast would

charge me," Ferris said. "Layton is a dandy and an irritating man, but he is not fainthearted. And he would not allow a bear to do his work when a pistol would suffice. He was frightened by the beast into inaction and afterward his vanity would not allow him to admit he'd been afraid."

"Aye," Pegleg said, who, though hard on greenhorns, was slow to believe anything ill of a member of the brigade. "Layton may have been flattened—as we all have been at times—but he did not purposefully withhold fire."

"And it may have been a misfire," Ferris said.

"You saw the flash?" Glass asked Ferris.

"The beast's jaws were six inches from my nose," Ferris said.

"Wyeth?"

"I was firing myself. Layton was behind me. I saw nothing."

"You smelled powder?" Pegleg asked.

Ferris and I were both quiet.

"We were upwind. I smelled my own powder," I said.

"Whether he fired his rifle or not he still had the Collier," Branch pointed out. "He could have put eight balls into the beast. We'd do better to toss him and take our furs to Flathead Post. At least the Brits are men and not dandies."

Flathead Post was the Hudson's Bay Company's fort north and west of the Tetons.

"Wouldn't have to go that far," Grignon said.

"HB's got a brigade on the Snake River. Would be glad to take any American furs."

"And aid in the transference of this land to the Brits?" Ferris said. "I'd rather dump my furs in some drainage."

"Didn't know you were such a patriot," Grignon said. "The rest of us will trade with the highest bidder."

Pegleg was stitching a skin into a willow hoop. He motioned with his bone needle.

"If it was a question of no return or return from the Brits, I'd take the Brits."

"Anyone would," Grignon said.

"I wouldn't," Ferris said again.

"I wouldn't either," Glass said.

"If we must trade with the Brits, which none of us do willingly, we do it at the season's end, not at the beginning," Pegleg said.

There were nods and murmurs from all except Bridger. He was the youngest in the brigade, the most docile, and gave little thought to disputes in camp. He would go along with the other men.

"Even if we all decided to scatter, Captain Smith wouldn't go along," Ferris said. "We'd have to fight him as well."

"Then we put a ball in him along with Layton," Grignon said, but this was met with scowls from Pegleg and Branch.

"We will put a ball in your back before we put

one in Captain Smith's," Glass said. "We will do nothing to Captain Smith. And you won't, either."

"Aye," Pegleg said.

"Smith won't buck once it's done," Branch said. "If the man is disposed of and the pelts remain, Smith will arrange matters to sell the pelts. Not happily, but he will do it. And I can assure you he has no love for Layton. But no one will touch Smith unless he wants to face me."

"And me," Glass said.

"That's settled," Pegleg said. "Quiet. Here he comes."

Below us we could see Layton riding up the grassy drainage.

"We do nothing for now," Branch said. "We gather the pelts. We wait. Maybe the elements do our work for us."

And then Layton was riding into camp.

Through the entire negotiations I had not spoken. As a part owner of the brigade I was against any mutiny. It would be disastrous financially for me. But if it came to the thing actually happening, I'd be damned if I'd toss my fortune into a river. Ferris could do that. He had a rich father. I'd take my furs to the Brits or attempt to transport them back to St. Louis.

As Layton arrived at the north end of the encampment, Ferris and I left to saddle our horses on the south end. When we were out of earshot of the others, I said, "Would you really toss your pelts?"

"What I told them is true," Ferris said. "I'd not trade with the Brits. Though more likely I'd try to get them back to St. Louis."

"As would I," I said.

Ferris wrapped his picket in a dirty cloth and stored it in his saddlebag.

"But blast it, Wyeth. All my fortune is in this company. We must stay together. And Layton must hold his tongue."

"He isn't capable of it, even to save his life."

"Well his life is what is at stake," Ferris said.

We were silent as Layton was walking near.

"Hello, Ferris," Layton called. "You are looking unusually diligent."

"Wonderfully pleasant to see you," Ferris said back.

Layton strode into camp in a boisterous manner, knowing we'd all been talking about him. Seven men and stony silence greeted him. A moment later we all rode out to check our traps. No one wanted to linger in camp if Layton was there.

Several weeks passed and there was little change in Layton's unpleasant manner, but there was a change in the brigade's organization which improved relations. Noting our extreme discontent, Smith, being a shrewd and able leader, began to send Layton out to set traps like the rest of us. Layton complained at first, saying he did not fund an entire brigade to be a common laborer, but Smith insisted that it was necessary to increase productivity. This change in organization had the effect of connecting Layton to the men in industry and in fatigue as well as in profit, and after a day on the march Layton was, if not more agreeable, at least less able to express his disagreeable qualities as he was half silenced by excessive fatigue, as we all were after fourteen or sixteen hours of wading through icy water and riding from creek to creek.

A month passed in this way, with Layton learning the art of trapping. Then, in late June, we were riding together as a brigade in the rolling foothills north of the Crow village when we came across three Snake natives stranded on a grassy hilltop. There were two dead horses nearby with packs of pelts still cinched to their backs. The dead horses had halters with the iron rings welded together and unornamented leather like the British used. By the prints there had been many other horses, at least fifteen, some of them shoed. There were no live horses. Up the slope a dead native lay in the tall grass, a piece of his scalp missing and hatcheted below the knee. Smith motioned for Glass and Ferris to scout the area. The rest of us took up defensive positions on the hilltop. Branch walked down the grassy slope and Pegleg followed at some distance with his musket and long gun, though there was little need for this, as the natives seemed utterly defeated.

Branch knelt next to the closest native, who had an arrow wound in his bicep, and the two conversed for at least a quarter of an hour. Then Branch walked back to where we had secured ourselves on the hilltop and said, "There's a Hudson's Bay brigade half a day's ride to the north. These Snake are employees of that brigade and were sent to trap these mountains."

"On Crow land?" Smith asked.

"On our land," Branch said. "The Crow have tongues like everyone else. The Brits heard of our bargain and sent the Snake to poach. They were returning when a party of eight Gros Ventre came across them. They have lost their horses and one man is dead. They want transport back to the HBC brigade."

"And who leads the brigade?" Smith asked.

"Captain Pike."

Smith held still for a moment, considering this. Sebastian Pike was the most powerful man in the trapping regions, second in the hierarchy of the western arm of the Hudson's Bay Company, the world's largest corporation at the time. He was a feared man in all the west, known for his iron will and ill humor.

"The natives say they'll pay twenty pelts for the use of horses and an escort," Branch said. "And we'll receive Pike's goodwill for the favor."

Smith began to agree to the arrangement, but Layton said, "The British are here on American territory and were too cowardly to try to trap on this land themselves, but sent the Snake natives to do it for them. And now we'll reward them for their attempted theft by returning their furs to the brigade? No. We will not take twenty pelts. We will take all the furs the Snake gathered. But will spare their lives."

"Pike will be displeased," Smith said.

"I am not concerned with his state of mind," Layton said.

Branch and Pegleg grinned at each other. They had writhed under Layton's tongue and peevishness enough that it pleased them to think that same quality would be turned on one of their enemies.

Smith motioned disapprovingly, as there was an unspoken rule of accommodation to anyone in distress no matter which company they worked for. Two years earlier Smith and his entire brigade had been sheltered for a whole winter at Fort Vancouver after trying to poach on the HBC's territory on the west coast.

Smith said, "The Brits are weary of giving us sustenance so we can survive to compete with them. They were generous with me two years past. We must be generous in return."

"They are on our territory and are poaching on our drainages," Layton said.

"As I was on theirs when given hospitality," Smith said. "I cannot return their hospitality by stealing their furs."

"Which they have already stolen from us," Layton said. "I absolve you from all responsibility. It is not your decision. I am the majority owner of the company. They are on the wrong side of the mountains and they know it. It is true we have had little chance to be generous but also little chance to show our displeasure. They move arrogantly in large brigades and cross into our territory because we can do nothing about it. They squash our livelihood and leave a fur desert behind and then boast that this land will be theirs. I am not so much a gentleman that I am not offended by this policy. We'll take the British furs but aid the natives by returning them to safety."

Smith looked off toward the north and said, "Pike won't be happy."

"I am not in the habit of asking the British permission to make my decisions. Who will accompany me to return the natives to the British encampment?"

All of us volunteered. No one wanted to miss a confrontation between the St. Louis dandy and the hot-tempered British brigade leader.

"Good," Layton said. "Tell the natives the terms. We leave instantly."

Branch broke off a piece of pemmican from a sack of provisions, and then another, and then a third. He walked back down the slope and handed each of the three natives a piece of the sustenance, and while they were eating Branch sat near them and made them understand what he offered. They seemed indifferent to the terms as long as they were returned to the brigade. After ten minutes Branch waved for three horses.

"Ask them what they want to do with the body," Layton said.

"I don't need to ask," Branch said. "They're Snake. They leave the body where it fell and don't touch it."

Glass and Bridger stayed with the supplies and the rest of the horses and furs and Layton, Smith, Branch, Ferris, Pegleg, Grignon, and I started north. As we passed the dead native I saw where his body had begun to bloat and decompose with flies buzzing over him, and the leg hatcheted and the bone protruding. We left this body in the grass and rode over rolling hills and through rocky lowlands, heading north.

The Hudson's Bay encampment was on the southern bank of a creek we called Big Rock. This was on the plains just north of the Wind River Mountains and it was debatable whether this was American or British territory, as the borders described by the Treaty of 1818 were vague at best and were based on inaccurate maps.

As we rode, Smith, who was normally the most stolid of riders, was nervy and impatient, barking out orders when it was not necessary to do so. There had been skirmishes between British and American brigades in the past, and the jockeying for position among the brigades had escalated as the land became trapped out and as the stakes for the continuing renegotiation of the Treaty of 1818 became clearly connected to returns from the trapping brigades. We were just about to confiscate half a season's worth of pelts from three natives commissioned to a brigade run by the second-in-command of the most powerful company in the world. Smith knew that Pike would not be pleased and that John McLoughlin, the administrator for all of North America who had shown him hospitality at Fort Vancouver two years earlier, would hear of his ingratitude. It rankled.

Layton, on the other hand, was particularly jovial. He detested drudgery and monotony but enjoyed confrontation and battles of any sort. Furthermore, he reveled in any situation that gave vent to his able tongue. We had been on the trail for three months and now there was something to do other than wade through icy water and scrape the pelts. The men responded to Layton's mood, taking many jibes at the Brits.

The ride took four hours.

As we neared the rolling, scrubby grasslands where the British were encamped we saw a hundred sailcloth and native lodges and three hundred horses in a makeshift corral. Layton motioned for the Snake to get off their horses and they did. They did not wait for Layton's signal but simply walked down the slope toward the native encampment. Smith motioned for Ferris and Pegleg to stay back. They got off their horses and tied them off to a scrubby tree and tied off the three horses the Snake had been riding and positioned themselves in a natural fortification to make a stand if necessary. Layton, Smith, Grignon, Branch, and I rode down to the encampment of clean-shaven Brits and bearded French trappers, and as we neared the encampment Pike emerged from his lodging and spoke briefly with the three natives.

Sebastian Pike was a brisk, efficient man in his mid-thirties. He had been on the march since he was sixteen and knew the western lands and the life of a trapper like few others. Above all else, he hated American trapping companies. He knew, as we all did, that the struggle over the fur-bearing creatures would likely decide whether that land became American or British, and he knew that in many respects the British had the upper hand. They had superior forts, superior supply lines, and superior support from their government. I am sure he felt they had superior men as well. The British were ordered and hierarchical, and the Americans were impulsive and scattered. But America was closer to the trapping lands, and the waves of Americans willing to risk their lives for profit must have seemed endless.

Still, it was undoubtedly true that the large Hudson's Bay expeditions led by Pike were the most powerful force in the mountains. It was rare that a trapper defied him openly, as Pike's word was law beyond the Missouri.

When Pike heard the terms of the native's rescue he stood in place for a moment, then turned briskly and strode toward us.

"Smith! Jedediah Smith! You have stolen two packs of high-quality beaver and muskrat that belong to the Hudson's Bay Company and the British Crown."

Smith blanched and Layton moved his bay forward.

"They belonged to those three Snake Indians," Layton said. "Our agreement was with them. If they broke their agreement with you, then that is not our worry."

"Whoever you are, you have stolen British property, you have had the gall to come into my camp and do it, and you have trespassed on British territory."

"You're east of the mountains."

"I'm east of these mountains. But west of others." Pike turned on Smith. "Smith, speak. You wintered with us two years past and were given every convenience, including the generous offer to lead a brigade. You foolishly refused and were released in the spring to return to your country. Now you have chosen to repay our generosity by stealing from these natives who are our employees."

Smith would have given much, I think, to say he had argued against taking all the furs.

"I have taken a leave from the Rocky Mountain Fur Company and am here only as a scout and captain for the Market Street Fur Company."

"The what?"

"The Market Street Fur Company."

"It's my company," Layton said. "I am captain and owner of the brigade."

"Well that at least explains your impertinence, if not your audacity. What is the name of the company again?"

"The Market Street Fur Company. Based on Market Street in St. Louis. And it is owned by me and several others in the brigade. Smith is our captain and scout."

Pike paused at this news. He seemed genuinely interested. Here was this twenty-six-year-old with dimples and a St. Louis accent, out in the wilds of North America, saying he was a brigade leader and company owner. The Hudson's Bay Company was a model of order, organization, and regulation. No captain would receive a command before spending at least five years in the mountains, and usually much longer. The belief among the British was that the incapacity of the Americans to work cohesively would result in the land reverting to the British. But Smith was seen as an exception. His Rocky Mountain Fur Company had trapped successfully for three seasons, competing and even out-trapping the British.

"And who are you?"

"Henry Layton," Layton said, reaching down. "Pleased to meet you."

Pike ignored his hand. "I know your father."

"Glad to hear it," Layton said.

"It was not my pleasure. I had a shipping dispute with him five years ago. You are the admirable son who was bringing such joy to his life at the time, now here to brighten my day. Thank you for visiting."

Pike turned abruptly and started back for his camp. Smith motioned for us to withdraw, but Layton could not help himself.

"We have returned three natives who were stranded on the slopes of our drainages, encouraged by you no doubt to poach on our lands."

"The Crow lands are hardly your drainages," Pike said, turning back.

"They are for these months."

"Because, against all treaties and agreements, you have armed them with long guns that even my lieutenants cannot afford."

"You arm your own allies. We have armed ours."

"We arm our allies with Northwest Trade guns. Muskets. Not long guns. And in accordance with long-standing custom."

"It is your habit to believe any of your own actions are sanctioned by custom and any of ours are egregious. Captain Smith is a gentleman and an honorable man and would have returned the natives for the cost of twenty pelts."

"An acceptable sum."

"I am not a gentleman when the agreements are all to the advantage of my enemies who are poaching on my land and hide behind custom to try to steal my furs. These natives were stealing from us. Despite that fact, we rescued them and returned them to safety. It is not my custom to help my enemies steal from me. Yet we saved their lives. I am waiting for our thanks."

Smith, Branch, and I all stifled laughter. Pike turned white with anger.

"Your aid was hardly worth half a season's returns."

"That was the negotiated price for guiding them back."

"Three Snake natives who were born in these hills hardly need guiding from a St. Louis dandy out on a wander. It was extortion and theft."

"It was the price of their survival," Layton said. "Perhaps it is not worth the cost to you, though I imagine it was to them. Good day."

Pike reached for his hip and I found my pistol

pointing at Pike's chest. I had followed the argument with growing admiration for Layton. He could be an impatient, ill-tempered dandy, as we all had witnessed, and he undoubtedly had a poisonous tongue in his worst moments, but he was wonderfully energetic when it came to defending his position, and he had said openly what we all believed about the British brigades but had never dared say in their hearing: that under the guise of custom, and with the implicit threat of their government-funded forts and giant brigades, the British had muscled their way into our territory, and when confronted with their encroachment had fallen back on what they called protocol or custom. I resented this encroachment, as all American trappers did, but we were cowed by their numbers. Layton was never cowed by anyone. And in that moment we all admired him.

Immediately after I drew my pistol to protect Layton at least eighty of Pike's trappers swung their rifles toward me. Layton, Smith, and Branch all pulled out their pistols. Only Grignon held his hands up.

"Lower your weapons," Smith said from behind me, very calmly. "No need to have a massacre over two packs. You see my men here. They are armed and will gladly pull their triggers."

"I see five men who will be dead within the minute if we battle," Pike said.

195

"We will all die, as you will, and more to the point, London and Washington will hear of this. It will be good for neither of us, but particularly not for you, as you will perish. You know this," Smith said, his eyes scanning the eighty rifles pointed at us. "Your interests are to not incite a battle that will echo through Washington and London and disrupt the Treaty of 1818. Lower your weapons. And we will lower ours."

"Your man must lower his first," Pike said, motioning to me.

"His name's Wyeth. He is a free trapper and part owner of the company."

"Pleased to meet you," I said.

Pike's eyes moved to me for a moment, then to Ferris on the hilltop, who had a bead on him. Slowly Pike took his hand from his holster. I lowered my gun. Pike's men lowered their weapons, though with some grumbling.

Grignon pretended he was lowering his weapon, though he had never raised it.

The entire camp was watching this confrontation, including the natives, among whom I noticed Red Elk, the Blackfoot chieftain whom I had first seen at the surround a year ago, and who was the reason the Crow had agreed to the treaty with us. I had heard he was scouting for the HBC. I saw now that it was true. I felt him watching me, and after a moment, seeing that Pike would not release his men to fire, the native chieftain turned away, disdainful that the Americans had gotten the better of Pike in his own encampment.

"You cannot be a willing party to this," Pike said to Smith.

"And he wasn't," Layton answered for him. "Captain Smith argued for your men not because of the rightness of their cause but because of the personal generosity shown to him in the past. I judged against it because of the pervasive encroachment of your brigade and many like it. If you are looking for someone to blame, blame me."

"You need not worry about that," Pike said. Then to Smith, "I know better than to appeal to your companion's better instincts, which I am sure he does not possess. But I appeal to yours."

"I am only the scout and captain. Not an owner," Smith said. "Good day."

"We are camped half a day's ride south of here," Layton said. "If you wish to attempt to take back the furs that are now ours, you can come and try. I look forward to your visit."

"It may come to that someday," Pike said. "And if we choose to determine the right to take furs solely on who is the strongest, we will see who triumphs."

"That we will," Layton said. "In the meantime, I wouldn't fly a British flag on American soil, which this is."

"You have aligned yourself with pleasant company," Pike said to Smith.

"I am beginning to like the company more and more," Smith said, and by the nodding and grinning of Branch and Grignon I saw that he echoed the sentiments of the entire company. That was Layton's finest hour.

Layton wheeled his horse and started off. The rest of us followed. As we passed the little hillock, Ferris and Pegleg joined us, grinning broadly.

"Oh, that was pleasing," Smith said. "Bravo, Layton. I can think of no other man who could have done that. Sebastian Pike's arrogance has met its match."

"I will take that as a compliment," Layton said.

"It is," Smith said.

Pegleg jostled me, almost knocking me from my horse.

"You had eighty Northwesters pointed at your chest. How's that feel, Wyeth?"

"Better now that it didn't come to battling," I said.

"And that was a swift draw," Smith said to Grignon. That sent the men jeering, as Grignon had not drawn his pistol at all.

We rode on and reached the original encampment just before dark, where we rested until moonrise, then rode all night until we were back in the high mountains. We did not see the British brigade again that spring, but over the next few weeks we heard the Blackfoot were attacking the Crow at the edges of their stronghold using

Northwest Trade guns supplied by the British, and that the Sioux were peppering the American supply lines also using Northwest guns that they had not had before. But that was outside of our protected slopes. In the Wind River Mountains all was calm and the story of Layton's confrontation with Pike was told again and again, with much exaggeration and pleasure that calmed the distemper of the brigade.

Then it was high summer and we had our mid-season accounting. The year before the average trapping party had gathered ninety-six pelts in the entire year. We had gathered a hundred and forty pelts apiece in half a season.

Late July 1828, and Ferris and I left the Wind River Mountains heading east, riding out through dry runnels and up onto a volcanic ridge that ran like a black spine through the barren plains. We had a pack horse and some jerked meat in case game was scarce and only a vague destination of "mountains to the northeast."

In the warmest weather the furs were thin and of less value, and Smith and most of the men had gone for supplies at a trapper rendezvous near Bear Lake. Layton had joined a party of Snake and planned to negotiate for the right to trap their drainages the following year. Ferris and I, after half a season of industry and forced companionship, had petitioned to "scout for fertile waterways," but were really just off on a wander.

Midmorning, and we were six hours from our encampment, the mountains to the north distant gray silhouettes, when Ferris stopped and looked behind us and studied the vast, scrubby, barren land to the south. He started up again. Fifteen minutes later he stopped again and scanned the land behind us.

"You see that dust?" he said.

There was a faint, thin tail of dust rising up.

"Anyone heading north or east'd come this way. Doesn't have to mean anything," I said.

"Nope. Doesn't have to," he said.

We started up. After half a mile Ferris stopped once again.

"Someone's coming after us," he said.

Just to the east there was a jagged black rock shaped like a pyramid, maybe forty feet high. Ferris turned and looked at it.

"There's forage on the other side of that rock lump. We can rest the horses. Hide in the crags. See who's coming."

I held out my powder horn.

"Give them a welcome."

"Might come to that," he said.

It was just the two of us and the horses and no one else in sight. We rode across the plain and around the triangular black rock. In the shade on the far side the rocks were covered with green and orange lichens that seemed very bright against the

200

dark surface. There was a seep off the east side and the water gathered in a bowl that looked like it had been cut out with hand tools. Black pollywogs hovered in the depths of the pooled water, which overflowed the bowl and dripped off the edge of the rock through bright green moss and formed into a trickle that meandered in a channel of ferns. We picketed the horses in the shade with the lead ropes long enough for them to forage. Ferris and I filled our gourds and then he grabbed his rifle and I grabbed mine and we climbed up the back end of that rock lump and eased around to the west side. We dropped into a cavity and stood with our elbows resting on the flat surface and our guns in front of us. If Ferris was afraid he did not show it. He had his customary, flat, calm, cheerful manner that had been seen as being naïve and innocent when he had first joined the brigade but later was understood to be something else entirely: love of the wilderness, indifference to danger, willingness to battle if it came to that, and above all, love of the life of a trapper. It gave him a kind of confidence that I believe was simply the result of knowing that he was doing exactly what he wanted.

We waited. Fifteen minutes passed. We could see the rising dust from approaching horses.

"Is it natives?" I asked.

"Look at the way they ride. Spread out. Don't care who sees. It's natives."

"Not a war party."

"Not yet," Ferris said.

We watched as the horsemen came over a small rise and rode past the point where we'd turned off. There were about twenty of them and they were dragging lodges and had at least forty ponies. Dogs weaved among them. They went on along the crest of the ridge and were almost out of sight when the riders stopped and consulted among themselves and then one of the riders turned back along the path they'd made and stopped at the point where we'd turned off. The rider jumped down and looked at the prints and looked off toward the rock where we hid.

"You still think they aren't following us?" Ferris said.

"I don't think that one's a native," I said.

"Why?"

"I don't know. I don't think he is."

He was far enough away that it was hard to tell.

"Like to have that glass in the pack saddle now," Ferris said.

"Yep," I said.

Ferris and I waited with our rifles resting on the flat rock.

A few of the other horsemen in the party had turned back and trotted up to where the first horseman had stopped. They all looked off in our direction. We knew they could not see us in the shade of the great rock, but we lowered ourselves and watched them and waited. After a few minutes I said, "It's Layton."

"I think it might be, too," Ferris said. "The way he stands there pontificating. It's Layton."

"Why's he following us?"

"Don't know. He said he was going with the Snake to 'negotiate.'"

I clambered out of the cavity and down the back end of the flat, angular rock. Ferris followed me. We got back to the seep and I mounted my horse and Ferris mounted his and as soon as we came around that dark rock the horseman held a hand up in greeting and Ferris said, "Yeah, it's Layton."

We rode out and met him in the middle of that barren expanse in the midday sun. Behind Layton we could see two of the braves in his party lounging in the dust, smoking a pipe. A squaw on horseback watched us.

Layton said, "I saw some natives with HBC saddle packs to the south. Not far. It was three men. Riding fast. They know I glassed them."

"Which way?" I asked.

Layton pointed to the south.

"They were heading northeast. Not far from here. Snake said it was Red Elk."

"You think he's after us?" I asked.

"I don't know if he is or if he isn't but I know the Brits don't want us here. And Red Elk was in their encampment. You tell me. What else are three Blackfoot doing way out here on British horses?"

Ferris and I glanced at each other and said nothing. Layton took off his deerskin cap and wiped his forehead and replaced the cap on his head. I looked back east. Ferris did, too. It was wide-open land. Vast, desolate, and empty. It was very quiet.

"Hard land to hide in," I said, finally.

"Hard land to get away in, too," Layton said.

"What do you think?" Ferris said to Layton.

"I'd rather hunt than be hunted," Layton said.

"That would be a story to tell in St. Louis," Ferris said.

Layton got a peevish look. "I'm hardly thinking of that, Ferris."

"And what would we do if we found them?" I asked.

"See what they want. Fight if it comes to that," Layton said. "Better to choose the battle than have it chosen for us."

Dark shadows of clouds moved slowly over the black rock to the south.

"Lot of land," I said. "Even if they are looking for us."

"Maybe if you ride off alone they'll follow you," Ferris said, grinning. "We can get 'em after they stick a spear in you."

"It might come to that," Layton said.

"So why go looking for it?" Ferris said. "Most

likely it's something else." Layton was quiet. So was I. Ferris added, "We'll keep our eyes open, take our chances."

"Wyeth?" Layton said.

"We'll take our chances," I said.

Layton said nothing more but I could tell he wanted us to abandon our plans and ride south with him.

"Just thought you should know they were out there," he said.

"Thanks," Ferris said.

"Thanks," I said.

Layton tipped his hat and rode back to the natives. Something a little dismissive and impatient in his movements.

"He wanted us to invite him with us," I said, when he was out of earshot.

"I think you're right," Ferris said. "We get two weeks without him and he follows us into the desert. Can't stand that we get away for a minute. Thinks he's our captain and has to 'manage' us."

I looked back again at the land behind us. That barren rocky table with the sparse grass and the brown path running up the middle and meandering as it went south.

"You think he even saw those savages?" Ferris asked.

"I guess he probably did. Now if it was really Red Elk, and if they're really after us, that's another question."

We scanned the land behind us with the spyglass but saw nothing. It would have been a hard land to move in without being spotted.

We started up again, stopping to look behind us now and then. After an hour we passed Layton's party. We gave them a wide berth because of the dogs. Layton had taken his deerskin shirt off and was just in the white cloth with his rifle across the pommel. He yelled, "Keep a lookout," and we said do the same. The squaw rode alongside him, proud and haughty. She turned and glanced at us and then looked away, chin high, showing her profile. She was very pretty.

We rode on all afternoon, Ferris and I, along the crest of that rounded low ridge. Each time we looked back Layton's party was a little farther behind us. Near the end of the day we slid off the ridge and rode east, down into a river valley that we'd been paralleling all day. We crossed at a sandy bottom with green ferns waving in the current and the water cold and the air cool around it. We rode up the far side through reeds that were as tall as the horses and swished their underbellies. We climbed the bank and were suddenly back in the sparse hills with the sun behind us. The mountains seemed much closer once we were on that side of the valley. The land was greener.

By sundown we'd reached the foothills of snow-covered mountains. We could feel the snow above us in the cool air that swept down from the mountains. I was just unrolling my buffalo robe and Ferris was cooking over the fire when we saw dust rising in the dusk light. I took out my glass and watched.

"It's Layton, right?" Ferris said, without looking up from the pot.

"Yep."

"I'd know his horse anywhere," Ferris said. "We don't invite him but he can't take no for an answer. Has to do whatever he wants. Has to follow us. Now we'll have to invite him. And if we don't do it, he'll ask himself."

Ferris was rarely put out by anything, but he seemed genuinely annoyed by Layton's appearance. He had been looking forward to that wander and leaving the brigade behind.

"Damned blackguard. Thinks if we don't mutiny it means we're friends."

After fifteen minutes Layton arrived, trailing a pack horse.

"Those natives told me of another way back," he said as he dismounted. "Safer, they said. Not on that ridge. Thought you should know."

"I thought you were negotiating with them for fertile land for next season," Ferris said.

"I cut it short. It was more important that you knew of the safe route," he said a little sheepishly. "I can catch up with them tomorrow."

I felt Ferris's eyes slide to me.

"Well, obliged for the warning," Ferris said.

"Gotta keep the brigade safe," Layton said, with false jocularity.

"You hungry?" I asked.

Layton picketed his horse near the water and sat.

"I wouldn't turn down a meal. And I got some provisions."

He pulled out a flask. Ferris grinned when he saw that.

"The man comes prepared," he said with a little more enthusiasm.

Ferris took the bottle and pulled the cork out and Layton sat down by the fire. Ferris offered me a swallow before he had one himself, then lifted a pot that rested near the fire and took a large wooden spoon resting in it.

"You came all that way. Have some dinner," he said.

Layton stayed with us that night and the next morning made halfhearted preparations to return to the Snake until we asked if he'd like to join us on our wander. By his ease in accepting it was obvious that was what he had wanted all along.

That morning the three of us started up into the high mountains and within a few hours were in dense alpine forests dotted with cold blue lakes and bounded by steeply sloping rock walls. We made camp at the prettiest of the high mountain lakes and stayed up in those mountains for two weeks, during which time we hunted and fished and explored the surrounding peaks. Ferris sketched the land and the trees and the flowers and I scribbled out my impressions from the spring season, taking much care to note my emotions in a way that only a young man can feel is necessary. And though it was unlikely that there would be any chance to send it, I scribbled out a long letter to Alene, telling her of our take for the first half of the season and of Layton's glorious feud with Pike, which I was sure would interest her, and made vague references to the initial discord in the brigade that seemed to have faded, though not vanished entirely. It was strange to write her from that wild and distant place. I knew that my real life and my future were with her, and that she was the single most important person in my life, yet I had not thought of her much over the previous months, and it was only late at night when I felt close to her, or that my mind returned to our life together. I am not saying my heart was not hers, but only noting a curious fact. When you are on a trapping brigade, engaged in constant struggle with constant danger, it is hard to imagine any other life, and it is easy to forget the civilized world and your connection to it. Alene had certainly known of this phenomenon, which was why she had extracted my promise to return at the end of the season. It did not seem so farfetched now that I might want another year in the savage country. I was both glad for the promise and felt half constricted by it, though I knew she was wise to have asked for it.

The days passed easily, and in the middle of the second week, as we sat around the fire, Layton spoke of his plans for the following year.

"I have had my pick of the chaff up till now, but I mean to remedy that. Once I return to St. Louis I'll find a woman of quality."

"You are going about it in the right way," Ferris said, and Layton said, "How right you are, Ferris. I am making a fortune, which is exactly the thing to do. Women don't resent anything so much as not having money."

"I am sure that has been your experience," Ferris said.

"As it will be yours," Layton said.

"As far as I have seen money matters little to Alene," I said.

"And yet she married Horace Bailey," Layton said.

"Of course that could only be because of the riches?" I said.

"Can you deny his riches were persuasive?" Layton said. I began to answer but he cut me off. "Don't misunderstand me, Wyeth. I don't blame her for marrying into money. I'm glad it was her and not someone else. I am simply stating the facts. She chose Horace Bailey over all others because he was the richest of the men courting her."

"Richer than you?" Ferris asked.

"Far richer."

"It couldn't have been that she simply preferred Bailey," I said.

"I am not saying it could not have been. I am saying it wasn't. Can you deny the money was persuasive?"

"I can deny she chose him because of it," I said. "And I can give you proof. Despite the fact that you tried to persuade her with the aid of money in the settlement, she was never partial to you, not before Bailey and not afterward."

Layton's eyes blazed. "That money I gave her in the settlement was hardly meant to court her. She was in need of charity and unlike all the others surrounding her I managed to get her to accept aid. None can deny that."

"They could deny it was meant disinterestedly," Ferris said, after a moment.

"It is true that I cannot prove that it was done disinterestedly," Layton said. "And given my past conduct I am sure I deserve your suspicion. But I can assure you that it was done without any motive except to aid her in a time of need. I did court her at one point. Like all who have come into contact with Alene, I have seen her to be a fine woman. But my hopes for her ended with Bailey's marriage. In the settlement when I gave her that money it was simply to aid her, nothing more. Though it is true I hoped that she would see that I helped her disinterestedly and would judge me to be a changed man."

"She is far from thinking so right now," I said.

Layton looked into the fire. "Well, I hope you will speak to her in my favor, Wyeth. If you feel I deserve it," he added.

Ferris laughed. "You want Wyeth to woo her for you?"

"I told you already. My hopes in that direction died a long time ago, long before Wyeth was joined to her. I want him to speak against the false beliefs she has of me. I was a scoundrel at one time. But I am no longer. You must see that."

"The case is not so definitive as you present it," Ferris said. "We see that at moments you recognize your bad behavior, but that does not mean you have changed it."

Layton continued to look unhappily into the flames. "In time you will see that I have."

"Why care what Alene thinks of you?" I asked.

"Because she is a good woman who saw me at my worst. If I can change her opinion of me I will know I have remedied my life. Until then it is just something I wish for. Not something I know to be true."

Ferris and I were both silent, embarrassed to hear irreverent Layton speak so earnestly of another's opinion of him. I understood something that night. As I lived against my father's imprecations, so Layton lived against Alene's hard judgments of him. At least that is the way he explained his need to impress her. Given Alene's absolute and nearly illogical hatred of Layton, I felt this desire to win her approval was a much more difficult task than he imagined. Alene blamed Layton for Bailey's death. I could not see that anything he did would change that.

After a moment, Layton said, "I devised a method for aiding Alene. I did it disinterestedly. Or with the intent only of improving her opinion of me. Don't judge me harshly until I have done something to justify it."

"We could hold your entire previous life as justification," Ferris said, laughing. "But we will withhold judgment in this particular case until you have given us the needed ammunition. Then we will pin you to the wall with it."

"I expect nothing less," Layton said.

The subject was not mentioned again, but several times over the next week I wondered whether his vehemence on the subject was because he had remedied his behavior or because he desperately wanted to believe that he had.

Those two weeks in the high country passed with the most amicable feeling between us, and it was not until the last day that Layton showed the unpleasant side of his personality that we all knew existed. On that day it was as if Layton purposefully went out of his way to spoil all the goodwill he had built up over the previous weeks. Our planned diversion for the day was to ride to a teardrop-shaped lake that we had spotted from a high ridge. We set out at noon and for the entire ride Layton was in an irritable, poisonous frame of mind. This ought not to have been surprising. One of Layton's peculiarities was that as soon as he'd had an enjoyable time, he reacted against the good feeling it produced, as if this feeling were a bind or restriction. I do not quite understand the mechanism—perhaps it was a barrier against the bonds of friendship, perhaps some form of self-hatred or self-sabotage—but he inevitably became insufferable after having an enjoyable time, as if to balance out what was pleasant with a dose of poison.

As we rode that day Layton complained of the route, his horse, the dust kicked up, the idea of the ride itself. He complained of the pace Ferris set and of how I sat in the saddle and of both our horses. He complained of every aspect of the ride and the day and our conveyance. He reverted to that high-toned, simpering, superior manner that all found aggravating, and by the time we arrived at our destination, we were both ready to turn our guns on him to shut him up.

On reaching the edge of the lake, Ferris leaped from his horse, I thought to get away from Layton, but after thrashing through reeds Ferris emerged hauling a vessel made from three roughly planed logs and bound with twisted sinews and horsehair. He floated the vessel to a sandy beach and stood admiring it. We thought it most likely that some trapper had constructed it earlier that summer.

"All aboard," Ferris shouted, and climbed on top of the makeshift craft, sending small waves out over the mountain lake. He found a long piece of driftwood that could serve as a pole and began moving the craft back and forth in the shallows. I found a split branch that could be used as a paddle. Layton, who at first looked as if he would not join us, waded through the water, climbed on, and stood in the center, feet spread wide. He had not taken a pole or an oar, but just stood there as if waiting for us to ferry him. Ferris, who noted this complacence, took his pole and shoved the raft so Layton fell.

"Captain's down," Ferris said. "What a pity."

I stepped on the raft at the exact point where Layton had fallen so the water sloshed on him. Layton scrambled up unsteadily, half doused, which did nothing to improve his ill temper. I got on the raft, holding my oar. Ferris pointed at a rocky island in the center of the lake.

"Onward," he said.

"Double time. Captain's orders," Layton said.

Ferris caught my eye at the words *Captain's orders*. I could see he imagined that was the way Layton thought of himself, as the captain, and us as the subjects. We both hated that.

Ferris began poling. I paddled. Layton balanced in the center of the raft, not trying to help in any way but calling us "slaves" and telling us to paddle faster.

Once free of the shore the raft glided slowly and smoothly over the surface of the lake. I could see the stones and rocks and old submerged trees angling deeper as we drifted outward. The lake was entirely bound by gray rock walls. It was very still at that hour and every sound seemed clear and distinct and even a normal voice resounded. With each movement the makeshift vessel sent small, rounded swells slowly toward the edge of the lake. I could see the swells reaching the reeds on shore and see the rocking tips of the reeds as the waves passed through them.

"Are we poling fast enough for you?" Ferris said to Layton.

"Heave ho, deckhand," Layton said.

The raft approached the small island and moved between two jutting rocks that formed a sort of inlet. Green ferns swirled beneath the water as the oar and the pole passed over them. The sand rose to meet us. We grated ashore.

"Land ho," Layton said. He leaped onto the beach.

Beyond the sand of that island there was a small strip of grass and crooked-trunked aspens that lined a grove of evergreens. The rocks that formed the two arms of the "bay" were white-stained

216

from birds. The steeply sloping walls of the abrupt valley seemed larger and grander and more ominous from the island. I could see snow overhead. I had not been able to see that from the shore of the lake.

"I'll yell if I find buried treasure," Layton said, and walked off into the aspen grove. Ferris and I were quiet until he was out of sight, and then, when we could no longer see him, Ferris said, " 'Heave ho, deckhand.' You know that's what he really believes. That he's our king and we're the slaves. We should make him swim."

"That would be a fair punishment," I said.

"The deckhands rise up against tyranny!" Ferris said.

He reached for the pole and I took the paddle and we jumped back on the raft and without another word shoved off toward the center of the lake, leaving Layton on the island without means of returning to shore.

The sun was low in the sky and the air was thicker and duller now. The tops of the granite peaks were pink and I could see a few wispy clouds near them. We were fifty yards off the island when Layton walked back onto the beach and saw we'd abandoned him. I noticed he was carrying a long branch that could be used to pole and I understood that he had walked off to find a pole so he could help us propel the raft on the return. When he saw we had left him he understood in an instant what had happened: his ill-temper had driven us away. Layton stood beneath that towering gray rock at the silvery water's edge. I did not exactly pity him. Layton was too annoying and overbearing to truly pity. But seeing him alone out there, abandoned by his friends, I felt a twinge of remorse.

Layton saw us out in the lake. He did not call to us but strode along the beach, jumped up onto one of the high rocks that jutted out over the small bay, put a hand to his chest, and gave a fierce, guttural cry. His voice resounded and echoed among the gray rock walls. He gave another cry, and then, surprising both of us, he began to sing. It was the aria from *Il trionfo di Clelia* and his voice was magnificent. I had not known he could sing but it was a true, resonant baritone, echoing and amplifying against the rock walls. It was rich and glorious. And it was all so unexpected. I can see him still, a red sash about his neck, a lone man standing on the perch over that silvery lake against the rising rock walls, booming out into the grainy air, in Italian.

Ferris and I held our pole and paddle very still, the deep, rich, lovely sound reverberating all around us in the rocky amphitheater. His singing went on for two minutes and it was wonderful. When the sound faded against the granite walls, without a word, Ferris and I started back, not to the beach but to the rock outcropping where

Layton was perched. As we neared Layton leaped off the elevated rock. He seemed to hover in the air for a moment then landed in the center of the vessel with a violent thud, sending steep, rounded swells toward shore.

"Onward, gentlemen," he said, and as he said this he stepped to the edge and began to pole vigorously, driving the raft on by himself.

His irritable nature, which had risen up for half a day, dissipated instantly, and for the entire trip back Layton poled with extra vigor, as if to show his "captain" comment had only been a joke. But it had not been a joke exactly. I would call it a confrontation, a rising up of the ugly part of his nature, the dark force inside him that he was constantly battling with. It was the part that felt superior and the part that yearned for companionship struggling with each other. One part of Layton rebelled against any stricture, including the binds that friendship imposes, but another part desired companionship, wanted to be part of the brigade and had struggled to save the goodwill that had built up between us over the past weeks. And I believe he did save it, but barely.

By the time we reached the shore we were all on the best of terms again, and I understood something about Layton: there was a vain, poisonous part of him, but it was not the only part or even the truest part of him, and that he was in a battle with himself to rein in the ugly side of his nature. I thought the survival of the brigade depended on this struggle.

The next morning, very early, we slipped out of the mountains, rode across the desert valley, and by sundown the following day were back in the Wind River Mountains where the rest of the brigade had already gathered. We had taken Layton's route that the Snake had told him was safer, and when we arrived we heard that three trappers from a St. Louis Company brigade had been found dead on the ridge that we would have taken to return if we had not heeded Layton's advice.

I want to speak for a moment more about Max Grignon, who was the one wholly disagreeable element in our brigade. Grignon had pretensions of being a gentleman, which every man in the brigade found laughable. With his unkempt red hair and his torn calico shirt he seemed about as likely to become a gentleman as Pegleg or Bridger. And in the second half of the season, as the relations with the rest of the brigade improved, Layton began to ridicule Grignon's pretensions openly, much to the amusement of the rest of the brigade. It was as if Layton felt responsible for recruiting Grignon, who was not an able trapper and certainly not a fine companion, and seemed to be attempting to apologize for bringing him along by ridiculing him. But like everything Layton did, he carried that ridicule to the extreme, and by mid-fall his mockery of Grignon had reached merciless and ridiculous proportions.

When Layton was having trouble with some calculations he very seriously asked Grignon if he could come to his aid, which sent the other men snickering. Another time, when Layton had climbed to a pinnacle and was asked what he saw, Layton yelled down that he saw Grignon on bended knee to some maiden in the Rocky Mountain House. Another time Layton asked Grignon if he could borrow his vest as he wanted to impress some natives. Later that same day he called to some squaws just as Grignon had dropped his leggins to relieve himself. There were these jests, and a dozen others, and I suppose we all joined in the ridicule. Grignon was a lazy, bragging wheedler, full of shallow cunning and low, poisonous opinions. We all agreed he was an entirely unpleasant character, and yet for all his unpleasantness, there was a sort of yearning in Grignon for companionship and camaraderie, and I suppose we ought to have pitied the man and done what we could to make him feel a part of the brigade. Though he was at times a pathetic creature, Grignon was also a dangerous one. We all would have done better to remember this.

Still, all this is with the benefit of hindsight. In the placid fall season we were distracted by the general good humor of the brigade, the fertility of the land, and the glimmering promise of our future riches.

On a warm, windy late-August afternoon the brigade was interrupted in its labor by gunshots. We could hear them faintly, first one shot, then a series of them, echoing up from the east. Minutes later we saw smoke rising and knew that men were battling on the dusty flats east of the mountains. An hour later three natives appeared on horseback outside of our encampment, bare-chested and wearing deerskin leggins. One of the natives was bleeding from a gash across his chest, and the others carried both rifles and bows.

They stopped just out of rifle range and Layton, Smith, and Branch walked out to meet them. They spoke for a quarter of an hour. When they were finished the natives wheeled and rode off, not hurrying, and Smith, Layton, and Branch came back and stood at the edge of the fire.

"The Crow have some Blackfoot trapped up on a rock, Red Elk among them," Smith said. "The Blackfoot have fortified their position and the Crow want our help in dislodging them. They say if we're good friends to them here and give assistance they'll be good friends to us by trading two packs of pelts for a few horns of powder."

"What assistance?" Pegleg asked.

"There are natural bastions three hundred yards

from the spot the Blackfoot have fortified. The Crow can't make that shot. We can. They want our help to pin them down while they ride in to overwhelm them."

Glass, the oldest and the most experienced member of the brigade, stood and began filling his powder horn. This was unusual, as Glass rarely presumed to make decisions for the group. He was a silent, watchful, unpresuming fellow, and the most taciturn man I have ever met.

"I see you think it's an advantageous exchange," Smith said.

"Advantageous or not, I see we have no choice," Glass said. "We're on Crow land, and despite their excessive pride about their warfaring abilities, they've humbled themselves and asked for our aid. If we don't help them now they'll be humiliated, call us ungrateful, and we'll never make it out of these mountains with our pelts."

The other men nodded, agreeing with his judgment—we were their guests and they had asked us for help. We had no choice.

The men in the brigade began to stand one by one, reaching for their weapons. I stood, too. Only Ferris remained sitting, looking sullenly into the fire.

"I didn't sign on to be a mercenary," Ferris said.

"You signed on to get rich," Grignon said. "Two more packs for killing savages. What opposition could you have?"

"None that you would understand," Ferris said.

Smith sat next to Ferris and said, "There are others who will join in willingly. Wave your weapon and make some noise. That's all that's required. And bring your quill. It will be a spectacle."

Ferris considered this, then nodded, and after a moment stashed his notebook in his jacket and began preparing for departure with the rest of us.

Ten minutes later Smith, Branch, Bridger, Grignon, Pegleg, and Glass rode down to the flats. Layton, Ferris, and I were left to secure the furs in a nearby cave. We trailed the others by at least an hour, and I thought we might miss the battle entirely, but when we crested the last hilltop that overlooked the flats we saw that the Blackfoot were still encamped on their rock and the Crow were still making preparations to dislodge them. We stopped at that elevated spot and tied our horses off and Ferris sat and quickly began to sketch the scene that lay beneath us.

The rock on which the Blackfoot had fortified themselves had vertical sides and was surrounded by featureless land for at least half a mile in all directions except for three rock outcroppings rising at a distance of about three hundred yards to the north. Footholds on the back end of these outcroppings made excellent aeries. Pegleg, Grignon, and Glass had been placed in the aeries, and as we arrived they were peppering the

Blackfoot, who were well hidden but could not fire without exposing themselves. The shots from the long guns could not penetrate the Blackfoot defenses but did keep the Blackfoot from exposing themselves in order to fire on the Crow. From our elevated overlook I scanned the Blackfoot in my spyglass—men and women and children were crouched behind rocks, most cowering and terrified, but a few, including Red Elk, whom I recognized, were laying out balls and powder and arrows and other weapons, preparing for battle.

Meanwhile, Long Hair's band had gathered to the north and were dashing about on horses, waving their weapons, and beyond these warriors, riders in a makeshift corral were dividing several hundred horses into two separate groups.

Ferris sketched all this quickly, and when he'd completed his first study, Layton instructed him to hold his work up.

"Wonderfully accurate and lively," Layton said. "Bravo. A year from now you'll be snubbing us on Market Street, the famous physician and artist."

Ferris gestured dismissively with his bit of graphite.

"Physician? I'll hardly be that. Taking the pulse of rich dowagers is no life for a man. When this season's over I'll squander whatever riches I've managed to accumulate, complete several studies, then continue my wandering. You two will be gentlemen in St. Louis while I'm still scraping the drainages."

"And loving the life," Layton said. "While I'll be bored senseless in some drawing room, settled into the occupation of destroying my father's business."

"An occupation for which you have long been in training," Ferris said.

"Since birth," Layton agreed. "It's Wyeth who'll be most envied of the three of us. Comfortably settled with Alene and living on Bailey's fortune with the footman calling, 'Make way for the gentleman.'"

"I'll be settled on my own fortune," I said. "And I'll know that all my father's imprecations were groundless."

Ferris's hand paused in its scratching. Layton gave me a skeptical look.

"Whether you make a fortune or not, the accusations about your mettle were groundless. You see that, do you not?" Layton said.

"I will see it when I succeed," I said, and Layton gave a knowing look.

"Your father's drunken bile has made an ambitious man of you. I will remember that method of motivation when I have legitimate children of my own."

Ferris was about to reply with some inflammatory remark, but was silenced, as the real battle had begun.

The first of the two tightly packed groups of churning horseflesh were being driven toward the field of battle by native handlers. From that distance we could see the riders dashing about the horses, waving strips of knotted leather, driving the riderless horses past the fortified rock and then urging them to circle around again and again. The Blackfoot fired into the horses, but with as much effect as firing into a pool of minnows. When the Blackfoot had wasted much of their ammunition, the second, smaller herd of horses was then sent out at a slight angle to the rock. Most of the horses in this second wave were riderless as well, but a few carried natives with their bodies pressed to the side so they could not be hit with a bullet or arrow. With the dust and the many riderless horses and the shots from the long guns making exposure dangerous, it would have been impossible for the trapped Blackfoot to tell which horses had riders and which did not.

The Crow women from the village had gathered at five hundred yards and begun to yip and let out high-pitched shrieks. The waiting warriors beat their shields and let out high cries. The air was filled with the thunder of hooves and the cries of warriors and the shots from the men.

The first riders approached the gray rock and one by one they leaped from the backs of the horses directly onto the rock. Within several seconds we could see nothing because of the smoke and dust surrounding the rock and could only see the flashes of gunshots, like lightning inside a cloud. Pegleg and Glass and Grignon left their perches and ran toward the rock, pistols drawn. The three of us clambered off our promontory and made our way toward the gray rock, which was completely enclosed in a dense cloud of dust and smoke.

As we approached the rock we saw abandoned horses wandering about everywhere, many of them bleeding from gunshots. The base of the rock was literally clogged with bloodstained horses, some of them with bodies beneath them. By the time we managed to clamber up to the flat area at the top of the rock, the battle was over. The Crow had overwhelmed the Blackfoot and were dispatching those who were still alive by crushing their skulls with the barrels of their rifles.

We had lost Layton in the dust and as Ferris and I wandered back out to the flats we saw him standing among five Crow who were holding two Blackfoot captive. One of the Blackfoot was an old man and another was a boy. Layton was offering his spyglass in return for the two captives. Perhaps Layton meant to take the prisoners and negotiate with the Blackfoot village in return for a favor, but I believe he acted at that moment out of compassion.

The Crow listened indifferently to Layton's pleadings. They had lost eight men in the battle and were in no mood to show mercy. Grignon airily watched Layton's futile pleading, and after a moment, seeing it would do no good, took his pistol, put it to the boy's head, and fired. The boy slumped to the side. Layton looked as if he'd strangle Grignon, and Grignon, who'd said he'd always wanted to kill a native, gave him an odd, complacent smile and skittered away. A moment later one of the Crow raised his club and brained the old man, and Layton, still holding the spyglass, walked out into the smoke and dust and we did not see him again for at least half an hour.

At the edge of the field, Pegleg had cut one of the packs of furs open that Smith had received for our participation. Pegleg examined the contents. He held a pelt to Ferris, to show him. Ferris took the pelt and winged it away without looking at it and sat in the scrubland, staring out at the battlefield.

Within minutes the magpies and vultures flapped over the field in growing multitudes. The remains of the mangled bodies were attached to rope harnesses fitted to Indian dogs and dragged through the dust. The women were wandering about the field thrashing the dead Blackfoot with thorns. Some of the women had their faces blackened and were missing the first joints of their little fingers.

A while later I saw two dead Crow on a travois. These two natives had been sent in pursuit of

Chief Red Elk, who had leaped off the rock and escaped on one of the Crow horses. The horses these men had ridden were not found.

Far off in the field of battle, near the gray rock, I saw the Crow chief Long Hair being carried away on another travois. He had fallen off his horse a hundred yards from the battle site and been trampled. He had been a shrewd, reliable leader and was the man we had made our agreement with to trap those mountains. Now he was dead.

We had arrived at the battlefield in mid-afternoon. By dusk we were riding back to our encampment with two more packs of furs and with much speculation about what Long Hair's death would mean for us.

For several days we kept double sentries and cached our pelts in various hidden spots, but nothing happened. Just as before, the natives left us unmolested and we went on gathering our pelts in the protection of the Wind River Mountains.

It was mid-September, and with Long Hair dead we had decided to trap the most remote reaches of the mountains, as far from the native villages as possible. This section of high country was not far from land trapped by other companies, and one morning Branch rode into camp, leaped off his horse, and told us that he had met with a Western Company trapper named Clybourne who said a free trapper named Jenks was bivouacked at a nearby lake and was offering his Spanish thoroughbred as a prize in a horse race.

"Sold his outfit and pelts and is offering up the horse," Branch said.

Jenks's horse was renowned for being the most noble creature west of the Mississippi.

"Why in the name of God would Jenks give up that magnificent thoroughbred?" Ferris asked.

"Because he can't bring it back with him on a keelboat, so he figures he'll have some fun. Buy-in's one pelt or three dollars."

Ferris slapped his hands together. "I think I'll set some traps in the lowland today."

"As will I," Branch said.

Soon all were vying for the low-lying water-ways, which would be close to the flats where the race was planned, then any thoughts of trapping at all were set aside.

That morning, to a man, the brigade rode out of the mountains and by noon had arrived at a mixed encampment of trappers and natives along a shallow lake in the arid sagebrush steppe east of the Wind River Mountains.

There were already fifty trappers and a dozen natives at the encampment when we arrived, with more arriving every minute. A skinny, gesticulating trader in leggins with a thick black mustache and otter skins wrapped about his plaited hair was yelling, "Three dollars or one adult pelt for the buy-in. Winner gets the horse and I get the pot."

This was Jenks, a swaggering, resourceful man. With the tip of his knife, he pointed south to a rock pinnacle where a flag hung, a dot of color in the distance.

"To that rock lump and back. Any way you want to go, not my concern. It'll be a scramble. First one back gets the horse. Rest of you can scatter."

A stocky trapper with a limp carried lime paint in a barrel with a leather handle looped into two rough holes. The trapper was drunk, and using a makeshift brush, he left a wavering line in the dust. Ferris, Layton, and I stepped over the lime and walked down the hill to get a look at the horse. It really was a handsome creature. Sixteen hands high and beautifully shaped, mild-tempered, and statuesque.

"I'll let you boys admire him after I win," Layton said. "Might even let you hold the bridle."

"Damned generous of you," Ferris said.

"Maybe feed him a carrot once we get back east," Layton added.

There was a scuffling at the edge of the knotted group of trappers surrounding the horse. I turned to see natives pushing their way through the crowd. There were eight or ten of them and Chief Red Elk was at the front. It was three weeks since that battle on the rock and he still bore a gash across his forehead.

When Red Elk saw Layton and Ferris and me at the horse he slowed and struck his chest and pointed at the horse and said some words in native dialect. His meaning was clear. He was saying it was his horse.

"Ain't so," Jenks said. "I got it off Harris in a card game."

"My horse," Red Elk said in English. "Mine! Mine!"

"Straight flush. Most miraculous luck of my life," Jenks said.

"Mine!"

"Yours if you win the race," Jenks said. "Not before."

"Which you won't," Layton said. "Because no horse is faster than my Uncle Bill."

"Mine . . . mine . . . mine," Red Elk was saying.

Layton ignored him, stroking the horse's neck, saying, "Oh, you sweet thing, you are all horse, nothing else, just a fine, beautiful creature, and you will be mine. . . ."

Layton went on stroking the horse and smiled at Red Elk in that irritating way of his, which sent a current of laughter through the other trappers, who were alive to the comic elements of the moment, particularly those who knew Layton: the St. Louis dandy mocking the Blackfoot savage. Red Elk fingered the smoothed wooden handle of his hatchet, while Layton went on mincing, pretending to be oblivious. After a moment Red

Elk simply gestured at him with his hatchet and walked off toward where he'd left his horse.

"You made a friend," I said.

"He'll be an even better friend when I ride off with this magnificent creature," Layton said.

"Think he's in love," Ferris said.

The race was to begin at noon. In the time before the race Ferris and Bridger and I rode out to survey the course. Between the starting line and the rock pinnacle there was a mile of arid scrubby land with a few small rises. About a third of the way to the pinnacle the navigable land dropped into a drainage for about fifty yards and then wound up the far side. After that, the most direct route went up a small hill lying in between the canyon and the pinnacle. I rode down into the canyon and back up the far side and to the top of that hill, which was dotted with prickly pear and sage. Far in the distance I could see the trappers and natives at the edge of the blue oval of the lake. There were at least a hundred horses to the south in a natural corral, writhing and jostling. Above them, white pelicans turned and wheeled silently in the midday light. I mapped out a route in my mind, then rode back to where the trappers were lining up at the white lime. Red Elk was already there on a magnificent black horse almost the equal of the horse that was being offered as the prize. He turned and looked at me as I went by, and gave me the same mute, questioning, half-displeased look that he'd given me in the British encampment. I rode past him and found a space next to Ferris, who made room for me, as everyone in the line of horses was jockeying for position. A moment later Layton rode up on his Uncle Bill and edged into the line right next to Red Elk. Ripples of amusement went up and down the line of men.

There were around seventy-five contestants, consisting of native horsemen and various white trappers—Frenchmen, Brits, Americans, Spanish, Scotsmen, a Swede—all of us crammed together, joking, vowing to win the race, edging for position. There were squaws to the side decked out in porcupine quills and white sheepskin dresses, and in the center of this writhing throng Red Elk and Layton cursed each other, threatening to battle before the race even began.

A flask was being passed down the line. It was handed to me and I drank from it and handed it on and it continued from hand to hand until it reached Grignon, who turned the flask upside down and drank until it was gone, then handed the empty flask to Layton, who tossed it over his shoulder.

"Wonderfully generous of you, Grignon," he said.

"Much obliged, Captain," he said.

Jenks waddled out in front of the line of jockeying horses.

"Well all you lard-eaters! You corncracking

flatlanders! You pork-eating greenhorns! I'm heading back to the States by way of a flatboat on the Missouri and I can't bring my horse. This marvelous creature saved me in many a scrape and I hate to part with her. She'll go to the best rider, who won't deserve her. This scramble is around the pinnacle and back. Take any route you want. First one back gets the horse." He gripped a pistol and checked to make sure it was primed. "You had enough of my palavering?"

"Naw, we want more speeches," someone yelled from the crowd.

"Tell us some mountain philosophy, Jenks," another yelled.

"I got it right here," he bawled, waving the pistol.

There were drunken guffaws and harsh yells and coughs and cries and all the men elbowing and pushing and shoving.

"On the sound of the gunshot," Jenks yelled, and walked to the side where squaws and a few trappers too drunk to ride and Smith, who saw no profit in racing, watched. The rest of us were lined up, thigh to thigh, seventy-five men on horseback in the middle of those desert wastes.

The shadow of a hawk passed over us slowly. We waited and waited and waited and someone coughed and then Jenks raised the gun and . . .

BANG!

We were off.

Seventy-five tightly packed horses leaped forward at once. Grignon's horse veered and stumbled and other horses fell over it and then there were pileups all down the line. My mare Sophie stepped nimbly among the fallen riders and was then galloping out into the open flatlands, fading cries and whinnies and curses behind me. Ahead of me there was a red-haired Scotsman named Frazier. To my left I saw Ferris and Bridger. To my right there was a trapper named Oates. I glanced back beneath my arm and saw Red Elk on his enormous Spanish stallion emerging from the dust, then Layton a little behind him, low in the saddle, perfectly poised. Some stragglers emerged from the dust far behind them but that was it. Almost all the other riders were entangled. In an instant it was a race between fifteen horses and not seventy-five.

Frazier had pulled his stirrups high so he rode crouched on top, charging across the desert. I could hear soft hoof beats behind me and looked beneath my arm to see Red Elk urging his horse on. There was a different sound to his horse, which was unshod. He was twenty feet behind me. Then ten. Then he was past me. Red Elk was a wonderful rider, thigh muscles tight, his body flowing easily with the motion of his magnificent horse.

Red Elk approached Frazier. He tried to pass him but Frazier cut him off. He tried to pass again, but Frazier moved to cut him off again and Red Elk's horse stumbled and lost a step and Frazier inched farther ahead. Red Elk was two steps behind him. They were twenty feet ahead of Ferris, Bridger, and I. Red Elk reached behind his head where his cudgel rested in a leather holster. He gripped the club and . . . Smack!

Frazier tumbled from his horse and in an instant had disappeared behind us. His riderless horse veered off.

"Bastard," I heard Ferris shout.

"Don't have my gun," I heard Layton yell from somewhere behind me.

I glanced back and saw Frazier limping away.

It was Red Elk in front now. Ferris had inched ahead of me on his mare. Layton was to my right, hanging back just behind me, though I felt certain he could have passed me if he'd wanted to. His Uncle Bill was the equal of any horse in the west.

We rode around that first hill, down the canyon and along sandy soil at the bottom, then on hard, red rock where it was suddenly very hot and still and the hoof beats echoed off the rock walls. We rode back up the far side of the canyon, weaving among enormous boulders on the slope, and emerged on the open flatlands.

It was Red Elk in front, then Ferris, me, Layton, Bridger, and behind him a Brit on a mottled pony. The others had fallen far behind.

The group of us entered a low channel around

the rock pinnacle. As I curved around the pinnacle, in a spot where a dry streambed ran up right along the base of the rock and made a three-foot channel, I came upon Ferris just getting back on his horse. He must have fallen as he made the turn. "Aggh," I jeered as I raced past. He waved a hand to ward off someone behind me and I looked back to see Layton collide with Ferris, the two entangled, all legs and dust and whinnying, and then Bridger and the Brit raced past, and I was back out on the flats. Halfway there.

Red Elk was fifteen yards in front. I was second. Bridger and the Brit were ten yards behind me. I looked back and saw Layton and Ferris emerge from behind the pinnacle, not injured but far behind after having collided with each other.

I was approaching the small hill from where I had surveyed the route. Red Elk had turned to the left of the hill. I began to follow in his path but at the last moment went up over the top of the hill rather than around it, weaving among sage and scrub. When I emerged over the crest I passed the spot where I had surveyed the landscape. The blue lake was spread out in front of me with the pelicans wheeling and the white triangles of the native lodges to the west of the lake and the horses in the corral, all of it magnificently lit in the autumn light. I slipped down the back end of the hill, and as my path converged with Red Elk's I realized I had made up some ground. We were neck and neck now, three feet separating us, close enough to touch each other. As we rode Red Elk turned and looked at me and reached behind his head as if he'd swipe at me with his cudgel but he did not. He just kept pace with me, the two of us riding alongside each other, Red Elk casting glances at me and then slowly inching past.

I spurred my horse, and for a moment I gained ground and oh, how I wanted to win, to prove myself to all those men, and to myself, to know that I was equal to any man in the west, with that unquenchable desire for accomplishment, for recognition, for glory. I urged Sophie on, but even as I yearned for victory, Red Elk was gaining ground. Sophie gave everything she had, but Red Elk had the better horse and was the better rider. He was soon several lengths ahead of me.

I glanced beneath my arm and saw Layton passing Bridger and the Brit. In front, Red Elk slipped farther ahead. We were approaching the small canyon that came in from the right and angled southwest. We'd all calculated the quickest route was to ride down the south side of the canyon and along the bottom, then come up on the north side through a dry channel and ride in the last quarter mile over the flatlands. But at that moment, as I galloped behind Red Elk, as I felt the possibility of winning slipping away, I did not follow him into the canyon but rode high along the white rock lip to a point where the canyon cut steeply through a narrow channel and the two banks were fifteen feet apart. I veered from the south bank and then rode straight for the precipice. I felt Sophie resisting but then she caught my intention and being an eager, obedient animal, burst forward with mad enthusiasm. We charged at the canyon and just as we reached the precipice I heard Alene say my name: *William.* I cannot explain this but can only say I heard it clearly, as if she'd whispered it in my ear to bring me back to reason—but too late. We were just on the precipice. Sophie leaped and I rose with her.

There was a moment where I was forty feet over the canyon, where my shadow and Sophie's shadow crossed the canyon floor beneath me and Red Elk looked up to see a horse and rider sailing overhead, crosswise. And then, the *thunk thunk* of the front hooves. We landed heavily, stumbled but stayed upright, and were galloping on toward the wildly gesticulating drunken band of trappers and squaws and spectating savages that were waiting at the finish line. Red Elk emerged from the canyon and drove his stallion desperately, but I was too far ahead, and I, William Wyeth, on a third-year mare, had beaten all the other trappers and the natives in the race for that thoroughbred.

I pierced the waiting crowd and the men practically lifted me off my horse. Jenks took the halter of the prize horse and thrust it at me.

Beyond the shrieking throng, Layton pulled up short and turned away, furious. He was terribly competitive and an awful loser. Pegleg had begun to bait him when the halter was jerked from my hand and Red Elk was in front of me.

"Mine!" he was saying. "Mine! Mine!"

I reached to grab the halter. Red Elk raised his cudgel but was struck from the side and knocked into the dust. Layton stood over him.

"Wyeth won, you beast!" he shouted.

Red Elk moved to rise, but Layton was standing over him and would have kicked him if Red Elk had not rolled aside. A moment later Red Elk was up, gripping his cudgel, but Pegleg was there holding a pistol two inches from Red Elk's head. Within another two seconds forty guns were pointed at Red Elk, who stood with the cudgel half raised, understanding the madness of his actions. Slowly he lowered the cudgel and casually slid it in the loop of his deerskin holster. He brushed dust from his chest and looked at Layton and then at me and spoke slowly, with Branch translating: "You are the men who aided the Crow in the massacre of the Blackfoot. Now you have stolen my horse."

"Won the horse. Not stole," Layton said in his imperious tone.

Red Elk studied Layton, then me. "I know where you trap. I know the country you must cross with your pelts."

With that, he turned and walked off. There was a moment of silence, and then Pegleg held a bottle to Layton.

"Drink up. Tomorrow you'll be under Red Elk's scalping knife."

That sent the men chattering and jesting and the crowd closed around us again and the celebration resumed, but all the while that look from Red Elk crackled inside me.

By late afternoon we had left the flats and started back to the mountains. I was leading my new black thoroughbred, which was a marvelous creature but wholly impractical for the trapping land. We half expected an ambush by Red Elk and his men, but it did not come, and by evening we were back in our protected mountains.

By mid-fall we knew we would accomplish what I had not thought possible: We would average somewhere between two hundred fifty to three hundred pelts a man, which was the largest take for a small brigade in the history of the fur trade. We knew that if we could bring those pelts to market, it would change all our lives and possibly the borders of the west, but as the season's end approached our enormous return provided little satisfaction, as having those furs in the mountains and having them in St. Louis were two different things. The Blackfoot had vowed revenge against us and Captain Pike had placed a bounty on our furs and it seemed every trapper in the west knew that we carried a fortune.

One night that October, just as Ferris and I were settling down to eat from a burbling pot of fat and meat, Layton came into the firelight and sat with an utterly self-satisfied and complacent expression.

"What is it?" Ferris said. "You've come here to say something. Out with it."

"You don't think I came to enjoy the company?"

"God," Ferris said, turning to me. "Does he think us simpletons? What is it?"

Layton took a taste from the pot, smacked his lips, and said, "Eat your wonderful potage. Tomorrow we wander."

"Guess these drainages aren't rich enough for you," Ferris said.

"Aren't looking for drainages," Layton said. "But looking for a way out of them."

Ferris considered this. So did I. We understood his meaning.

"Through Spanish land?" I guessed.

"Why not?"

"Not the quickest way," Ferris said.

"But maybe the safest. Not a lot of Brits to the south," Layton said. "And not everyone knowing what we carry in that direction either." Then, seeing Ferris's reluctance, "The others can scrape up the dregs. If we find safe passage we save the brigade. And you can bring your quill and parchment and record land that's never been put to paper. What possible argument could you have against it?"

Ferris seemed to resist the idea for a moment, as if he felt we were shirking by leaving the brigade behind while they worked, then seeing the sense in it, leaned back on his elbows, and said, "When were you thinking we'd start?"

"Tomorrow at dawn. Can you be ready?"

"Of course."

"Wyeth?"

"I'd rather sleep till midday," I said, and Layton tossed a stick at me.

The next morning, much to the envy of the rest of the brigade, Layton, Ferris, and I set out to survey for the possibility of an alternate, more hidden route out of the western mountains. We started south, and for ten days we traveled across rolling, deserty slopes and up through high, snowbound passes, sleeping in shrubs or dense woodland and passing through numerous barren valleys. It was fall, and very dry and cold for that time of year. The valleys we passed through were occupied by native and American and Spanish trappers, all of them half starving and with few returns. The farther south we traveled the more trapping parties we encountered, and the more barren the land became. Everywhere we found the animals diminished and the men impoverished. I thought of the piles of beaver flesh we had left behind, the rotting buffalo after the surround, the waste that was involved in the industry, not overwhelming as long as we were trapping in empty, open country, but in those crowded drainages the effect of trapping brigades passing through year after year was clear. It had been a wild and untamed and beautiful country, but very quickly, in several years, it was becoming something else—mapped, over-trapped, and hostile. In ten years' time there would be few who remembered the land as it had been in all its pure and savage glory. I was glad I had been there to see it. I was glad I had not spent my last season in waterways where the men were desperate and starving.

On the tenth day of our wander, as the mountains had begun to diminish and the air became gentler, we crested a dry ridge to see a green valley spread out beneath us, dotted with horses and cattle and regular squares of plowed land. We could hear cowbells rising faintly from the rivulets, a sound I had not heard for more than two years. Beyond the fields was a white steeple and the whitewashed walls of a church.

"Whatta you say we take a ride down there and give our regards to the conquistadores?" Layton said. "Gentlemen like us. They'll probably give us dinner and brandy in crystal glasses."

Ferris took a deep breath and looked away. "They're Spanish, Layton. They arrest American trappers."

"But we're not trappers," Layton said. "We're gentlemen adventurers from St. Louis, seeking safe passage to Santa Fe."

"Good God," Ferris said.

"And they're not Spanish anymore," Layton said. "They're Mexicans. Completely different thing."

"Same people," Ferris said. "Different name."

Layton made an impatient sound in his throat. "We have ridden ten days to determine our chances of safe passage to the south. I can see no other way of determining those chances than meeting the men we would certainly encounter if we passed through with a brigade and pack train. I am going to pay them a visit. Who is coming with me?"

Layton started down the slope. I looked at Ferris.

"Not a good idea," he said.

"Nope," I said, and the two of us followed Layton down into the valley.

We had been riding for less than ten minutes when a group of five men on horses started out from the settlement toward us. They wore steel helmets and carried long staffs with curved blades. Three greyhounds streaked across the plowed land toward us, then curved around behind and came running back, making our horses skitter. Two hundred yards off natives plowing by hand stopped and watched silently as the five horsemen flanked us on either side and held their lances out, poised, as if to gut the horses. A man with a thick black beard on a black horse trotted up. He wore a curved sword on his belt and had a haughty expression.

"*Hola,*" Layton said in a cheerful, entirely false tone.

"*Ustedes están ingresando a las tierras de San Cristóbal.*"

"*Somos caballeros de la carretera y venimos a ver al administrador para pedirle permiso para pasar por sus tierras. Nos dirigimos rumbo a Santa Fe,*" Layton said in a halting Spanish.

"*Usted es francés.*"

"Americans," Layton said. Then to us, "I told him we're gentlemen of the road, asking for directions to Santa Fe. I think it worked."

"Undoubtedly," Ferris said.

The man with the sword said something to one of the men behind him, then the men with the lances moved closer and motioned for us to follow.

We rode on hard-packed trails between plowed fields where natives stopped to watch us go by. When I looked back they were still watching. I could hear bells ringing from the church.

After fifteen minutes we arrived at the settlement, which had a hardened mud wall around it, painted white. Inside the walls were apple and pear trees and the church had the large white cross on top that we'd seen from the mountainside. There was a square in the center with an oak tree and native children playing a game with colored hoops.

The riders motioned for us to halt in the square. Four of the soldiers got off their horses and we dismounted as well. The halters were taken from us and handed to natives who led them away. The four soldiers walked off and sat in the shade of the oak tree and lay their lances in the roots and sat and watched us.

"What now?" I asked Layton.

"We wait."

"You got this all worked out, don't you?" Ferris said. Then to me, "We're dressed like trappers and we came from the trapping lands. They're going to say we're trying to open up trade through Santa Fe, which we are, and arrest us."

I stepped to the side and saw our horses being fed grain and rubbed down.

"They're feeding our horses," Layton said.

"They're Spanish," Ferris said. "They like horses. They don't like Americans."

One of the soldiers ambled over and motioned for us to hand over our rifles and we did. As an afterthought he took our pistols, too. He walked back to the shade and handed Layton's Collier pistol to the soldier next to him and the second soldier looked at it and held it up and sighted with it, and he handed it to the next soldier and it went all around until it came back to the first soldier, who walked back over and held it up and made a motion like shooting. Then he waved his hand to indicate there was no flash pan and Layton nodded that was the case. The soldier walked back to the others, speaking animatedly, holding the pistol high.

"What are the chances I get that back?" Layton said.

"Zero," Ferris said.

"We agree on something," Layton said.

Four more soldiers walked from the stables. There was the clinking of chains and five natives in shackles were led out into the square from a stone lockup. A Spaniard with a black beard and a very white shirt began flogging one of the natives laconically until the native collapsed and was dragged off. The man with the white shirt wiped his forehead and had started in on a second native when the door to the main house opened and the flogging stopped. A tall, thin, elegant-looking man with a closely clipped beard and thin hands walked out. Layton walked over, smiling, and said, "*Hola. Gracias por su hospitalidad.*"

This man squinted against the sunlight and winced at Layton's Spanish.

"I speak English as well as you do," he said, in a cool, crisp tone.

"I am relieved to hear it," Layton said.

"Follow me."

We followed him up the steps of his dwelling and into a house with dark wood and panes of glass, white lace tablecloths and crystal chandeliers. The servants were native women in European clothing. The furniture was from Spain.

The administrator, as he was called, sat behind a desk with an ink pen and a pad of parchment and a large book on a page half filled with scribblings.

"I am Emilio Echevaria, an administrator, formerly of New Spain, now the Republic of Mexico. You three are American trappers, trespassing on Mexican soil, invading our country in violation of the Adams-Onis Treaty, and will be detained until further clarification from the capital. I should hear a reply within a month's time."

He said this succinctly and dipped his quill in ink.

"What are your names?" he asked.

"My name is Henry Layton and I am hardly a trapper," Layton began. "My father is a landowner and manufacturer from St. Louis, and we are adventurers and students of nature. We were connected to a trapping brigade, were waylaid by misfortune, and are now washed up on your shores. We ask for nothing except safe passage to Santa Fe and back to our country. Any imprisonment will be heard of in Washington and will be forcefully resented and resisted."

Echevaria's pen remained poised, and after a long moment, in a sarcastic tone he said, "You are what?"

"We are three gentlemen travelers. I am a student of nature."

"I can see you have immersed yourself in it," Echevaria said, and began writing again. As he did, he said, "You look like trappers and I believe you are trappers. American trappers who are looking to establish trade with Santa Fe. Trade which, if established, will overrun the region with your compatriots."

"We look like trappers because we traveled with a trapping brigade," Layton said. "Beastly men among whom we suffered numerous privations. We have arrived here at this oasis of civilization by the will of God. I am a gentleman. And my companion here"—he motioned to me—"is a law student and writer of verse."

"Worthless occupation."

"You are not alone in that estimation," I said. "My father would agree with you."

Echevaria smiled briefly and mirthlessly. He wore a frock that went up to his neck. He had languid movements.

"We stumbled upon your magnificent settle-ment—" Layton began.

"I do not agree with your estimation of the settlement. I am fifteen hundred miles from the capital and surrounded by barbaric wilds."

"It is far superior to any of the American settlements."

"I don't doubt that. And yet it does not meet Spanish standards, which are different from Americans'."

"Perhaps that is the case," Layton said.

"It is the case," he said.

"I see that it is," Layton said. "We put ourselves at your mercy."

"I would like nothing better than to show mercy," Echevaria said dryly. "But you understand the position in which I sit in front of you is not as caretaker of an estate but as administrator of an entire region and with specific instructions on how to treat invaders."

"We are hardly invaders," Layton said. "We have washed up on your shores inadvertently. We appeal to your benevolence."

"Benevolence whose bounds are constantly tested," he said. "I am the administrator of a borderland territory far from any real civilization and not connected to the capital by anything but the most rudimentary of dirt paths. I have British forts on my northern edge. I have French trappers in the mountains and Russians across the desert. I have your American counterparts in the interior, endlessly rapacious. Of all these threats, the Americans are the most worrisome. Once they begin to come they will not stop. I know this. Sickness and starvation do not stop them. Threats and imprisonment seem inducements. The only real defense I have are the beastly Comanche who have done more to protect our borders than all the soldiers. But even those ghastly natives will be no match for the hordes of greedy settlers if an easy and safe route is found to Santa Fe. I have been ordered to detain any foreigners, but particularly Americans, and particularly those who seek to establish a trading route with Santa Fe."

"We did not seek to establish a route, but have sought to avoid it," Layton said. "And the tales of our hardship and the hostility of the natives will discourage any who try to follow in our path. My friend here"—he gestured to me—"will write about it for all to read. But we must be given safe passage if our story is to be told."

The administrator looked at us silently. There was no way to hide that we had been in the wilderness for months. Echevaria had begun to write again when Ferris stood and said, "May I borrow a sheet of parchment?," and without waiting for a reply, took the paper and his quill and very quickly, very expertly, sketched Echevaria sitting at his desk. It was a striking resemblance, and it entirely surprised him.

"I had my training in medicine," Ferris said. "But I have disappointed my father by taking off for the fur country to pursue my study of the arts."

"Au natural," Echevaria said.

"Precisely," Ferris said.

Ferris finished the sketch and placed it in front of him, then reached in his jacket and produced his sketchbook, which had the marvelous studies inside it.

"This is a portion of my work completed while among the trappers, which I mean to turn into full oil paintings when I return to my studio in St. Louis."

Echevaria took the book reluctantly and opened the first page. He looked up at Ferris, surprised, and began to page through the various sketches.

"These are unexpectedly excellent," he said.

"I appreciate your discernment," Ferris said. "We have taken to the road for inspiration. We have almost lost our lives. We are begging hospitality and safe passage."

Echevaria shut the notebook, turned, and said something in Spanish to one of the maids. A moment later a glass of water was placed before me and one before Layton and one before Ferris. The glass was crystal, heavy, and the water was cool and fresh. I tried to drink slowly.

"You must forgive me. I have so many troubles," Echevaria said.

"We have only one. We beg safe passage," Layton said.

"You may get your passage," Echevaria said. "It will be for once, and it will not be free. And it will not be in the direction you hoped. But you will not be detained."

I heard Ferris let out a long, slow breath. Echevaria began writing again. After a moment, without looking up, he said to a footman, "Bring them to the kitchen and feed them. And don't lead them through the front rooms when they go out."

An hour later we were led around to the dirt square where we'd first been detained. The flogged natives were now lolling beneath the oak tree. Our horses were waiting for us. Echevaria emerged from the front of the house and motioned to the soldiers who walked over. Our knives were given back and our rifles and all the pistols, except for the Collier, which was handed to Echevaria, who turned it over and heard some explanation in Spanish. He examined it closely.

"Ingenious," he said. "Barbaric. Ingenious."

He put the Collier in his shirt.

"We will escort you to the edge of our land and point you to a route that leads to the west and north where, in two days' ride, you will come across a company of trappers that has gathered illegally on the wrong side of the border. You can encamp with them and find safe passage back to your country. I am sending out messengers this afternoon. If you stray from your route, you will be arrested. If you attempt to bring any furs to market in this direction, you will be tried and sentenced to death for espionage. If you show up in Santa Fe or try to recruit men or if I see you again for any reason, you will be cut down. Good day."

Echevaria turned and started inside and Layton said, "What did the natives do to deserve such treatment?"

"They traded horses with an American trapping company," he said.

Five minutes later we were riding on a well-worn path down the valley. The five soldiers rode behind us, close at first, then further away, and when I looked back a third time they were far in the distance riding back toward the settlement.

"Gentlemen of the road," I said. "Wonderfully inventive, Layton."

"It was not my tongue but Ferris's quill that saved us. Bravo, Ferris," Layton said.

"I believe it was the combined effect of the three of us together," Ferris said. "We hardly seem like trappers, grouped as we are."

"But we will appear exactly like trappers if we pass with horses and pelts," I said. "What chance do we have of heading this way again with the brigade?"

"We have accurately assessed the possibility," Layton said. "There is none. We cannot bring our fortune in this direction."

"At least we know," Ferris said.

"Yep," Layton said. "Now we know."

In the distance we could see that the road turned to the north and beyond the road were the jagged peaks of the high mountains. It was late afternoon. It was a warm, still day, more like fall than winter. The hills around us were green and we could hear many birds in the shrubs. After some time Ferris began singing "The Banks of Newfoundland." Layton and I joined in and the three of us sang as we rode:

> We'll scrape her and we'll scrub her
> With holy stone and sand
> For there blows some cold northwesters
> On the banks of Newfoundland.

We had ridden ten days until we were at the southern edge of the high mountains. On that afternoon we turned northerly again toward the high peaks and the three of us sang our way back into that vast wilderness.

The next morning Layton rose in a poisonous mood. He complained of the lack of fuel for the fire. He complained of the uselessness of our voyage, the letdown of heading back to the drudgery and monotony of the brigade, and the depression of even thinking of returning to St. Louis and his father's company. He complained of the difficulty in moving our furs, and the stupidity and risks of the fur trade in general, and the heavy loans he had taken on to fund the brigade, and all the dangers and pitfalls of that desperate business, and how it was worse for him than for any of us, as he had gambled more on it and had more to lose, and how his life was unending misery and toil.

Ferris and I listened to these complaints without comment, as we'd learned that any engagement in his commentary when he was in that poisonous mood only heightened his bile. A few times he seemed to struggle with himself, understanding he was being a foolish, insufferable fellow, but he did not seem able to check his tongue and kept up his unpleasant commentary all morning and into the afternoon until Ferris and I were ready to turn our guns on him. In these moments he seemed the most vain, self-involved, comtemptuous creature imaginable.

Late that afternoon we arrived at the encampment that Echevaria had spoken of. It was a congregation of various trapping companies and free trappers and at least five hundred natives who had settled down in a long, thin valley on the border between Mexico and the United States. Eight or nine merchants, undoubtedly from Santa Fe, had illegally carried their goods out on ponies and set up booths where powder, lead, smelting ladles, bullet molds, tobacco, hatchets, knives, and many other items were sold for a thousand percent increase on Santa Fe prices. The traders' goods were spread out on gray blankets, and drunken trappers were squandering their year's salaries on Taos Whiskey and gifts for squaws.

Ferris had stopped at the first of the traders and

begun to barter for a flask when we heard the cries and shouts of men in the distance. The three of us turned toward this tumult, which seemed to come from beyond some cottonwoods, and a Swedish trader with beaver skins piled up in a lodge behind him, said, "Da mountain men play gladiator, yes they do."

"Play what?" Layton said.

"Gladiator," he said.

There was another distant roar and Ferris paid for the flask and the three of us rode on through the grove of cottonwoods and past three trappers snoring in the shrubbery and emerged to see a clump of two or three hundred men surrounding a makeshift corral. Inside the corral, chained to a boulder, was a large bear. At the far end of the corral, tottering, stood an enormous black bull with a series of inch-deep gashes on its side. One of the bull's horns was missing and blood oozed from the spot where the horn should have been. On the near side of the corral, facedown in the dust, lay a young Spaniard in an embroidered wool bolero. A group of young men, also in boleros, stood at the edge of the corral, looking silently at the young man who appeared to be trampled and gored.

"What in God's name is this?" Layton asked a bearded trapper who stood at the edge of the corral.

"Bull-bear brawl," the trapper said. "What you see is what it is. You get in there and touch that beast's head you get a sack of gold." I noticed the bear had a patch of lime on its forehead. "That pup in there's the second who tried."

"Where's the first?" Ferris asked.

The trapper motioned to a lump wrapped up in a buffalo robe. "That's the first."

At that moment the young men in boleros leaped into the corral and dragged the lifeless Spaniard off. Meanwhile, Layton had gotten off his horse and thrust his weapons at me.

"Hold these for me, will you, Wyeth?" he said.

"You're not serious?" I said.

"But I am," he said in a small voice.

"You'll be torn limb from limb."

"Then the bile will run out of me and I'll die a fine fellow and not a blackguard," he said. I began to speak, and in that self-pitying tone he employed in his worst humor, he said, "I have not had the proper training. I cannot restrain myself. My demons have overtaken me. You hardly need deny it. I have not the will to conquer them on my own but I will conquer them with the help of this contest."

"Getting yourself killed is hardly the solution, Layton"

"But risking death is," he said in a pointed tone. "Danger subdues the ill humor. Adventure and camaraderie are a remedy."

"You will perish and we'll all be stranded without a captain."

"Then you and Ferris will benefit, as you ought," he said. I began to say that I hardly hoped for that, but he interrupted, "This is the cure for my ill humor. I have no choice."

Layton tossed his weapons at me, then pushed his way toward the barker, shouting out, "If there are no brave men here I suppose I'll have to do!"

I heard Ferris laugh loudly behind me. "Good God. Is he volunteering?"

"I believe he is," I said.

"Stop him," Ferris said, but it was too late. The men had crowded around Layton to get a look at him. He was puffed up now that he was at the center of the crowd. He began parading back and forth in that mincing way of his, baiting the men.

"Am I the only brave man here? I guess I am."

There were roars and clapping. Layton went on, "I thought I'd heard they had men in the south. I guess I was wrong."

Money began to change hands.

"He's mad," Ferris said.

"He said it was the cure for his ill temper," I said.

"Of course it will be a cure. He'll be dead," Ferris said.

The crowd around Layton grew. More bets were placed. Then a bell was rung and Layton walked to the edge of the corral, wrapping a red sash about his hand. The throng of men—French and British employees of the HBC, American free trappers, Spanish from Santa Fe, and natives from at least five different tribes, all in various stages of drunkenness—crowded around that makeshift corral to watch. They had had other volunteers for the bull-bear fight but never a self-satisfied St. Louis dandy. They were all jostling for position. Layton put a foot on a cross slat and for a moment I wasn't sure he was really going to do it. I waved for him to come back, but he only shook his head, swung a leg over the fence, and dropped into the corral.

As soon as Layton landed in the dirt the bear swung around to face him and the bull raised its head. Layton unwound the red cloth from his hand and bent on one knee and took a handful of dust, then stepped toward the bear slowly, stopping several times to mark the bull, then moved on again. The bear strained toward Layton and the boulder with the chain attached to it rocked forward. Layton checked the bull again, then turned back to the bear. He took another step forward and the bear lunged to the length of its chain, reaching with one outstretched paw. The bear moved elastically and reached much farther than I expected. The swipe of the claw crossed Layton's chest. Tiny fragments of his shirt flew.

"Ah ha," the crowd yelled.

Layton held his arm to his gut. He stumbled back then steadied himself. Blood dripped from beneath his arm. Behind Layton, the bull began trotting, unsteadily at first. It moved not toward Layton but along the edge of the makeshift enclosure. Ferris raised his gun and aimed at the bull, but seeing Ferris with the gun, Layton motioned violently. He would not go on until Ferris lowered his weapon.

"Damn him," Ferris said.

The bull passed behind Layton and went on around the corral and when the bull passed us I could see the pulse of blood from its wounds, which left a trail in the dust. The bear turned to follow the progress of the bull, straining against the chain. The boulder turned slowly leaving deep brown grooves in the dust.

The bull came all the way around and as it did it veered from the edge of the corral and trotted toward Layton, who turned to the bull and held out the red sash. The bull ran for the cloth and Layton jerked the cloth away from the bull and put it in reach of the bear, who caught a segment in its claws, jolting Layton forward. The sash tore. Layton fell. The bull wheeled and turned on Layton, who rolled out of the way. The bull was carried close to the bear, who raked the bull's side with an awful tearing sound. The bull tottered. The bear turned back to Layton and Layton threw dust in the bear's eyes and moved suddenly to touch the lime, but the bear felt Layton's presence and snapped at him and Layton dropped. The jaws went an inch over Layton's head. The bull wheeled and was thundering toward Layton, who lay flat in the dust. The bear, hearing the thunder of the bull's hooves, swatted out blindly, smacking the bull on the head. The other horn was knocked sideways and the bull's head twisted. At that moment Layton leaped up and put his hand on the bear's forehead, then dropped and rolled out of the bear's reach. Then he was sprinting back toward the edge of the corral. The bull tottered toward Layton, hornless, but Layton was already leaping the fence headlong into the arms of the waiting men. He thrust his lime-covered hand in the air and a singular cheer went up from the crowd.

A moment later the men hefted Layton on their shoulders and carried him about, shoving a sack of coins into his hands. I could see Layton grinning complacently, pleased with himself, as if for once the world was treating him in the manner he deserved, but he was also pale and his hands shook. Blood oozed from the gashes in his gut.

"We'll hear about this for the rest of the season," Ferris said.

"For the rest of our lives," I said.

After Layton was set down he reached inside his shirt and wrapped the sash around his torso to bandage himself. Meanwhile, the bull had staggered to the far end of the corral. It had been raked deeply by the bear and its guts bulged from the wounds. Layton consulted with two Spaniards.

He gave them each a coin from his sack and they walked off and returned with eight-foot lances with gleaming triangular blades. They entered the corral and walked up carefully to the bull, positioning themselves, lances raised. The bull watched them dully, not moving. In a sudden gleaming flash of metal the bull's throat was slit twice and it collapsed, dead.

The lancers turned to the bear but Layton yelled out, waving his purse. The men with the lances walked back and Layton gave them each another coin. The men set aside their lances and came back with sections of rope and reentered the corral on horseback with two other riders. The lead rider swung the rope in the air, and when the bear reached out the swinging rope circled the paw, catching it. The first rider backed up gently with his horse, stretching the bear with the weight of the horse. The same was done with the other paw, and then the back legs, so all four limbs were bound. The riders backed up carefully with their large Spanish horses until the bear was stretched out along the dust, grunting and thrashing but powerless.

At a signal from the lead rider Layton ran in, inserted a gray key at the bear's neck, unlocking the clasp of the chain and then hurried off. The crowd, who had watched all this with interest, began drifting away nervously. The bear was now held only by the riders, but was not chained to the rock. Men with rifles positioned themselves. The gate to the corral was opened. Layton, with difficulty, got on horseback. He nodded to my horse, and said, "I'd get ready, Wyeth. You too, Ferris."

Ferris put a hand on the neck of Layton's horse. "That was worth the ride out here."

"I thought that would please you," Layton said. "And I saved the beast's life. You can congratulate yourself, Ferris. You've made a naturalist of me."

"I'd hardly call you that," Ferris said.

"Henry Layton," he intoned. "Friend to all creatures."

Before Ferris moved on, he opened the front of Layton's jacket and peeled back the sash. Blood was seeping into Layton's leggins. Ferris looked as if he wanted to treat Layton right there, but Layton waved him off.

"Later," Layton said. "Horseback."

Ferris got on his horse and Layton motioned to the four horsemen who were holding the bear outstretched. At a sign they let go of their ropes and galloped out of the corral. The bear, suddenly unbound, leaped up in an explosion of twisted rope and dust. A moment later it had flung the binds and loped out the open gate. It lurched at a drunken Frenchman, snapped air, and moved off through a marshy area and between two lodges. A minute later the bear was seen on a far slope, lumbering up the mountain.

"That will be a story to tell the ladies," I said.

"I am looking forward to not having to exaggerate for once," Layton said.

We rode fifteen minutes outside the encampment and settled at a pleasant spot along a creek where Layton dismounted and Ferris stitched his belly with deer sinews and a bone needle. Layton's ribs were bruised as well as gashed, and though I had not seen it happen, apparently Layton's foot had been trod on by the bull. He winced and hobbled his way through the next few days, needing help to get up and down from his buffalo robe and unable to raise his left arm over his head. I was unsure if Layton would be able to travel, or if he did, what sort of black mood the injuries would put him in. I need not have worried about that. Once we resumed our journey, Layton hardly spoke of his ailments and, if anything, seemed in a better mood because of them.

I understood something about Layton that day. He was peevish and voluble about any slight irritation or discomfort but took real physical harm indifferently, as it calmed his inner churning. And what's more, though he had relapses into distemper from time to time, his desire to remedy his life was genuine, and was succeeding. I was not surprised by this improvement. There is little that ails a man, particularly a St. Louis dandy, that is not remedied by a season in the mountains.

Twenty-five days after first leaving our brigade

we returned to report that there was no safe passage to the south and that if we were to bring our furs to market we'd have to make a run for Fort Ashley across that no-man's-land east of the Wind River Mountains.

In late November the Crow, who had mostly ignored us, began passing through our camp on a daily basis, apparently friendly but surveying our position, and noting the number of our pack horses and, if possible, the location and number of our furs. Branch, who had a wife in the Crow village, told us that many of the young men in the village blamed Layton for the Brits arming the Blackfoot and wanted to renegotiate the contract that Long Hair had made with the brigade or, more likely, to take all the furs from us by force and sell them to the British for more guns and powder. It was rumored that some of these Crow braves had received gifts from Pike's emissaries with promises of much more if the American furs were brought to trade at Flathead Post. These rumors filtered into camp for a few weeks. Then one morning Branch galloped into camp and said that the Crow were gathering their weapons and an attack was imminent.

The packs of furs were hastily gathered and loaded on ponies. We all bedded down, as if to retire for the night, but as soon as it was dark and the fire dwindled we rose again and as silently as possible, and without a word of parting to the Crow, left our encampment and wound our way out of the mountains, nine men and thirty laden horses. We rode all night, hid ourselves in shrubbery before dawn, rested through the short daylight hours, and rode north and east during the long winter night with only the stars to guide us.

The land to the east of the Wind River Mountains is arid sagebrush country and high-desert steppe, and for four days we made no fires and survived on dried meat and berries and the horses survived on what they could forage while picketed. When we rode, the white horses were covered with dark saddle blankets and we abstained from calling to one another or firing our weapons. On the evening of the fifth day the land became too broken to travel by night. We rested half that night and were up before dawn on the following day, the sixth, in which we began traveling by daylight.

On this day we passed through an arid land of many low waterways, and among enormous gray rock lumps, the largest of which was at least five hundred feet high. All of these stones had gray sloping sides and were faced the same direction and we called these rocks "elephants" because of their size and shape and gray color, and that afternoon, from the top of one of the elephants, we saw the smoke from a large native encampment to the south that Branch said held Red Elk and his men.

"Can they see us from there?" Smith asked.

"They can see our dust. No way they don't."

"Guns on the pommel," Smith said.

That afternoon Ferris and I were managing the rear of the pack train when he scoped the land behind us and kept the glass at his eye for a long time. A while after that I saw him glassing the land again. I rode back and he handed me the spyglass and pointed to the west and I saw what he had been seeing: dust rising in the afternoon light.

"Could be a herd of elk stranded out of the mountains," I said.

"Could be a lot of things," Ferris said. "But no herd of elk's going to follow us like that. You know that as well as I do."

Smith and Pegleg rode back and surveyed the land but already the dust had diminished and it was hard now to tell what we'd seen.

We rode all afternoon and stopped at a dirt crater with a small spring at the bottom of it. The spring was ice-rimmed and meandered off into a narrow, jagged canyon. Smith ordered the packs to be unloaded and set up as fortifications around the edge of the water hole. That took about forty minutes. After we arranged the packs Ferris glassed the land to the west again and we both saw the dust, closer now. Pegleg walked over and looked to the west with the spyglass and then held the glass to Layton, who looked, and then handed the glass back to Ferris.

"Whoever it is has been following us all day," Ferris said.

"Probably some of the squaws back in the Crow camp," Pegleg said. "Didn't get enough of Old Peggy during the season."

"Undoubtedly," Layton said. Then to Ferris, "What do you see?"

"I see dust that could be made by anything. But there is little out here besides men on horseback that would follow us for half a day."

All agreed with his assessment and there was little discussion about it. Only two years before Ferris had been considered a greenhorn trapper with the regrettable habit of sketching whatever he saw. Now he was one of the most trusted men in the brigade.

Pegleg handed his horn around and we all loaded our weapons and then Pegleg refilled his horn and afterward went down with Grignon to corral the horses in a narrow canyon that ran off to the east from the water hole. The rest of us stood at the south end of the crater and waited. We knew that British and Americans alike thirsted after our furs, but we were all good shots with the long guns, and if we had a favorable position, which we had in that location, we knew we could hold off a much larger brigade.

There was maybe an hour of daylight left. We watched the land to the south as the rising dust formed itself into a vague line and then became the wavery image of a single rider on horseback and then a man wearing a beaver hat and a native sheepskin jacket. Layton, Smith, Ferris, Branch, Bridger, Glass, and I stood at the edge of the crater. Behind us we could hear Pegleg and Grignon driving the horses into the protection of the canyon.

The man in the sheepskin jacket approached. He stopped at two hundred yards, waved once with his gun, then rode in slowly.

It was not until he neared that I was sure he was a white man.

He was riding an unshod native pony with a wooden saddle that seemed to be fashioned out of a stump and hempen rope. He carried only a small roll behind him that held, among other things, a tattered buffalo robe. We scanned the desert flats all around but it was just the one man. He rode in past us and went to the edge of the crater and rode along the edge, looking down at our gathered take for the season, then rode back in a loop and came to a stop in front of us, and said, "Hiya."

"Howdy," Layton said, not friendly.

The rider had long brown hair that fell around his face. There were scars on the right side of his face and the hair of his beard did not entirely cover it. He carried a Sheffield knife at the side and a smaller dagger at the front. There were feathers hanging from either side of his cap and beaded sheepskin on the fringes.

"You searching us?" Branch asked.

"Following your path. I'm going up to the big lake near the Tetons."

"Ain't going in the right direction for that," Glass said.

"Savages sent me scattering."

"Red Elk's band?" Branch said.

"I veered from them, same as you did."

"But we're not going to the same place," Smith said. "Our path makes sense for us. Not for you if you're going to the big lake."

"Took a roundy way to be safe," he said.

He had only one pack horse with few provisions and no lodge and no meat or furs to speak of.

"Traveling light for a long trip," Branch said.

"I move quicker that way."

"Not much quicker than us. We saw you this morning."

"I'm steady," he said, and grinned. He was missing some teeth in front. As he spoke his eyes were moving all over our position. He was taking in our weapons, our fur, each of our faces, and casting glances over the edge of the crater into the gloom of the canyon where the horses were jostling and snorting.

"Took in quite a haul," he said.

"Passable," Layton said. "Native furs of little worth."

Glass thrust a gourd with a cork stopper at him. "Drink."

"I'll have a swaller. Long as it's not poisoned," he said.

He gave a gap-toothed grin as he said this. Glass did not smile back but just kept holding the gourd out. The trapper hesitated, then took the gourd and pried the stopper off and drank one swallow. Then he capped the gourd and handed it back.

"Are you the owner?" he said to Layton.

"I am," Layton said and held his hand out. "Henry Layton."

The man shook his hand.

"Bill Callahan," he said.

"Never heard of a trapper by that name," Glass said.

"Now you have," he said.

"You're free to ride with us," Layton said.

"Just the drink," he said.

"Stay the night."

"Nope. Gotta keep moving," he said.

To arrive at dusk and not stay the night with a larger brigade was unheard of. The rider was already turning his horse.

"Just passing through. Thanks for the hospitality."

He started off slowly, all of us watching him. We knew we'd just been surveyed. We could have stopped him by shooting him, but that was the only way. Branch raised his weapon but Smith waved him off. The rider had taken account of our position and fortifications and the number of packs we carried. We could only hope that what he saw of our preparations would prevent any attack.

The man rode for ten minutes to the north and he was just a speck on the horizon when he turned west. After another ten minutes he'd turned back south, making a large loop around us. He must have known we were watching. I guessed at that point he didn't care.

"You see any sign of anyone else?" Layton asked.

"Nope," Smith said. He looked to the west and then back to the south.

"Don't mean they're not out there," Glass said.

"Nope," Smith said, again.

"That dust we saw wasn't from just one man," Ferris said.

"Nope," Smith said.

Through all this Glass gazed at the ground two feet in front of him. Ferris also seemed puzzled by something. Smith looked over at them and after a moment said, "What is it, Ferris?"

"I know him," Ferris said.

"Had the same feeling," Glass said.

"He was a friend of Grignon's," Ferris said slowly. "Do you remember? At the surround. Grignon was tormenting a wounded buffalo. He had a friend."

"Bouchet," Glass said.

"Didn't have the scars or the long hair then. But it's the same man."

The rest of us all remembered at once.

"Branch. Get that blackguard Grignon up here," Smith said, but Bridger and Branch were already sidestepping down the edge of the crater. They made their way into the canyon and at the same moment both cried out.

Ten steps into the canyon Pegleg lay facedown with his throat slit, a large splash of blood in the dirt. By the prints we understood that there had been many natives hidden in the canyon before our arrival. There were no horses left in the canyon. They had all been taken. Every one. We had not a single horse left. Grignon had vanished.

We remembered that it was Grignon who had informed us of the location of that water hole and had guided us there. In a single moment I realized I'd lost a good friend, my fortune, and my future happiness with Alene, as without horses I would not make it back to the settlement before spring-time.

As it grew dark Smith arranged us into defensive positions and we watched as fires appeared to the east and north. Many drums and savage cries and chanting filled the night. I lay there, gun pointed into the darkness, and thought how close we had come to succeeding, and how a single man, if well placed and sufficiently treacherous, can bring down the good work and preparation of much better men.

After midnight Smith came to my fortification and said, "Stretch your limbs, Wyeth, or are you afraid of a little scraping?"

I was led into the narrow arm of the canyon where the horses had been corralled and Ferris and Layton were already waiting. Smith and Branch had dug a grave for Pegleg using a knife and an iron bar from a pannier and the one shovel. Layton, Ferris, and I took over, and for several hours we expanded a hollow in the bank. It was pitch black in the canyon, and as we worked we cursed Grignon and invented methods of torment for him—scalping, cutting off limbs, cooking his innards—and with each imagined atrocity we laughed and then laughed some more and were then overtaken by a giddy, manic, abject hilarity. Odd. Pegleg dead and us on the scaffold and my future happiness dashed. Mostly, I remember laughing.

After several hours we were relieved by Bridger and Branch and just before dawn we gathered to bury Pegleg. In the dim light I looked into the face of my dead friend for the last time, and I thought that if Grignon were in front of me I would have committed depredations that would have out-done those of the savages.

Having interred Pegleg, we took half the pelts and piled them in the hastily constructed cache and covered it with dirt, which was stomped down and smoothed with branches from a shrub. We threw the remaining dirt into the stream and wiped out our footprints and tried to smooth away any sign that anyone had been there. We thought, perhaps, it would be the means of salvaging half the season, if we could survive.

As the light rose we saw what we were up against. There were more than a hundred natives in a half circle around our encampment, some waiting with their lances raised, others dashing back and forth, but none approaching the crater.

Beyond the natives, about half a mile away, there was a low point we could not see, but by the dust and the smoke from fires we could tell it was occupied by many men.

After an hour of waiting the natives quieted and a gap formed in the ring and a single man on horseback started out from the main body. Smith glassed the rider and something settled over his features. He handed the glass to Layton who looked for a moment, moved his mouth around, and lowered the glass.

"Pike," he said. Then, "Come on, Wyeth. You pointed a gun at him last time you saw him. You can do it again with the savages behind him."

Layton, Smith, and I started out across the desert on foot. We stopped a hundred yards out from the crater and Pike rode toward us slowly. I could see that he was enjoying himself. He dismounted and took his time picketing his horse. As he did it five British trappers in deerskins rode out and stopped behind him, muskets pointed toward us, in case we had thoughts of blasting him and ending his life with our own.

"Henry Layton," Pike said as he walked up, extending his hand. "How good to see you."

"I believe it must be pleasant for you," Layton said, ignoring his hand.

"Our company was passing through these territories, which will soon be ours, and we saw what appeared to be a brigade of trappers stranded without horses. We have come to your aid just as you came to the aid of my men."

"Wonderfully coincidental," Layton said.

"I have some influence with the natives. I can transport you to safety at Flathead Post for the customary price that you have already established."

"Two packs of fur is the customary price," Layton said.

"The price, which you established, is all the pelts gathered in exchange for your lives. I will take all your pelts. You are free to accompany us to safety."

"I'd rather slit my throat," Layton said.

"I believe the natives will accommodate you in that," Pike said. Then to Smith, "I apologize Jedediah. You are in bad company."

"I have grown to appreciate my company more than ever," Smith said. "In the spring we inadvertently came upon three Snake natives who were stealing from us on your orders. We saved them from the Gros Ventre at the cost of two packs of fur. You have purposefully lured us into a trap at the cost of many times that amount of pelts and at the cost of a good man's life."

"I did not sanction that."

"It happened all the same. He lies back in the drainage with his throat slit. Pegleg Cummins, from Mississippi."

"It was not my doing," Pike said.

"It was the result of your treachery."

"The treachery was not mine but one of your own brigade. I was simply invited to profit from it, same as you were before."

Smith looked away and spoke bitterly. "We may have taken too many pelts from the Snake, but it was not by design, and there was no treachery involved. You realize that."

"Of course he realizes it," Layton said acidly. "Why even talk to the blackguard? He simply wants our furs."

"And I will have them," Pike said. He turned on Layton with a sudden, steely annoyance. "Henry Layton, winner of friends and protector of old ladies. Since our last encounter I have made inquiries and heard of your adventures along the wharfs in St. Louis. You of all people should not talk of leading others to their demise. You are not well remembered, either at home or abroad."

"I cannot speak for others," Smith said, "but he is well-liked in this brigade among those who know him best."

Layton nodded to Smith with genuine gratitude. "Thank you, Jedediah."

"What I have said is true," Smith said. "You have become an able captain and trapper. All have noted it."

Even at that moment, Layton beamed with pleasure.

"I thank you again."

"You two will have much time to bask in your mutual appreciation," Pike said. "Step away from your weapons and let my men approach or we will cut you down."

Smith began to step away but at that moment a horseman broke from the ranks of natives and rode toward us. Pike waved the horseman off, but the rider kept coming. It was Grignon. He was wearing a new deerskin jacket and his cheeks were clean-shaven and he had gotten oil from somewhere for his mustache. In a day he had transformed himself into a British dandy.

Layton and I reached for our weapons, but Smith made a hissing sound and we lowered them reluctantly.

"Morning, Layton. Morning, Captain," Grignon said in a particularly jaunty tone.

"Back in the ranks," Pike said.

"You ought to be thanking me, not giving orders," Grignon said airily to Pike. "I have just made you a fortune."

"And yourself one," Pike said.

Smith watched Grignon steadily with absolute hatred.

"Pegleg lies with his throat slit," Smith said. "He was a good man and a loyal friend. I will make it my life's work to repay that treachery."

It was said simply and with absolute conviction. Grignon tried to appear unaffected, though his voice shook.

"Pegleg was given a choice," Grignon said.

"I know the sort of choice you gave him. He would not betray his friends or his country so you killed him for it. I will track you down, Grignon."

"And if Smith doesn't find you, I will," Layton said.

Grignon sniffed and looked away. "I will make it easy for both of you. You can find me next in London at the Manor House. Good day," he said.

Grignon started back. Pike held his mouth shut, displeased. He had not wanted that interchange and it was clear he disliked Grignon.

"Now it is you who have aligned yourself with savory companions," Smith said sarcastically to Pike. "You will regret it."

"Perhaps I will regret having to associate with your pleasant countryman. I already regret his tone and will correct that when I have the chance. I feel he will never be a true member of our brigade. I will make up for the unpleasant association with a successful return on the season and the knowledge that the boundaries of this region will be redrawn in our favor. Very soon I will no longer have to debate about where I place my flag. I repeat what I said before, Jedediah. You are a solid fellow. When the land officially changes ownership I expect to find you looking for a job and will gladly hire you."

"You are overly optimistic about the new borders."

"I am optimistic, but understandably so," Pike said. "We control all the land between the mountains and have just secured the largest return in the history of the entire country. You can leave your companions and come with us now, if you like. Or you can return to this country in several years' time. A British brigade awaits you."

Smith turned and looked away. He said nothing.

"Then I leave you to your fate," Pike said, and turned to go, but Layton stopped him, saying, "We gave your natives horses when we rescued them. If you mean to offer a fair exchange, leave us seven horses so we can return to our country."

"There are seven of you. Seven horses will guarantee that you will make mischief. I will leave you four. That is enough to go for help, but not enough to make a nuisance of yourself, as the other three will be at our mercy."

"There was a black thoroughbred among the horses," Layton said. "Make that one of the four. We will need it if we are to survive the winter."

"The black thoroughbred that was among the

horses is a fine creature and is now picketed next to my lodging," Pike said.

"That horse belongs to the son of Chief Long Hair," Layton said. "It was loaned for the trip, and was to be returned by the mulatto Branch after our journey. It is not our horse."

This was untrue, and Pike could have confirmed this by asking Grignon, but he did not want to see Grignon again and did not call him.

"It appears we will be wintering in the Crow encampment," Layton said. "It will make their charity to us more palatable if we have not lost their prized animal."

"I hardly need worry about your discomfort with the natives."

"You do need to worry about their displeasure when they discover you have stolen their prized animal. That thoroughbred was the property of Chief Long Hair and is now the property of his son. The Crow will know you took it despite being informed of its true owner."

Pike considered this silently. He knew it was foolish to unnecessarily anger a native chieftain. Without a word he walked back to his horse, unpicketed it, mounted, and said, "Agreed. Four horses. One of them the black. You will temporarily surrender your arms and withdraw from your positions. You see that single tree out in the flats." He pointed at a scraggly cottonwood. "You wait there. My men will hold your weapons during that time and will extract payment for your lives. Any variation and I will release the natives to do as they please."

Pike wheeled slowly and rode away.

Smith turned to Layton. "I am glad you can still think of horseflesh."

"I'm thinking of retrieving our furs."

"With four horses?"

"Yes."

"Explain," Smith said.

"Let's see if they find the cache first," Layton said.

Smith did not question him further, and we all walked back to the crater. Smith advised the men to surrender their weapons and to walk out to the tree indicated. A minute later Pike's men marched in with twenty-five beasts, and one by one led off our spoils from the entire year. At first they only found half of the pelts, the other half being hidden in the cache, but Grignon knew the size of our take and rode in and walked about inside the crater and into the canyon and through all its various channels and found the newly dug spot. Layton looked off at the wastelands cursing Grignon. Smith sat leaden and silent. That return had meant a secure life and many comforts for the entire brigade, and for me it represented a happy future with Alene. All of it was carried away in less than an hour.

After the last furs and most of our supplies had

been removed, and only a few lead bars and dregs of a barrel of powder remained, Pike returned with two men leading four horses, one of which was the black thoroughbred I had won in the horse race. Pike rode past us and said to Layton, "It was truly a remarkable return for a season. Thank you for taking the trouble of gathering it for us. If I see you again my men will dispatch you. Good day."

He motioned to the riders behind him. The first horseman rode up and tossed the halter of the black and struck Layton in the face with it. Layton reached for his pistol but it was not on his hip, as it had been surrendered. When the men were a hundred yards out one of them unrolled a robe and our guns and knives and pistols and hatchets clattered out onto the scrubland, all of them without powder or balls.

We waited until the riders were a smudge on the horizon and then we started out and gathered our weapons and returned to the crater. Our belongings were scattered and tossed into the muddy water. Many of our personal items had been taken. In the canyon we saw the Brits had trampled over Pegleg's shallow grave.

When I talk about this now—I mean, this story of my friendship with Ferris and Layton and our unexpected foray into international affairs—this is the moment when men doubt my story. There are royalists who say that a respected and honored man like Sebastian Pike, second-in-command of the western branch of the Hudson's Bay Company, would never risk an international conflict over the spoils of a single season of pelts from an obscure trapping company. All I can say is that it happened and it was not an illogical decision on his part. The greatest fear of the British was that an American brigade would arrive in St. Louis with an enormous return, which would set off a stampede to the trapping lands by the impulsive Americans, who seemed incapable of judging a situation accurately if there was the smallest possibility of making a fortune. And though the British government denied the assault happened, it did in fact happen just as I have written here. One man died from it, Pegleg Cummins, and we were left stranded in the wasteland, seven men with four horses and little in the way of powder or balls. But Layton, with his habitual scheming, had considered a way to use the four horses, and particularly the black thoroughbred, to regain our fortune. As it turned out the future of the western half of our country, the best part of the country, I believe, may have rested on my horse, Ferris's shot, and Layton's powers of persuasion.

By midmorning, Layton, Ferris, Branch, and I were dashing back across the scrubland and by midafternoon we'd arrived at that region of rock elephants that we'd passed through the day before.

We crept up the sloping back of the southern-most of the elephants and glassed the native encampment we had seen previously. It held fifty or sixty lodges and many horses in a corral beyond. After we had all taken a look, Layton said, "Three ride in. One stays behind and observes. You're the fastest, Wyeth. If we perish you go north and east and find an American trapping company. You could be back here in a week with reinforcements and save the remains of the brigade."

"And leave you to the natives?"

"If it comes to that, yes," Layton said. "Whether we are three or four, we're still hopelessly outnumbered. If we perish you can be the means of aiding the rest of the brigade."

"The others have ample food and water," I said. "They will be discovered regardless of whether I bring horses or not."

"There is no certainty of that," Layton said. "And if you keep yourself hidden we are assured that at least one of us will survive. You could still make it back to Fort Ashley before the turn of the year. Alene awaits—"

"Do you think I'd use Alene as an excuse to abandon the brigade in its most desperate moment?" I said.

"I am certain you wouldn't, Wyeth, which is why I am attempting to reason with you, knowing you would not suggest it yourself."

Layton caught Ferris's eye and I understood they had spoken of it beforehand.

"There would be no shame in staying hidden, and much good sense," Ferris said. "The fortune you'd receive from Alene is far greater than anything we've gathered here. These pelts mean less for you than they do for us. And another's happiness depends on your survival. Stay hidden. Observe the parley. And if we are slain you remain with a horse to go for help."

"Do you think I'd be such a coward as to let you three go without me? Smith, Glass, and Bridger will be discovered regardless. You know that. And if anyone is to stay at a distance it ought to be Ferris, as he has the best shot. I will not remove my gun from the negotiations out of self-interest."

"Then do it for Alene," Layton said. "If you perish you ruin two people's lives. If I die I will make several parties exceedingly happy, including my father."

"I hardly believe that," I said.

"I feel it is more true than you know," he said.

"I will not burrow into some hole while you risk your life," I said.

"Well, someone ought to stay back," Ferris said. "If it were Layton in your position he would have ridden off already, leaving us to our fate."

"That is untrue and unjust," Layton shouted. "Untrue and unjust and I resent the implication, Ferris. I demand you take it back. I am trying to save Wyeth's life and using all means to persuade him, but I cannot say I would scatter at this desperate moment. I would not and I cannot say I would."

"You are wonderfully persuasive," Ferris said.

Layton puffed himself up. "Persuasion is one thing. Self-incrimination is another. We are in the greatest wilderness known to man on the verge of dashing after a murderous rascal who has stolen our fortune. I can truly say I have never looked forward to any expedition more in my entire life. I would never leave the brigade at such a moment. Captain Smith has placed his trust in me and has given me the great honor of saying I've become an able trapper. Do you think I'd repay that compliment with personal cowardice? I'd rather die. I expected Wyeth would refuse. I was simply giving him the opportunity to be sensible. But I suppose none of us would be here at all if we had that malady. Bravo, Wyeth."

Ferris made a derisive clicking sound as this bit of bravado did little to convince me to hold myself apart and much to aggrandize our desperate action. Henry Layton, who was known as a self-satisfied St. Louis dandy, was surprising us all by risking his life for the brigade, though he was also boasting about it shamelessly. That combination of bravery and puffing himself up with his own oratory had the distinctive imprint of Layton's personality, containing equal parts daring, foolishness, and bragging. But for once Layton did not exaggerate about our situation. It was true that we were at the very center and tipping point of the world's interest, and all our lives hung in the balance.

"You corncrackers ready?" Branch asked after a moment. He'd been on his elbows, surveying the native village. "Their scouts will spot us. It's better if we approach on our own rather than being impelled."

"If we ride to our death, let's do it grandly," Layton said.

We descended the back end of the "elephant" and mounted our horses and rode out with a sort of swagger, bolstered for a moment by Layton's romantic bluster.

At five hundred yards Ferris was left in a natural fortification between two rocks and Layton, Branch, and I rode on another two hundred yards, and then dismounted and waited. Squaws and children had run out to the edge of the village. Dogs coursed around us, barking. Men on horseback, armed with muskets and bows, arrived at the outskirts of the village. Then the line of natives parted and a delegation rode out. They came slowly, on horseback, four men, wrapped in furs hats and buffalo robes, with another fifteen warriors following behind. Branch walked out to meet them and there was much gesturing and striking of chests and pointing at the black thoroughbred. This conversation, half in sign language, half in various native dialects, went on for ten minutes. Then Branch walked back to where Layton and I waited and said, "They're willing to listen before they begin the depredations."

"I'm glad to hear it," Layton said.

"But make no mistake. Red Elk means to eat your liver for dinner, Layton. You too, Wyeth. Save a bullet for yourself."

The first native in the delegation had broken from the others and started toward us. I saw it was Red Elk, riding the same horse he had ridden in the race several months before.

When he arrived at our windswept spot he jumped off his horse and left it there without picketing it. He reached inside his furs and took out a pipe and lit it. He puffed on it slowly, then handed it to Layton who smoked and then handed it to Branch who smoked and then handed it to me and I smoked and then handed it to Red Elk who bent down slowly and turned it over and tapped it on the ground a few times, then stood and refilled it and passed it around again, all in silence.

The pipe was secreted back in Red Elk's robe, and Layton stepped forward and said, "I am certain your spies have told you that we have lost our horses and our furs. But I do not think you understand why we are here now, so give us time to speak."

Branch translated, and when he was finished Red Elk waved at the picketed thoroughbred behind me, and spoke briefly. Branch translated.

"He says, 'Chief Pike has taken your pelts and now you have come to offer me something that is already mine to try to get me to help you get back what Pike has taken from you.'"

Layton made an impatient huffing sound, and said, "Tell him the horse is not to bargain for. The horse is a gift. Tell him that."

"I was just about to," Branch said.

Branch spoke in the native tongue, and then Red Elk spoke at some length.

"He says he can take the horse whether it is a gift or not," Branch translated. "And offering something to persuade can hardly be called a gift. He means to slit your throat, Layton."

Layton turned to Red Elk.

"We are enemies. That is true. But you are also enemies with Pike. Am I right? You worked for Pike, and you wanted long guns, but he has not given them."

Branch translated this to Red Elk, who said nothing, but by his silence we saw this was the case. This was Layton's real gamble. He was sure that Pike would not have given Red Elk long guns, and that Red Elk would have resented it.

"Your land is being overrun," Layton said. "You have only one choice. To fight and align yourself with the victor."

"It appears that will be Pike," Red Elk said in return.

"It appears that way but it will not be," Layton said. "His men travel in large groups like antelope, numerous but skittish. We are like wolves. We travel in small packs and we hunt like you and sleep in the open like you and go where we please like you. The owners of the British company are in London, far away. Fat men who have never seen these mountains. We own our company. We work together and fight together and profit together. Just like you. Pike and his men will not leave the protection of a large company, but we go wherever we want and battle where we choose. And who we battle, we battle for ourselves. We ask you to join us in our fight against Pike, in retaking what is ours, and we will return the favor by giving you our long guns."

Layton held up his Hawken.

"I give this now as a sign of goodwill. Ten more weapons will follow. Ten long guns and all the powder we possess, and all the guns you can take from the British after you help us retrieve our furs."

Red Elk said nothing. He filled the pipe again and smoked from it and handed it to Layton who smoked and gave it to Branch who smoked and passed it to me. Red Elk's manner had not changed but I thought that if the proposition did not at least interest him we would have all been dead by then.

When I returned the pipe, Red Elk turned it over and said, "The last time I saw you, you stole my horse and had just participated in the massacre of my friends."

"We were impelled to be present at the battle against your friends," Layton said. "We did not actively participate in it and I argued to save the captives."

Red Elk looked at him silently. I had the feeling he knew this to be true.

"But we did aid Chief Long Hair with long guns because he was a friend to us. We will be good to you if you become our friend. And if you kill us here, which you could certainly do, your men will only get the guns we do not manage to destroy before you kill us. And you will also lose your life."

Layton motioned to Ferris out in the snowy waste.

"My man has four loaded weapons with him and you are in his sights. He will kill you at the first hostility."

Red Elk turned and looked out at Ferris—a small dot in the vast, snow-swept expanse. Red Elk laughed.

"That man?"

"Yes," Layton said.

"He is too far away to hit a horse. I could kill you and take your weapons and then kill him and take his weapons."

"You and at least three of your men would be dead before you got to him."

"Your man cannot hit me from there," Red Elk said.

"He could choose which eye to put a bullet through," Layton said.

Red Elk said something to his counselors and they murmured and looked at Ferris far out in the plain and shook their heads and laughed among themselves.

Layton walked over to one of Red Elk's counselors and reached up slowly and took an arrow from a quiver. He held the arrow up to show it to them, then walked some distance away and pushed the arrow into the frozen ground. It had a red shaft and three yellow feathers and stood out against the frozen prairie. Layton pointed at the arrow and then pointed out at Ferris.

"Wyeth, go tell Ferris to split this arrow."

"He can't make that shot," I said.

"Don't argue about it. Just go tell him." Then to Branch, "Tell the chief here that if Ferris splits this arrow from where he is right now, he joins us to fight Pike and enrich himself. If Ferris misses, he can do what he wants with us."

I began to protest but Layton waved for me to be silent. Branch translated. Red Elk motioned noncommittally, and Layton waved for me to ride out to Ferris.

I got on my horse and rode out and told Ferris

what was required of him. Ferris had been lying there beneath a buffalo robe for half an hour in the frozen flats.

"He wants me to do what?" Ferris said.

"Can you see the red arrow with the yellow feathers against the white snow?"

Ferris looked up at me. "I can't make that shot."

"He already told them you could. He wants to show what can be done with a long gun. He said you'd split it in half."

"Well, of all the idiotic things Layton has done this is the stupidest. I can't make that shot. What's going to happen when I miss?"

"Massacre, probably," I said. "If we are overtaken, don't waste time defending us. Ride north in Pike's path. Perhaps you'll escape with your life."

Ferris lay there beneath his robes sighting the tiny red dot in the distance.

"Has he really rested our hopes on this?"

"He has," I said. "Good luck, Ferris."

"It is you who will need luck when I miss this impossible shot," he said.

I rode back and said that Ferris would fire presently and we waited. It was me and Layton and Branch and Red Elk and his counselors out on the snowy, windswept plain. The entire population of his village stood to the side watching, anticipating the massacre they were sure would follow. Far out in the wastes Ferris stood and shook his arms out and stepped about to warm himself. Then he lay back down and aimed for a long time. A minute passed with just the high whistling of the wind and the distant barking of dogs in the native encampment. Then there was a puff of smoke and the delayed sound of a gunshot seared across the icy wastes. I turned to see the shaft of the arrow was half as long as it had been and the top piece had tumbled off ten feet away into bits of stubbled grass sticking out of the snow.

Red Elk walked to the arrow and retrieved the feathered end and examined it. He looked out at the puff of smoke drifting away. Ferris was already reloading his weapon. Red Elk said something to the three counselors, who stood dumbfounded. After a moment one of them mounted and started back toward the encampment. The two others followed, leading the thoroughbred. Red Elk said some words to Branch, then mounted his horse and rode off slowly. When he was out of hearing Branch said, "He'll join us with thirty men. They will keep whatever spoils they gather from the Brits other than the pelts. And they will take our guns and powder as payment. He says the trappers with Pike are not warriors and the natives are mostly Flathead and are worthless in battle. He says we should not have given up our weapons when we were surrounded as even seven men could have repulsed them. He says the large brigades move slowly and we will overtake them tomorrow. He says in two days he will have our furs back. The only question is if any of us will live to carry them."

We overtook Pike's brigade the following evening, just as Red Elk had said, and the morning after that Layton and I were hidden in shrubbery in a wide, sloping valley with a burbling spring running up the middle. Four HBC trappers were positioned near the spring listening to the distant gunshots of a diversionary assault that had been launched by Red Elk and his men against the main body of the HBC. The horses had been secured in a natural corral of dense shrubbery half a mile from the battle, and only these four drivers were left to watch over the horses, as the British knew that even if the horses were somehow diverted, it would be impossible for the thieves, so encumbered, to get very far without being overtaken. Pike had more than a hundred men in his brigade, plus at least that many natives. He could overwhelm any force in the west.

The sound of gunfire rose and Layton and I crept to the edge of the shrubbery in which we were hidden. Ferris was separate from us, up on the slope somewhere in the trees with the long guns. Smith, Branch, Bridger, and Glass were with the diversionary assault, but said they would return in time to come to our aid.

Layton and I studied the drivers, knowing that

we must disarm them, take control of our pelts, and make a dash east with the pack train before the bulk of the brigade was alerted. There were four men we had to overcome: a large, knobby-nosed captain whom I knew from St. Louis, an old-timer with gray hair who looked like he'd spent his life on the march, and two French trappers, one with a thick blond beard and the other clean-shaven.

These four men were all turned downhill toward the forest as another volley of fire sent a large cloud of smoke drifting over the trees. At this same moment a rider appeared out of the forest and moved up the slope and when he neared I saw it was Grignon. He spoke to the knobby-nosed captain, who motioned to the loaded pack horses wedged into the narrow enclosure made by the dense shrubbery. I understood Grignon was asking about the furs and the security of the horses. By the captain's careless gesture it was clear that he felt the furs were perfectly safe.

Grignon examined the natural corral and spring and then his eyes moved up and down the clearing and rested on the shrubbery where Layton and I were hidden. I knew he could not see us but his eyes stayed on the shrubbery for a long while.

The bearded Frenchman stood laconically and stretched and took two gourds hanging from a saddlebag on his horse and turned to the spring. The captain, the old-timer, and the clean-shaven

Frenchman watched the smoke rise above the trees to the west. The bearded Frenchman moved for the spring and Grignon held his flask out but the Frenchman pretended not to notice.

"They know he's worthless," Layton whispered.

"They know he betrayed his friends," I said.

The bearded Frenchman knelt at the spring and filled the gourds and then corked them by striking them with his palm. He handed one of the gourds to the captain who struggled with the cork stopper. It had been wedged deeply and the captain could not dislodge it. Grignon, meanwhile, had taken his own gourd and knelt at the edge of the spring. Layton nodded to me. There could be no better moment than that.

Layton and I eased our way out of the shrubbery, Layton holding his pistol in his left hand and a hatchet in the right. I was holding a pistol in each hand.

"Bet you wish you had that Collier now," I whispered.

"If I had the Collier I would not have the satisfaction of cleaving Grignon's skull with my blade," Layton said.

We crept side by side, Layton and I, shoulder to shoulder, moving slowly along the outside of the shrubbery, which ended twenty-five yards from the spring. I could hear the pop of gunfire now and now and now. Grignon sat back and listened to the fighting, then bent again to the spring, reaching his gourd far underwater. Layton and I stepped out into the open and Layton raised his hatchet and began to run. I followed.

In front of us Grignon held the gourd deep beneath the water. The stream trickled and the sun flared on the glistening snow. The captain had given up trying to unstopper his gourd and held it out to the clean-shaven Frenchman, who was pleased to help him, wanting to show his strength. We were fifteen steps away, close enough to see the white strands in Grignon's hair as he bent to the pool. I could see the straining muscles in his shoulder. Layton raised the hatchet high. When he was four steps from the spring Grignon looked up and Layton ran the last steps and swung with the hatchet. Grignon rolled and the blade hit not the top of his head, but severed his ear and grazed the scalp. The blade rung as it split a stone two inches thick.

The captain whirled and I fired and he fired at the same time. Both our bullets went wide. The bearded Frenchman was reaching for his rifle when the gourd was blown from his hand. Two thin streams of blood sprung forth where his fingers had been. That was Ferris in the trees with his long guns. The other Frenchman had fallen and was reaching for his pistol, but Layton kicked it away. The man looked up at Layton and said, "*Je suis un booshway comme toi*," and ran for the shrubbery. Layton did not fire on him but turned to look for Grignon, who had dashed off toward the far slope. Meanwhile, the captain had tossed his pistol and was reaching for his rifle when I fired with my other weapon. The captain fell back to the edge of the spring. I moved to leap on him but saw with surprise that there was no need. He was dead. I had killed him.

I turned about the clearing, but Layton and I were now alone at the spring. The captain was dead and the others had fled. The camp hands did not get a percentage of the returns of the profit of the brigade and were not going to die for the furs. In a matter of ten seconds it was only Layton and I at the edge of that burbling spring. I glanced at the dead captain again. The bullet had passed through his mouth and come out the back of his skull. His head lay to the side, his brown hair floating weightlessly in the clear water. A thread of blood trickled crosswise over his forehead and dripped off his nose into the water. I could see individual drops clouding the water. Years later, as all else fades, those drips of blood in the spring stay with me.

There was movement down the slope. Grignon had crossed the stream and was slipping across a snowfield. I retrieved the captain's rifle and sighted Grignon and fired and he fell. He got up and stumbled into some shrubbery. He was still alive, running down the slope.

"The horses," Layton said, and I turned to the

makeshift corral where a hundred and twenty fully laden pack horses and mules were gathered, jostling one another. Some of the animals held equipage, but about sixty of them held pelts. Not just our furs but the British profits from the entire season. As I went for the lead horse and began to separate the animals carrying furs from those that carried equipage, I realized that Layton was not behind me but had mounted one of the Frenchmen's horses and was riding down the slope.

"The pelts," I yelled but he was already gone in the direction Grignon had fled, holding his hatchet.

I turned back to the horses, found the lead pony, and led the beast out slowly. I tied the lead horse to a tree and led out another string. I tied that horse off to another tree. I had led out a quarter of the animals when something whooshed past my ear. I looked up to see that three rearguard soldiers had spotted me and were dashing back toward the spring. Suddenly, the three veered to the north, one of them lurching in his mount. Branch, Glass, Bridger, and Smith were coming down the far slope with eight natives. A moment after that Smith arrived and saw our pelts and the British pelts still bound to the horses. He had been afraid that the furs would be unpacked during the battle. He gave a wolfish grin.

"Where's that flatlander Layton?"

"After Grignon," I said.

"Damn him. Pike would thank him for slaying the blackguard. It's the pelts that cut him. The pelts!"

Smith turned back to the first string of ponies. He began urging them up the slope. Branch took another string. Glass a third. Ferris was still covering us from somewhere in the trees. More natives arrived and began driving the remaining horses onward. Within two minutes all sixty horses carrying pelts were cut from the rest and were being driven up the valley. As we reached the protection of a dense patch of trees, I was just about to turn back for Layton when he rode past me, blood up and down his deerskin shirt, his left bicep gouged.

"Damn you, Layton," Smith said.

"Pleasure before business," Layton said, and gripped a bloody bit of gore—a piece of red hair with scalp on the end—tucked under the loop of his watch guard.

An hour later we passed through a notch in the gray rock walls at the ridgetop just east of the spring where we had battled with the British. This notch was the only passage over that ridge for many miles in any direction, and as soon as the laden ponies passed through the rock channel, natives began filling the gap with wood and charcoal, then covering it with hot coals that had been prepared beforehand. In a matter of minutes a large fire blazed, blocking the passageway.

Meanwhile, the laden ponies continued down the east side of the slope and approached a rocky stream where sixty native horses loaded with twig and rock–filled packs awaited their arrival. The waiting ponies were connected from their lead ropes to a cinch ring on the pack saddle, in groups of four, so as to resemble the Hudson's Bay horses. Ferris, Glass, Branch, and I were at the head of the real pack train, with native handlers to aid us. As we guided our horses into the creek we turned them upstream, to the right. At the same time the diversionary pack animals were led out of the creek and downstream by native riders, accompanied by Smith and Bridger. This was the decisive moment. We needed to lead the animals with the actual pelts into the stream for five hundred yards and then send them up over a shrubby rise in the opposite direction from the false pack train, which would be led in the direction of Fort Ashley. If the ruse were successful, and the animals with the pelts managed to get over the rise and out of sight before the Brits passed through the rock passage, then it was unlikely that the British would realize their mistake for at least a day, if not much longer. But we needed an hour to cross the barren slope. Pike and his men were no more than fifteen minutes behind us.

The last of the real pack animals turned up the streambed and were hidden by the bank and foliage just as the British began arriving at the flaming logs in the rock passage. Through the streamside foliage I could see the Brits dashing back and forth, battling the flames. Twice I stopped to glass the passage. I saw that the British had placed wet robes on themselves and were running up to the blaze and using bent pickets as hooks to drag the logs away. Natives were shooting arrows attached to thin ropes into the logs and pulling burning logs from the fire.

Once they passed through the rock passage they could hardly fail to see the ruse.

Glass, Branch, Ferris, and I, along with natives from Red Elk's band, drove the horses as fast as we could up the barren slope. Far below us Layton straggled behind. He was not aiding with the pack train, as he was supposed to, but simply riding slowly, trying to keep up, wobbling in his saddle. I motioned to Ferris, then turned back and when I neared I saw that the bullet that had caused the gash in Layton's right arm had also entered his chest. I had not seen that before. With each breath pink bubbles frothed from the hole in his chest. His skin was gray and glistening and his saddle blanket was wet with blood.

"Give me your musket," he said weakly. "I cannot handle the ponies, but I can help the brigade by delaying our enemies." I looked him up and down silently for a moment. Ferris had turned and ridden down to join us. He only had to glance at Layton to understand the situation.

"You will die if you are not treated," Ferris said. "Ride to the foliage along the streambed. We will hide ourselves in shrubbery and I will treat your wounds. Wyeth will drive the horses."

Layton began to protest but Ferris cut him off.

"Without care you will be dead within the hour."

"Then let me die battling," Layton said.

He reached to take Ferris's rifle from his saddle harness. He missed and fell from his horse and lay panting in the dust. He tried to rise and could not.

"Damn you," Layton said weakly. "Help me on my horse. I can be the means of saving the brigade if I can get on my horse." Layton clung to the edge of his stirrup and tried to stand again and fell back. "Damn you. Help me."

Ferris motioned for me to leave him but Layton was too pitiful a sight, groping at his stirrup. I jumped down and lifted him into his saddle. As I did Layton took the firearm from my holster. It was a musket as Ferris had my long gun.

"Give me my weapon, you scoundrel," I said.

"Do you think I care for your curses? I will delay the British and save the brigade."

"What you're doing is impeding our progress," Ferris said. "Dismount. And I will attempt to save your life. You can hardly affect the outcome in your state."

"I can hardly do otherwise," Layton said, not with his usual self-aggrandizing bluster but in a matter-of-fact tone. "You can see the situation as well as I. But I can still be the means of helping the brigade."

Below us, the British were on the verge of crossing the stone passage. Ferris turned and saw this, and then turned back and studied Layton. He could barely sit on his horse.

"We will go back together. If we live through the hour, you will let me treat you."

"Gladly," Layton said.

Ferris motioned up the hill.

"Someone needs to drive the horses. No time to argue, Wyeth. You've had your heroics. Let us have ours."

Layton turned his horse and took my hand. "If I do not survive tell Alene I fought bravely."

"You will tell her of your escapades yourself," I said.

"Live well, old friend," he said, and bolted downhill.

Ferris held his rifle up. "Do not wait for us. We will find you," he said.

There was a sort of dropping inside as they rode off, but there was no time to consider it. I watched Ferris and Layton moving toward the burning embers in the stone gates, then turned to drive the pack animals, which were straggling. I stopped several times in the next half hour to scope the stone gates. I saw that Layton had positioned himself in some rocky crevice and was shooting into the opening, scattering the British. Ferris— with Layton covering him—dragged a large tree branch and toppled it into the opening. In a minute the fire had blazed up again and this branch, wedged between rocks, could not be dragged away so easily. The Brits came swinging their hooks and again Layton blasted the opening with his musket. The fire was blazing now, a bright eye in the gray rock that, if left burning, would hold them for hours.

I drove the beasts until they had crossed the ridgetop and dropped out of sight, then turned and glassed the stone gates one more time. British gunmen had set up at various angles beyond the flames, but Layton was in a natural fortification and was well protected, firing into the gap whenever the Brits exposed themselves.

From the top of the ridge I glassed Layton. He was sitting with his back to a flat rock, loading his musket, and I thought at first he was talking to himself, but then understood that he was singing. I could hear it faintly through the sound of shouting and gunshots. It was that wonderful aria he'd sung the last night of our wander. Layton, that reckless, aggravating, honorable man, was holding off the entire British brigade single-handedly and singing while he did it. I left him there and followed the pack train.

Branch, Glass, and I, and a dozen natives, drove the animals all night and into the next day, half expecting the Brits to show up on our trail at any moment, but they did not, and by the afternoon of the following day we began to hope the ruse had worked.

We slept for several hours that afternoon, then rode all night and the next morning a horse was sighted to the north. Half an hour later Ferris arrived in the encampment. He didn't bother getting off his horse, but simply lay down on top of it.

"Our enemies were delayed for hours by Layton, who perished in the night." There were cries of grief but Ferris, exhausted, barked at us in a horrible way. "Onward, or his sacrifice is meaningless."

From that moment on, in Captain Smith's absence, Ferris became our brigade leader.

Seven days later, after nearly constant travel, we crossed a ridge in the Bighorn Mountains and wound our way down to a small encampment of Crow and Arapahoe natives, French trappers, and mixed-blood children. This hidden, protected spot in a game-filled valley was a perfect winter encampment. In those first days we slept with our guns and expected to be overtaken at any moment, but Pike and his brigade did not arrive, and then the real winter storms began, which would have prevented their crossing, even if they had been on our trail.

We settled into that valley for the winter and Ferris passed the time by sketching the children and the natives, and these studies were the basis for his famous painting *Winter Encampment,* which now hangs in a gallery in Washington. I spent my time completing the notes and details that make up the bulk of this narrative. And as we all grieved for Layton, we honored him by perfecting the stories of his bravery that would be trumpeted about Market Street for the next decade. In these stories Layton's demons were completely forgotten, his arrogant pride was forgiven, and his glorious last act of courage blazed up and outshone all else. He had been a vain man—brash, overconfident, reckless, lucky for a long while, and in the end, when his luck ran out, he sacrificed himself for the rest of us, which surprised many, though not those who knew him. I like to think it reflects well on our brigade that even our most self-regarding member had sacrificed himself, that our most foppish had also become the most brave, but I do not mean to misrepresent the man, either. He was always an irritable, thorny presence, as incapable of acting in a cowardly manner as he was of taking a small slight or inconvenience silently. Both his valiant and petty acts are remembered, though it is the good and the noble that shines brightest now. He had wanted to overcome his demons and I believe he did overcome them. What remains in memory is his vibrancy, his love of life, and his final act of self-sacrifice—and that is how it should be. In death, at least for our friends, we become what was best in us.

We stayed in that hidden spot all winter and one afternoon in early April, four months after we'd arrived, Smith and Bridger, who had ridden with Red Elk and the diversionary pack animals, arrived with twelve handlers, telling us how they'd been pursued by the British right up to the palisades of the fort. Pike had only relented at the threat of eighty American long guns, never understanding that he chased animals that carried sticks and rocks. Red Elk and his men settled at the fort for the winter, and after a month of rest, Smith and Bridger had turned around with extra handlers and started back for the Bighorn. After many hardships they had arrived at the winter encampment, inordinately pleased to see our fortune intact, though grieved to hear of Layton's demise.

The day after Smith's arrival there was a storm that made travel impossible and it was not until the end of April that we started back with our horses and pelts. It was the springtime of 1829 now and the prairies were sodden and the rivers high and traveling was slow, but because of the deep snow in the mountains and the difficulty in

314

moving we felt certain that if the Brits had wintered on the other side of the mountains, which we were sure they had, they could not cross so early in the season.

All that spring we passed trapping parties heading west, and they always gave a cheer when they understood we were the great Market Street Fur Company. The French, the British, and the Spanish had thirsted after our returns, as had other American companies, but now the men from these same American companies applauded us in a lusty way that was bewildering until we understood that exaggerated stories of our adventures had moved eastward since Smith arrived at Fort Ashley, and those stories had reached the States, where our battle with Pike and the Hudson's Bay Company had been published in the most romantic and gloriously patriotic terms that had little resemblance to truth, and would have satisfied even Layton's nearly bottomless desire for praise. Washington had taken our little skirmish and bent it for its own use. Our striving for pelts and fortune was painted as a patriotic endeavor. Layton had become a national hero. Every time we passed a brigade we were cheered by our countrymen for heroic acts that had no basis in fact, and Layton's bravery was compared to that of the Greeks at Thermopylae. All joined in the revelry, and it was a glorious time for everyone except me, as I had promised Alene I would be back by midwinter, and instead would be returning in late spring, by which time she had sworn she would be back in St. Louis.

So though I was pleased with the fortune we carried and the fame we'd won, I realized too late that all that was of little consequence in comparison to what I'd lost. Sadness and dread weighed heavily inside me. I questioned every brigade we passed if they had gone through Fort Burnham, and if so, had they seen or heard of a woman named Alene Bailey. No one seemed to have seen her and I was doubly sure she had returned to St. Louis. It seemed it was my ill fate to finally be ready to settle at the exact moment when the opportunity was taken away.

On the night before we arrived at Fort Ashley we met up with Red Elk and his men, who had ridden out to meet us. I do not know how they knew we were coming, but they did, and that night, a day's ride from the fort, Red Elk stepped into our encampment and demanded payment for his participation in the raid, which we complied with gladly, passing on our long guns and a small barrel of powder, and afterward, the remaining men of the Market Street Fur Company—me, Ferris, Glass, Branch, Smith, and Bridger—built a bonfire, and savages and trappers alike celebrated our success by drinking a jack of Taos Whiskey that Smith, of all people, had secreted in that spot for just that occasion.

Oh, how the fire flamed that night. Oh, how the drums boomed. The whiskey was passed around and the lot of us stomped and leaped and whooped and in general acted like wild beasts. Even the captain joined in, cavorting in a way I would not have thought possible of him. It was the last night of the brigade, the last night of the existence of the Market Street Fur Company, and we were all filled with affection for one another, and mourning for Layton and Pegleg, and were half wild with relief and sadness and the thrill of our riches.

The next morning Red Elk found me as I cared for my horse, and with Branch translating, told me that years before, as a young man, he'd had a dream that a white man would be the conduit to save his village, and when he'd first seen me bleeding on those grassy hills after the surround he knew I was that man, and that was why he had looked at me so curiously when I writhed on the hilltop. It was why, when I raced against him, he had not brained me as he had Frazier. And he said that it was not only Ferris's shot that had convinced him to join in the raid on the British but my presence, as he was sure I would bring salvation to his tribe. He told me all this in his indifferent, sullen manner, and even now I do not know what to make of it. I do not believe in native magic, but I suppose I do believe in fate, and I know that Red Elk had looked at me curiously long before our lives were connected, and that I felt a strange affinity for him from the beginning and still do, and do not know how to explain this other than to say it happened and it seems a mystery to me, too.

Minutes later Red Elk jumped on his horse, held up the long gun that would defend his people for the remainder of his life, and without a word of farewell departed, Branch riding with him, as there was no free place for him in the settlements.

A half a day after that the brigade and our fortune reached Fort Ashley and as we crossed the last low rise and the fort came in sight, we all let out a cheer, as there was a keelboat being loaded with pelts at that very moment. It meant that the river was free of ice and those who desired could be back in St. Louis in a month. I had just taken this in when I saw a slight figure dressed in white on the deck of that keelboat. I was a quarter mile off but something thumped inside me and I knew that it was Alene standing on the deck and looking to the west. Instead of going to St. Louis as she had promised, she had endured all manner of hardships to be out there at Fort Ashley in case I returned.

I can hardly describe the feelings that overcame me at that moment. It was a relief combined with a sort of dropping inside. Momentarily flustered, I rode not toward her but away, galloping several hundred yards off with my heart pounding and my hands shaking. I don't want to give the wrong impression. It was not regret I was feeling but the surprise of actually having survived and succeeded, and some other thing, too, that I can't quite name, something akin to the panic the mules get when they feel the yoke lowering, and perhaps, also, the glimmering thoughts of death that mingle with the conclusion of a great struggle. I had held myself steady for so long against failure and the imprecations of my father and the idea that my wandering nature was an unsteady and unsound foundation, and had been so certain of my eventual demise in some lonely place, that I hardly knew how to accept success. Alene had not left me but had ridden out to find me, and I felt my heart rising up to meet her sacrifice with my own. I understood that my days of adventure and wandering were over. It would be years before I understood how complete that ending would be, or how decisive.

By mid-spring we were back in St. Louis. Two months later we were married.

———

For a few months we were all famous men, but the brigade as a unit was never together again. Smith went back to his Rocky Mountain Fur Company and died two years later in an attack by the Comanche as he tried to open up a trade route with Santa Fe. Branch lived with the natives for many years and in his last days settled in a cottage to the west of the city with his Crow wife and was an emissary for the natives and their causes. Bridger became a scout for the government, a landowner, and father to at least fifteen native children. Glass retired to Oregon Territory and lives with his mule in the coastal mountains. And Ferris, as he'd promised, remained in St. Louis only to finish his studies, then returned to the mountains, and afterward has come back only infrequently, and increasingly unencumbered by pelts but laden instead with the wonderful canvases that are now spread across the galleries in the great cities of our nation. When I see him now, bent-backed and aging, but still with that winning, open, carefree manner, it makes my heart surge, as Ferris still embodies the recklessness and grandeur and camaraderie of those early years in the drainages, and he brings back the memory of Layton and his triumphant final act, which is recorded in Ferris's masterpiece, *Saving Grace*, where all can see the rock gates and the fire flaming and Layton in his fortification, brandishing his musket and defying the entire British brigade. Alene in particular admired this painting and several times remarked that as unlikely as it seemed, Layton had sacrificed himself for others, and must have been a much changed man after his year on the march.

As for me, with the returns from the company

and the fame of being in the papers and Alene's inheritance all coinciding, I'm afraid I paraded around for a few months, full of myself, and close enough to being intolerable that Alene once commented that she might as well have married Layton.

Several months after our marriage, Alene and I left for Pennsylvania to visit my family. Their correspondence had been full of misinformation about my glorious deeds, and I thought I ought to return while I was still worth something in their eyes. The journey home took three weeks on a paddleboat and another by cart, which I traded five miles from the farm for an expensive barouche. I put on a high collar and a Wellington hat and in that fancy carriage I sat next to Alene with my back straight and a stern expression. I could feel Alene scowling at me, thinking I was some puffed-up Grignon, hoping to lord my success over my poor relatives, but I told myself she did not know them, or know what I had suffered at their hands, and it was my dream to return in glory and riches and to impress them to no end. This will be my final triumph, I thought.

But as we passed the last bend of the county road and the old farm came into sight with its two oaks and little pond and orderly rows of greens, I felt my affected parading crumbling. Colonel, an old dog now, loped out to meet us. My brothers, portly and middle-aged, stepped out of the house, all smiles and excitement, eager to see their famous brother, and all my pretensions melted in an instant. My youthful exuberance surged and I leaped from the carriage and ran past that plodding horse, losing my hat, embracing them, one with each arm. I lifted my mother off the porch, and there was much free-flowing merriment on both sides, and I knew the barriers all along had not been in them but in myself, and I had conquered them at last, and I was happy and contented to be at home.

After a month we returned to St. Louis and Alene and I settled outside of the city on our own land to a life of comfort and industry that would make tedious recounting and does not belong on these pages. We have two sons. We have work to fill our days. I no longer yearn for the savage country, though I remember with satisfaction the adventures we had and the friends I made. I remember the days spent traversing the dark forests, the white rivers, and the far-off mountains. And though I have not forgotten our desperate moments, the dark times do not cling so much as the beauty and companionship, and this is as it should be. The compensation for youthful recklessness is contentedness and good nature in old age. Youth's bright flame sears the mind and leaves us glorying in the past with an unalloyed affection that does not dim the present but enhances it with fond memories untarnished by their unpleasant parts. Layton, who died magnificently, would appreciate that, as even at his best, he was always a vain man. The hardships and horrors are covered over with time and those hills are so pretty from a distance.

Acknowledgments

This is a work of fiction and readers with close knowledge of this time period will find much that is familiar and also much that is bent to the purposes of the narrative. The timing of some historical events has shifted slightly. For example, we see General Ashley, Jedediah Smith, and Jim Bridger in places where we know they did not go and doing things we know they did not do. Despite this fictionalization, I hope the spirit of their characters and of the time rings true. In short, though I have made every attempt to be as historically accurate as possible within the confines of the narrative, this is a work of fiction and should be considered as such.

The sources that were read for this book, if listed, would stretch for several pages. There were three books in particular that inspired me: John Tanner's *The Falcon*, W. A. Ferris's *Life in the Rocky Mountains*, and Francis Parkman's *The Oregon Trail*. I returned to these three books again and again to take in the spirit of adventure and curiosity that first attracted me to the trapping regions and the Indian country and the exploration of the west. Close readers of those three excellent books will find that I am indebted to them for many details of life on the trail. Diaries from the early trappers also make fine reading.

As always, I had the help of many generous readers who each improved this book. I'd like to thank in particular Tom Garrigus, Allison Glock, Chris Hebert, Michael Knight, Theresa Profant, Terry Shaw, Allen Weir, John Zomchick, and my family (Mom, Dad, Mike, Ian, and Erin), who all made this book better. I'd like to thank Jim Hardee at the Museum of the Mountain Man for offering his years of scholarship to minimize many foolish errors. I'd like to thank my agent David McCormick for believing in the book and my editor Deborah Garrison for her excellent advice and for shepherding the book to publication.

About the Author

Shannon Burke is the author of the novels *Safelight* and *Black Flies*, a *New York Times* Notable Book. He has also worked on several film projects, including *Syriana.*

Center Point Large Print
600 Brooks Road / PO Box 1
Thorndike, ME 04986-0001 USA

(207) 568-3717

US & Canada:
1 800 929-9108
www.centerpointlargeprint.com

4-15